I0663269

A VOICE SO SOFT

PATRICK LACEY

For Emily, who can make an imaginary microphone out of literally anything.

PROLOGUE
THE GIRL ON TV

OFFICER MIKE MALLORY SHINED HIS light into thick blackness. From the outside, the place was harmless enough: a two-story colonial with a newly finished front porch. It was the nicer part of town, homes much larger than necessary. Lawns trimmed to perfection. In-ground pools shimmering in the moonlight. But despite the well-to-do environment, the house in front of him made his skin crawl.

Every light was off save for one. The top left. The girl's room. He could tell from the stickers: pink and purple flowers faded from the sun. He shined the light toward the front door and saw his reflection staring back at him. But was there something else? Something behind the glare?

He'd responded to a domestic dispute call ten minutes prior, asking the dispatcher to confirm the address three times before he took off in this direction. Mike had answered plenty such calls during his six years on the force but never on this side of town. Cedar Drive was about as upper class as you could get.

Next door, an old woman stared from her screen door, eyes wide with something like fear. Probably the one who'd made the call. He caught her attention, nodded, let her know it was okay now that the police were here.

He cracked his neck and made his way up the drive. At the front door, he knocked and nearly yelped as the door pushed forward, creaking into the night. He reached for a light switch, felt the plastic button, pushed it.

Nothing. The room remained dark. A blown fuse, probably. Nothing more to it.

He stepped inside, shined the beam left, right, straight. Shadows danced on their own accord. He thought he heard something upstairs, some muffled voice that held dark promises. The air was heavy with the threat of a thunderstorm. He'd checked the weather earlier, though. Nothing but clear skies. An astronomer's wet dream, the shock jock had said on the radio.

Mike cleared his throat. "Hello? Is anyone home?"

Of course they're home, moron. They were just yelling at each other ten minutes ago. Probably hiding in their rooms.

He'd never been married himself—came close to it once, though—but Mike knew the way couples fought. His parents, together twenty years before being crushed by an eighteen-wheeler on a cool January night, had never shown anything close to affection in front of little Mikey. If they weren't arguing about bills or the way Dad looked at other women, they were playing the cold shoulder game, seeing who could outlast the other. Usually it was a tie. He recalled silences so dense he could hear his own pulse, make out with great detail how the faucet leaked once every twenty seconds or so.

That silence was a lot like this, only back then he hadn't felt such . . . what was the word?

Dread.

He walked through a large entryway. Fur coats were draped over hooks. A large mirror hung on the far wall. The reflected light blinded him for a moment. He shut his eyes, walked forward.

And slipped on something.

He went down hard, head hitting the floor. The backs of his eyes seared with pain and for a moment he wondered if he didn't have a concussion. He felt an egg already starting to form and he could've stayed down all night if it weren't for the creak above.

The ceiling buckled and the voice from earlier grew louder. He thought he heard music.

He tried to get up, slipped again. When he shined the light onto the floor he saw what looked like a slick puddle of oil. But the metallic, slightly sweet scent made him think of something else.

Blood.

There was blood everywhere.

It had leaked from around the corner, from the kitchen. It was all over him, soaking through the sleeves of his shirt. There were bits of something within the red. Something like skin and hair.

He backed away until he felt carpet, stood up, drew his nine millimeter pistol.

He called for backup, informing dispatch this was more than a domestic dispute. There may have been arguments but they'd turned to something sinister.

Pistol pointed toward the kitchen, he moved slowly.

"Hello?" he said again, louder but just as weak. "This is Officer Mike Mallory. If you can hear me, put your hands above your head and stay where you are."

No response. Unless you counted the noises above.

He took another step, hands shaking so badly the Mag became a strobe light. His equilibrium grew schizophrenic.

The blood trailed around the corner.

He lost the bowl of chili he'd eaten at Steve's Diner two hours earlier. Hot bile and half-digested beef made its way out of his throat and onto the tiled floor. Though the room was larger than Mike's entire apartment, he felt the walls closing in.

In the middle of the kitchen lay an island counter and on that counter lay two bodies. Faces up, staring at the ceiling with gouges that had once housed eyes. Someone had taken a chef's knife to them and they'd been in a hurry. There was nothing methodical about the wounds. They formed random patterns that reminded Mike of tiny mouths, the exposed bone a bit like teeth.

Get out and wait for backup. This is a double homicide and the killer is—

Upstairs. Footsteps again.

He thought of the faded flower stickers, raised his pistol, took the steps two at a time. On the second level, a small rectangle of light leaked beneath the girl's door. On the other side, music played. Something poppy, synths blaring over a catchy but lifeless tune.

"Hello? Is anyone in there?"

More footsteps.

And something like a giggle.

He tried the knob. Locked. He kneeled down, peered through the crack, and saw only one set of tiny feet. That didn't mean the killer wasn't in there, hiding inside the closet and instructing her to keep quiet.

"This is the police. I'm going to count to three before breaking down the door. Do you understand?"

A snort of laughter.

"One."

The volume on the television increasing.

"Two."

Words of some kind. The girl humming along with the tune.

"Three."

Mike stepped back and charged. The door slammed open, though he instantly wished it had stayed shut.

There was no killer inside, at least not the kind he'd been expecting. His mind had conjured a large man, filthy beard and tattered trench coat. Instead there was a girl of perhaps eight or nine. Unlike her parents downstairs, she was still alive, but they did have something in common.

Her eyes were gone.

Two jagged holes cried crimson tears down her cheeks and onto the carpet. The fabric was soaked through.

She danced around the room, head rocking back and forth like everything in the world was as it should be.

"Your eyes," Mike said. "Who did this to you?"

She stopped, giggled. "I did. Duh. Do you see anyone else?"

"Your parents."

She nodded. "They had it coming. That's what Angie said."

"Angie?"

The girl pointed to another girl. This one on the television screen. Some sort of reality game show, the kind where singers put their talent to the test in exchange for a record deal and a chunk of change. The girl on stage shook her hips with such primal force Mike felt his skin tingle despite the fear. She was beautiful, barely out of high school, and he could not deny the shiver along his spine.

"Isn't she pretty?" The eyeless girl kneeled down, felt along the floor until she found what she was looking for.

A chef's knife, the blade tinted red.

Mike shook his head, stepped back. "Drop it."

"I can't. She won't let me."

"She?"

"Haven't you been listening? What Angie wants, Angie gets."

Another step back. Out of the room now, his back touching the banister. "You mean the girl on the TV?"

"She has the best voice in the world and she says soon the world will be hers. Isn't that cool?" She held the knife forward.

"Don't move. I'm warning you."

"Angie said you'd say that. And you know what else she said?"

A murmur in the back of his throat was all he could manage.

"She said you're not above shooting a little girl in the chest." She charged forth, wound back—

And Mike pulled the trigger twice, both shots piercing the girl's ribs. She hit the banister and broke through the slats, tumbling downstairs and landing at an odd angle.

On the television, the beautiful girl sang her heart out.

♪

"You can do this," Miranda Irons said to the mirror.

In its reflection she saw a stranger, face covered in layers of make-up. Back home—home being LaPlace, Louisiana—she never even bothered to wear foundation. Her skin was flawless and she'd inherited her mother's ample bosom. She was, by all accounts, a natural beauty. Not quite a knockout but easy on the eyes in a simple sort of way. But on television, things were different. Singers couldn't be bumpkins. Country superstars had sex appeal. And tonight, staring at the stranger in the mirror, she couldn't help but smile.

"Not bad. Not bad at all."

Her parents had wished her luck moments before, telling her she'd do fine. She had this in the bag. For a while, she'd believed them.

Until Angie Everstein took the stage.

Miranda could sing her ass off but Angie's voice was something else entirely. It demanded your attention. Miranda had watched as the girl—eighteen years old, strawberry blond hair, eyes exotic yet accessible—sang her final song of the competition. She had the crowd in the palm of her perfect little hands.

Miranda's nerves set in shortly thereafter. She dry heaved into the toilet bowl. She hadn't eaten anything beyond a granola bar and a kale smoothie in the last two days. Her figure was great but her self-esteem was not.

Because one did not simply follow Angie Everstein. It would take an act of God to outsing her but Miranda couldn't give up now. She'd made it this far. The judges and viewers saw something in her.

She ought to march down to Angie's dressing room and congratulate her on a song well sung. That was the honorable thing to do. It might even calm her some.

She nodded at the mirror and the stranger didn't seem so strange anymore. She may have been covered in layers of make-up but her true self, the one her parents had raised her to be, was proud.

She spun around, marched toward the door, opened it—

And froze.

A figure stood before her. Tall and misshapen. Her eyes went out of focus, the details of the thing—for it was a *thing* and not a human—becoming obscure. She backed away, held her hands up in defense. The room turned from inferno to ice box. A cold draft blew from somewhere unseen and she cursed the wardrobe people for dressing her so skimpy. Every inch of her skin grew rigid. She shivered beyond control.

The temperature was the least of her worries.

She searched for a weapon but there was nothing more than a hair curler and a bottle of moisturizer.

"Stay away from me," she said. "I'll call for help."

The figure stepped closer. Her eyes grew fuzzier. A headache soared through her temples. Despite the chilly breeze, there came the scent of something burning. She imagined charred chicken wings, forgotten on a grill, only this was much more . . . human-like.

She backed away until she felt the wall on her shoulder blades. Cornered.

She opened her mouth to scream, vocal lessons be damned, when the thing touched her cheek. Its flesh was cold and smoldering at the same time. She closed her eyes, prepared for death.

When she looked again the thing was gone, replaced with the girl who'd been on television moments before.

"Everything okay?" Angie Everstein said. This close her green eyes were flawless. The irises went on for days and there was something inside her pupils, something that made Miranda's skin tingle.

Miranda rubbed her face, smearing professional make-up. "I thought you were a . . ."

"Monster?" Angie smiled.

Miranda laughed. "I must be going crazy."

Angie's smile widened. Miranda's tingling grew stronger. It covered much of her body, descended until it stopped just above her waist, not entirely unpleasant. "No offense taken." Angie brushed aside a strand of Miranda's hair. "I just wanted to give you a good luck kiss."

"A what?"

She leaned forward and placed her lips upon Miranda's. Just a peck but strong enough to take her breath away.

Even when the kiss was *over*, Miranda struggled for air. Her lungs worked overtime, throat swelling. She thrashed, begged Angie with her eyes.

Angie offered another million-dollar smile, pupils swirling with something like smoke. "Knock 'em dead, kid." She turned, flaunting a body that was the subject of countless thirteen-year-old boys' fantasies.

Miranda fell to her knees.

Just before her brain stopped talking to the rest of her body, she swore the *thing* was back. The thing from earlier with the dark skin and the misshapen limbs. And were those cloven hooves at the bottom of its contorted legs? And were those jagged horns on the top of its furry head?

Blood began to pour from her mouth, her nose, her eyes, and Miranda Irons lost the competition by default.

Making Angie Everstein the undisputed champion.

CHAPTER ONE
SETTING THE STAGE

"WHO THE FUCK IS ANGIE Everstein?" Josh Meyers held the CD, examined the neon cover with the half-naked girl. She looked manufactured, like she'd been squeezed from a mold and formed into a pop star. There was something off about her too. He could almost imagine her eyes turning black, her skin turning a pale gray.

"You really don't own a television, do you?" Trish said, reading through the list of new releases. "Or a radio for that matter."

"Only time I listen to the radio is for the weather. She have a new single or something?"

"Biggest song in the world. Number one on just about every chart. She won that singing contest show. The one where they have has-been celebrities judge you. *The Harmony Club* or something like that."

"Any good?"

"What do you think?" Trish rolled her eyes, hidden behind layers of black and green mascara that gave way to a nose ring, a lip ring, and, as Josh had speculated many a late night, probably nipple rings. She was beautiful in a non-traditional way, didn't give a shit about appearances. That was the reason he'd hired her in the first place.

Not that he'd be able to afford her—or the store for that matter—much longer.

He looked around the shop and could not help but notice a layer of dust resting over everything. Nobody bought physical music any-more. Why would you when you could click a mouse and have it hand delivered to you? Black Star Records, Salem's "premier" underground music store, specialized in everything that wasn't mainstream. You had your metal—black, death, thrash, and everything else that lay between. You had your punk—crust, hardcore, crossover, and so forth. Then there was the ska and the reggae, the jazz and garage. Anything that wasn't on the television or the radio. That's what Black Star was all about.

Which is why Josh couldn't make sense of the CDs.

He hadn't ordered them. Far from anything they carried and none of his regulars would be interested.

Angie Everstein. She could have been eighteen or twenty-three. Wore a sparkly dress that ended just below an anatomically perfect ass, which matched her legs and just about everything else about her. Josh despised pop stars and everything they represented but there was something about this one. He hated to admit it, but she was quite easy to look at.

He set the CD back into the box and scratched his beard. Long, unkempt, it matched the rest of his body. He didn't shower all that often these days. Not since the separation. Melissa had taken everything: his money, his house—even some of his beloved records.

Don't forget about your dignity. She took that and ran with it.

Truth be told, he'd lost *that* years ago, when he'd learned of his wife's extra-marital activities. Salem wasn't the world's smallest town but word still traveled quickly. At current count, Josh knew of five guys Melissa had fucked on the side. He'd met three, even traveled in some of the same circles. All losers. That seemed to be her type. Never mind her nice, if not smothering, husband. Little old Josh who'd saved every penny from his office job to follow his dreams and open a record store. No, she wanted the deadbeat, grungy pricks that so often frequented Black Star.

Not that he was bitter or anything.

The shop's speakers crackled with static, the record finishing up. A few moments later a voice began singing. Feminine, overly compressed, auto-tuned so it no longer sounded human. "What the hell is this?" He eyed Trish.

"This, Boss Man, is that little skank you're holding in your hands." She chewed at a nail covered in black polish. "Biggest song on the planet for three weeks and you're hearing it for the first time."

He closed the box of CDs and tried to drown out the lyrics, something about being young and in love, partying all night. The beat was your standard fare, constant and droning and it seemed to invade his mind. His eyes grew heavy and he could feel a migraine coming on.

Outside the sun was setting and the other stores were closing. He doubted anyone would mind if they closed for the night, but it would be irresponsible. It was late October in the country's Halloween capital. Someone might wander in from the streets and purchase a Darkthrone record or two.

Wishful thinking. Give it another three months and you'll be closed for good.
Still, closing up shop didn't sound bad right about now.

It would be a relief to get away from these CDs he hadn't ordered in the first place. He couldn't pinpoint exactly how the music—if you wanted to call it that—made him feel but the sensation went beyond annoyance. Made his hair stand straight up. That feeling when you were being watched. But that was silly, wasn't it? It was just a pop song.

"For the love of God, Trish, shut that shit off."

"Very funny." She carried a bag of trash into the back room.

"Seriously. I'm going to make you work all night if you don't turn it off."

She set the bag down and walked over to him. "I can't tell if you're joking."

"Joking about what?" The headache was perverse, spreading through his skull. His pulse became a snare drum, pounding harder and harder. He daydreamed of boring a hole through his skull just to relieve the pressure.

Angie's voice spouted within his mind, as if she'd found a way in through his ear canal. *Forever with you,* she sang. *I'll never leave your side.*

"Josh, I shut it off five minutes ago."

He rubbed his eyes and the headache receded, as did the internal beat. Only the hum of the air conditioner now. "What?"

"Are you okay?" Trish placed a hand on his forehead.

"Maybe I'm coming down with something. Why don't you get out of here? I'll see you in the morning."

"Get some sleep, will you?" She grabbed her backpack and headed outside. He watched her go and, despite the pain, couldn't help but wonder if he'd ever work up the nerve to ask her out.

Fat chance of that, Melissa said within his mind. She'd been out of his life for almost a year, yet she still riddled him with negativity. A brain tumor that wouldn't respond to treatment.

He tried not to look at the box on the counter, overflowing with

Angie Everstein CDs, tried to ignore the faint beat slowly creeping back into his head.

He wrote a note to find out who'd ordered those infernal things. Had he not been financially pinched, he'd fire them on the spot. He was jotting down the tracking number from the box when he heard the door open again.

"Miss me?" he said, turning around, certain he'd see Trish standing there.

No one and nothing but a cool breeze permeated through the store.

♪

"Pig face!"

Shawna Everstein ignored the comment. Not the first time, nor the last. Even in Salem, a town known for its Wiccan and Goth communities, she couldn't catch a break.

"Oink, oink," another onlooker said. She thought it was Brandon Matheson or perhaps Derek Sorrentino, the worst of her bullies.

She lifted both hands in unison and removed her hearing aids. The world faded to near nothingness. A bittersweet tradeoff. Her tormentors could no longer hurt her with words—sticks and stones, her ass—but other sounds faded too. Beautiful sounds. Distant traffic, fog horns, and crunching leaves—all of it vanished in exchange for a few moments of pure, unadulterated silence.

She climbed the hill, past the convenience store, past residential houses, until she arrived at her favorite spot in the world. Normally, Gallows Hill was packed with tourists during the days, teenagers during the nights, Brandon and Derek among them. But today, it was eerily void of activity.

She placed her hearing aids back in. The world returned, sounds registering once more. No matter how many times she repeated this process, it was always a shock. A small miracle and reminder she could still hear, no matter how poorly.

She sat on a bench and admired the scenery. The leaves had turned wonderful shades of bronze and gold and orange. She'd never traveled much, had only been to Canobie Lake Park, Water Country, and Dream Woods. But she was certain there was no place quite like Gallows Hill. Salem citizens took it for granted, a gold mine for tourists. To Shawna, it was a quiet place to sit and gather her thoughts.

And today she had a lot to think about.

Angie would be coming home soon. Life had been good these last few months. Shawna didn't have to feel inferior whenever her celebrity sister was in the same room. Didn't have to remember she was the ugly Everstein. Things would quickly go back to the way they were.

Or worse.

Because now Angie was a hometown hero.

Just thinking about it made her antsy. She stood and walked several steps before stopping suddenly.

Something caught her eye in the distance. A structure just beyond the line of trees. It hadn't been there the last time. Of that she was sure. This place was her private sanctuary. She knew every detail by heart.

A stage.

There was a stage behind the trees. A professional job. Lights and pyrotechnics and a large backdrop with words she couldn't make out. Had she been in the center of town, near the tourist shops, the revelation wouldn't have come as such a shock. Millions traveled to Salem for the season. On Halloween the place became a tornado of debauchery. Slutty costumes and cover bands for as far as you could see. But up here, away from the activity, there shouldn't have been a stage.

She took a few steps and stopped again. Something in her gut told her to turn around. The closer she got, the more the air seemed to change. She couldn't say exactly what had transpired but the atmosphere felt charged somehow.

Something moved behind the trees. Something misshapen. Its skin was eclipse-black and its legs ended in cloven feet. She smelled death, rotting things.

Someone grabbed her shoulder.

She turned toward her attacker.

But it wasn't an attacker after all. Just a construction worker whose breath smelled a bit like cold cuts. "You shouldn't be here." His voice sounded almost as tired as his raccoon eyes looked. "It's dangerous."

She nodded toward the woods, trying to catch her breath. "What's with the stage?"

"What about it?" He retrieved a crumpled cigarette from his pocket, lit it with a shaking hand. Something told her it wasn't from the temperature.

"Why up here, away from the festivities?"

The man looked around, studying Gallows Hill as if someone—

some*thing*—observed from nearby. Shawna's skin prickled as if to confirm the suspicion. "How the hell should I know? I just show up and do what they tell me."

"Who's *they*?" Shawna wasn't sure she wanted to know the answer.

"You'll find out soon enough." From the same pocket he produced a flask, unscrewed the cap, and drank for a long time.

Before she could ask another question, he walked toward the stage that should not have been there and was swallowed by the trees.

♪

That night, Shawna stared at her computer and tried not to cry. Her room was dark, the screen the only source of light. It washed the walls in a strange shade of blue as though she'd nodded off and entered a dream.

Or, to be more precise, a nightmare.

It wasn't just Gallows Hill that made her pulse speed. It was the Skype conversation from hell. On the screen, sitting on a bed twice the size of her own, was a girl that looked and acted like a stranger, though the two knew each other well.

"What do you want?" Mia said.

"I just wanted to hear your voice."

"Good luck with that." She laughed, touched her own *working* ears. Once upon a time, her giggles had been endearing but they'd turned mean-spirited in recent times. As had Mia herself.

Shawna rubbed her eyes, tired beyond return. She ought to turn in early. Tomorrow marked the beginning of the school week.

"Are we done here?" Mia said. "I hate it when you space out like that. It's creepy."

"Sorry, I was just thinking about—"

"About us. Yeah, you said that already. How many times do we have to go through this? There *is* no us. Not anymore. Not ever again."

"You can't mean that."

"I mean it. I promise." Mia rolled her eyes, as if she were addressing a teacher and not her ex-girlfriend. Three months prior, she'd been caring and loving but a change had taken place.

Change isn't strong enough of a word. It's like she's possessed.

The thought chilled Shawna. It wasn't the first time it had crossed her mind.

They'd dated mid-junior year through this past July, when the transition began. It took roughly three and a half weeks for Mia to transform into the girl on the other side of the screen. One day she'd worn her typical outfit: ripped jeans and an oversized metal shirt. The next, her pants were free from damage, more form fitting. The day after that, the band shirt (usually Cannibal Corpse or Metallica) was swapped for something boring: a halter top with reflective sequins. Then came the blond hair dye and the layers of make-up, until the girl Shawna had loved became someone else entirely.

It wasn't just her exterior, either. Something had changed *inside her*.

Their relationship, though short-lived, had been healthy. Mature. She didn't consider what they'd had to be puppy love. Mia had stopped answering Shawna's texts and calls. Near the end, when they *did* hang out, she was never in the moment. Something always on her mind. Infidelity perhaps. Mia was bisexual, Shawna queer. The former had more options. The latter felt like there was no one else in the world for her.

"Are we done here?" Mia said. "I've got plans tonight."

"What kind of plans?"

"None of your business." She stood from her bed and slipped on bright red shoes that looked fit for a runway model. Her shirt was bedazzled with sparkles and her lipstick made her face clown-like.

"Don't go," Shawna said. "Please."

"I have to. See you around. Maybe." Just before she ended their conversation, Shawna caught a glimpse of something hanging on her ex's wall. A poster that seemed even more out of place than Mia's new personality. Surely a trick of the light.

Surely she hadn't seen *you know who* holding a microphone and singing to a sea of fans.

Shawna slammed her laptop shut.

Her heart hammered. She wiped away equal doses of sweat and tears and almost screamed when her door opened.

Her mother, the glare from the hall blinding so she was just a shadow at first. She reached in and flipped the light switch. It took a long time for Shawna's eyes to adjust but when they did, she wished she was blind *and* deaf.

"Hi, sweetie. Dinner's almost ready."

She sniffled. "I'm not hungry."

"I think you will be when you find out who's here."

It can't be. I'm supposed to have another week before everything goes back to hell.

Her mother stepped aside and another figure appeared. The same figure she'd seen moments before hanging on Mia's wall.

The same figure she could not escape no matter how hard she tried.

Her room's temperature plummeted but her mother didn't seem to notice the change. No one ever did. It was like the general population was too hypnotized to see the beast that stood in front of them.

The second figure stepped forward, sat on the edge of the bed. Shawna recoiled as if she were face-to-face with a snake, only the truth was far worse.

That smile. Those eyes. The teeth.

Every feature a nightmare in and of itself.

"Hi, Sis," Angie said. "Miss me?"

CHAPTER TWO
YOU'RE INVITED

A KNOCK AT THE DOOR.

"We're closed," Harriet "Esmeralda" Hopkins said. "We open at nine tomorrow morning. Come back then." She did not look toward the door lest she see the idiot tourist, mouth hanging open, give her *that* look. The one that said *You are the palm reader and you will read my palm, O ghastly woman.*

It came with the territory. You couldn't own a magic shop in Witch City without drawing a crowd. Especially this time of year. And with crowds came exponential chances of encountering idiots like the one standing outside.

She'd be glad when the season was over. She loved Halloween. Loved the decorations and the horror movie marathons, not to mention pumpkin-flavored goodies, but it would be good to return to normalcy come November 1st.

Another knock, this one a bit insistent for her taste. She ignored them. Sometimes a cold shoulder did the trick.

She picked up a box of spell supplies (eye of newt and several other herbs that customers devoured) and carried them from the back room to the front counter. The books would need to be tidied up. A group of college kids had ruined the order earlier that day. The top shelf was reserved for rare leather-bound volumes, the middle for vampire literature. She didn't like stocking novels about sparkling immortals but she also didn't like the idea of being homeless. Girls ate the stuff up so she'd kept on ordering them. It seemed obscene, paranormal romance novels sitting next to Aleister Crowley texts, but she was too tired to care. It could wait until morning.

A third knock, loud enough to rouse her from her thoughts.

She dropped the box of supplies onto the counter too hard. One of the bottles within tumbled to the floor and shattered. Green powder erupted. "Son of a bitch."

She grabbed the broom and dustpan and set it near the counter. Then she turned her attention toward the door and gritted her teeth. "Like I said: we're closed."

No knock this time. In its place, a whisper. Make that *several* whispers. They seemed to come from everywhere and nowhere. Countless voices formed words too quiet to decipher. Her ears shuddered in response. Her skin went prickly and for the first time, not realizing what it meant, she was certain it was not a tourist standing outside Esmeralda's Ye Olde Magic Shoppe.

The light above the door flickered and burned out.

She'd replaced it just last week.

It thrust the front half of her store into darkness, like the night was a spreading disease.

Her heart rate tripled. Esmeralda had grown in size these last few years. Her doctors warned of ramifications. Cardiovascular disease and diabetes ran in her family—on both sides, mind you—and she'd surely follow in her parents' footsteps if she didn't make a change. The weight had not appeared miraculously. She liked to eat because it made her forget, if only for a moment, how much she hated her life.

But now, staring at the darkness and feeling lightheaded, she wished she'd taken her doctors seriously. Wished she'd kept up with her salads instead of Twinkies.

Wished she'd sold her business and moved to Florida like she'd always fantasized.

The whispers grew more persistent. Her mind raced with warnings.

Use the back exit. It's blocked with boxes but it won't take more than a minute to toss them aside and get the hell out of here. Whatever's out there isn't going to wait to be let in.

Whatever? When had it turned from tourist to something indefinable?

Around the time she began to make out what the whispers were saying.

At first she thought it was a poem of some sort. There was a rhythm to the words. A cadence. But the longer she listened she realized it wasn't a poem at all.

A song.

A song she recognized from the radio. Hard to escape these days, considering who sang it.

She walked toward the door in a trance, pushed along by an unseen breeze, until she was inches away from whatever lay on the other side.

Across the street, the lamp flickered for a moment. She feared it, too, would go out but it remained, the dim light not offering much in the way of visibility. It was dark out there. Darker than it should have been. Derby Street had grown too quiet. People passed by every few moments but the crowds had lessened drastically. It seemed unnatural. Halloween was two weeks away. The place had been mobbed earlier. But now it seemed Salem's offseason had arrived early.

She opened her mouth to scream, and though no words came out, something told her the passersby would not hear her voice even if they had.

The words (lyrics) grew louder.

One voice shined above the rest, angelic and demonic at the same time.

Forever with you, it said. *I'll never leave your side.*

Forever with you.

Don't ever try to hide.

She'd never heard the entire song, made it a point to shut it off during her commute. Still, she felt as though she knew every word by heart. Perhaps it had played while she was shopping or waiting in the dentist's office but the theory didn't feel right. Her jaw worked against her will as she opened her mouth and sang along with the chorus. Again she had the urge to scream.

Especially when the figure stepped up to the door.

It was impossible to make out its features in the darkness but just as she knew the song, she also knew the figure was horribly deformed. The shadows were a blessing. If she laid eyes upon whatever infernal thing had come to her shop, she would finally have that heart attack the doctors mentioned so often.

The figure lifted what looked like a hand. It wound back and slammed against the door. The glass groaned, a small crack appearing in its center. It cut through her name and the logo and somehow that seemed symbolic.

"*Forever with you*," she sang against her will. A single tear dripped from her left eye, tickling her cheek on its way down.

The hand pushed something against the door. A flyer or pamphlet. She couldn't make out the words. It turned and walked slowly into the neighboring alley. The piece of paper slipped to the ground, landing in a puddle between the cobblestones.

Her jaw became her own again. As did her voice. She rubbed her chin with one hand and her chest with the other. She stayed like that, certain the thing would come back. When it didn't, she kneeled down, opened the door, and grabbed the fallen paper.

The water had wrinkled much of the text but she could still make out the message.

A picture of a girl, the same girl who used to frequent the shop so often, asking about spells no one should've asked about. Revenge and mind control and, her favorite, conjuring spells.

Angie Everstein. The same girl who sang "Forever with You." Her skin glistened, lined with layers of sparkles. Eyes darker than the night. Esmeralda had the feeling the black orbs would follow her if she moved. Underneath Angie was an advertisement for her homecoming concert, to be held Halloween night on Gallows Hill.

The longer she stared at the image, the more she suspected she'd begin to hear the song again.

She crumpled the flyer and tossed it. Except that didn't seem final enough. She grabbed it once more, tore it into countless sections, and hurled them outside like confetti. The breeze carried them away into the night. For a moment she felt better. But the moment passed quickly.

Because Angie was back in town.

And she might come looking for more spells.

♪

"That one's mine," Melissa Meyers said, as though it were obvious.

"But I bought it." Josh's voice was barely a whisper. He set the skull-shaped candelabra down, unable to meet his soon-to-be exwife's stare.

"What was that?"

He opened his mouth but thought better of it. It was useless to challenge her. In the eight years they'd been together, he'd never once won an argument. Even when he'd been in the right, which was most of the time.

They sat on the living room floor of the condo they'd once shared. She'd never been fond of their home. The real estate listing had called it cozy. She'd called it microscopic. Not enough room for her clothes and shoes and those adult coloring books she insisted made her feel better. A stack of them stood on the kitchen counter, unused.

In between Josh and Melissa lay the remnants of several holidays: Halloween and Christmas and Thanksgiving decorations that had gathered dust. Tensions had been running high at the Meyers residence and neither Josh nor Melissa had been in the mood to decorate.

He'd been too busy trying to support her.

She'd been too busy sleeping with any guy that gave her a cursory glance.

He shuddered at the thought. That had been the hardest part. Thinking of his wife moaning, face growing flush, pearl-white teeth nibbling her lips as some stranger—and in many cases a familiar face—fucked her brains out.

He stared at the couch, where he'd first found her cheating, and tried to stop his throat from tightening.

"Well?"

He shook his head. "Sorry, what?"

She rolled her eyes, a look he'd grown accustomed to in recent times. "Are you going to give it to me or not?"

He'd bought the candelabra just after they'd moved in. The bulbs were mostly burned out and he'd never been able to find replacements that fit correctly. He knew for a fact she hated the thing but this wasn't about claiming items she liked. This was about power.

He sighed, slid it forward. "Take it."

Another roll of the eyes. "Not if you're going to be like that."

"No, really. There're plenty of other things we can divide." He compared their piles. His was roughly one-third the size. A few cardboard cutouts of vampires and werewolves. A porcelain coffin that had more chips than he could count. Melissa's bounty trumped his own. She had the remote-controlled rat and hanging bat and motion sensor witch candy bowl.

That stuff is yours. Hell, almost everything *in this place is yours.*

But he wouldn't speak up. Nothing new there. Melissa liked to say he was born without a backbone and though the expression hurt deeper than he cared to admit, it wasn't far from the truth. He'd never stood up for himself these last eight years, some of them good, most of them bad. Why start now?

"Oh, I meant to tell you. The real estate agent is coming this afternoon." Melissa stood up. Her sweat pants clung to her rear, reminding him of the skin that lay beneath. The skin he hadn't seen in so many months, though it had been shared with others without hesitation.

"Since when?"

"Since I called her yesterday." She opened the freezer, pulled out an ice cream sandwich which she devoured in three large bites. She'd insisted on eating healthier, her way of fishing for compliments, though her dietary habits rarely rose above junk food. They both knew her body was goddess-like, that she was light-years out of his league.

Hence the affairs.

"I can't make it today," he said, standing up and putting his measly Halloween pile into a crumpled cardboard box. "You know I have work."

She shrugged, chugged a Mountain Dew. "So don't. She's just checking the place out before she takes pictures."

"Don't you think I should be here?"

"What does it matter?"

"I just want to make sure she's being fair with assessing the place. In case you forgot, I lived here too."

Instead of answering, she opened one of the coloring books and flipped through the blank, colorless pages.

He scratched his back, made certain his spine was still intact.

♪

"Sorry I'm late," Josh said a half hour later when he entered the shop. "Traffic was hell." Once October rolled around, the city became a parking lot, only there was never any parking. Tourists flocked from every which way, crossing without looking, stepping into traffic like confused deer. He ought to take his bike from now on but his mind had been pre-occupied.

Melissa on that couch, covering a scream with her hand as the guy—had it been Rick from the Haunted Stirrings walking tour or was it the guy with the flaming phantom tattoo on his neck?—thrust deep into her.

Usually when he got to work, his problems faded but today they *grew* on account of the cardboard cutout standing just to the left of the door.

A cardboard cutout in the shape of Angie Everstein.

She stared at him, eyes mischievous and innocent at once. The board matched her likeness perfectly. It captured her hour-glass shape to a T. He shook his head.

"What the hell is this?" he finally said.

Trish shrugged from behind the counter. "Don't ask me. I thought you ordered it." The way she acted, perpetually disinterested, wasn't all that different from Melissa, yet he could not deny his attraction. At least they liked the same music.

"Don't even tell me." He studied Angie's cardboard eyes. They seemed to follow him. Probably just his nerves or a defect at the printing factory.

"It was here when I got in." Trish texted on her phone, giggled softly. He'd told her before to look more alert at work but this was hardly the time. There were more pressing issues.

Like who had stocked the Angie Everstein CDs. They'd been moved out of the back room and now occupied the front display, where the new releases should've been. Black and death and thrash metal were replaced with a manufactured, formulaic pop princess. He gritted his teeth.

"Who else had a key?" he said. "Besides you. I think I gave one to Tommy and one to Jeff a few months before he left."

"I doubt Tommy or Jeff would take the time to order a wholesale amount of that shit. Or maybe I'm wrong. Not my cup of tea but the girl can belt it out. Song gets stuck in your head after a while, you know?"

He *did* know. He'd only heard a sample yesterday but if he tried hard enough he could recall the melody. Could almost hear that soft, soothing voice as if Angie was living between his eardrums.

He rubbed the crown of his nose. It had been ages since his last full night's sleep. When he closed his eyes he saw Melissa and the life he'd wanted. "I don't have time for this." He hadn't realized how loud he'd been talking until a potential customer eyed him from the corner, set down a record, and made his way outside.

"Way to go, boss," Trish said. "Look, I don't know who ordered the stuff or set it up. It wasn't me—I swear. But what do you say we put that damned cutout in the backroom and swap the new releases back in?"

He calmed some but not all the way. *That* was impossible with the synthetic version of Angie staring him down with those dark orbs that passed for eyes. "Sounds like a plan. Thanks, Trish."

"Forever with you."

He tensed, nearly shoved her away. "What'd you just say?"

She held her hands up as if she were talking a jumper down from a building. "I said, 'Don't mention it.'"

He nodded, tried to catch his breath.

From behind them, one of the Angie CDs tumbled to the floor on its own accord.

CHAPTER THREE
AND THE WEEK BEGINS

MONDAY.

Shawna Everstein's stomach knotted. Monday signaled the beginning of the school week, which in turn signaled the beginning of hell.

She woke five minutes before her alarm sounded, as if the universe were laughing from nearby. A cosmic prank.

This too shall pass. Something her father once said before he left town on a business trip that turned out to be a permanent vacation.

The knot in her stomach remained.

Some things never passed.

She showered, dressed, and put in her hearing aids. From downstairs she heard bacon sizzling. It had been dry toast and cereal since Angie had left but now that Little Miss Perfect was back, her mother needed to keep up appearances. The smell churned her stomach as she made her way downstairs.

In the kitchen, Kristen Everstein huddled over the stove, flipping strips of bacon and scrambling eggs. It was the most maternal thing she'd done in ages. It was clear which daughter she favored. Angie was the angel, Shawna the ugly twin. It was also no secret that Kristen was beaming over Angie's success. She'd declared bankruptcy twice in fifteen years, handled money as well as a pre-teen.

The Eversteins were, for lack of a better term, broke as shit.

Nearly every purchase over these last few years had been made via plastic. But now, with a celebrity in the family, things were looking up. The debt would soon vanish with the money Angie was bringing in and Shawna would fade further into the background.

"That you, dear?" Kristen said, not turning around.

"Yeah." Shawna poured herself a glass of orange juice, drank it in three long gulps.

"Sit down. Breakfast is almost ready."

"What's the occasion? We run out of Pop-Tarts?"

Kristen ignored the insult and made a plate of food. She set it down on the table and fixed a cup of coffee, adding a half dozen Splenda so it became more of a milk shake.

"Where's the girl of the hour?" Shawna took a bite of eggs. Her stomach sizzled in response. Bile climbed her throat.

"You just missed her. Left right before you came downstairs."

"Finally going back to real school?" Angie had had personal teachers since she'd entered the competition. Shawna had begged to be homeschooled each year as her deafness grew worse yet she'd been denied. Apparently all it took was winning a national talent show.

Kristen shook her head. She held her mug with two hands as if it were something delicate, an infant or kitten. "She's meeting with her manager to go over the concert."

"Concert?" A bite of bacon, met with more bile.

Kristen nodded. "Her homecoming show."

"How come I didn't hear about this?"

"The details were being sorted out. Even I didn't know. It's going to be so much fun. Televised nationally. Can you believe that? Our baby girl is going to be a star." As if Angie wasn't already topping the charts. As if she'd never been on TV.

Shawna gave up on eating. "Why does she have to stay here? I mean, she can afford any hotel in town. I bet the Westin would pay *her* to stay there."

Kristen rolled her eyes. The dream-like sheen vanished, replaced by the unfit mother once again. "She wants to spend time with us. We're a *family* in case you didn't remember. Can't you at least pretend to be happy?"

"I'd deserve an Academy Award if I did," she said under her breath.

"What did you just say?"

"I have to get going. Don't want to be late for school." She tossed her food into the garbage disposal and flipped the switch before her mother could protest.

"Make sure you're home for supper," Kristen said. "Angie will be joining us. I'm making your favorite. Pork chops and apple sauce."

Her sister's favorite, she almost corrected. Her mother's pork chops tasted like shoe leather and the applesauce, often served at room temperature, reminded her of vomit.

She grabbed her backpack, covered with heavy metal patches: Iron Maiden and Slayer and Metallica. On her way out, her mother called her name.

"Oh, and dear?"

Shawna stopped in the doorway, torn between two hells: school and home. "Yeah?"

"This is going to be good. For all of us. Angie's going to make us the family we've always wanted to be."

Shawna cringed. She thought of the dark eyes, the devilish grins, all the torment Kristen had turned her head from.

And other things she told herself were just nightmares.

♪

Someone had drawn nasty things on her locker. The artist had the penmanship of a grade schooler, letters shaky and deformed. The pictures, though—those took skill.

There was a portrait of Shawna, her figure cartoonishly plump, though it wasn't far from reality. Angie had gotten the talent *and* the looks. On the ground beneath the animated Shawna were her ears, ripped from her head. A speech bubble hung in the air, just to the right of her face, which looked very much like a pig.

Deaf and dumb and ugly as fuck.

From behind she heard laughter. At first it was muffled, the owner trying to hide their glee, but eventually they gave up. Others joined in. She could sense them pointing.

She spun around. Within the sea of onlookers, she saw Derek Sorrentino and Brandon Matheson. Their faces said it all as they admired their artwork and then jogged in the opposite direction. The closest classroom door opened.

As the crowd dissipated, Shawna noticed one member linger for just a moment.

She and Mia locked eyes and for a nanosecond, things were the way they'd been last year. They were in love and for the first time in Shawna's pathetic life, she felt like *somebody*. But then Shawna noticed Mia's new outfit, the sparkles and tight-fitting clothing in place of the ripped jeans and oversized hoodie.

A hand touched Shawna's shoulder.

She spun, expecting to see her sister's dark, peering eyes, but it was only her English teacher, Mr. Fuller. "Rough day?"

"Horrible is more like it."

"Come on," he said, waving her into his classroom and shutting the door.

Miles Fuller had transferred from Somerville High last year. His parents were from Wales and his accent was somewhere between the homeland and a Boston drawl. He got his fair share of jokes but Shawna found it endearing. She found *everything* about him endearing. Her interest lay in girls but she could not deny the way Mr. Fuller gave her stomach a pleasant flutter every time their eyes met.

"Have a seat." He leaned on his desk, removed his blazer, and set it down beside him. He dressed much more professional than his colleagues, took pride in his work. On the board behind him was a set of written notes on *Catcher in the Rye*.

"Didn't they try to ban that book?" Shawna said. She rubbed her eyes, pretending she was just tired instead of wiping away stray tears.

"Some schools did. For a while, at least. But art usually prevails. That's the way it should be. I read your poem." Miles pulled a piece of paper from a folder and studied it for a moment. "It's quite good." This said with more of a Welsh accent for emphasis. "Really good, in fact."

Her cheeks reddened. "I just kind of threw it together." A lie. She wasn't the world's greatest student, but when it came to Mr. Fuller, she couldn't help but give her all.

"You should think about submitting it somewhere. There are plenty of journals that would love this sort of thing. I can give you a list if you'd like."

She smiled. "I'd love that."

He grabbed a blank sheet of paper and wrote for a few moments. "Don't listen to them," he said without looking up. "The students, I mean. They're just being cruel for the sake of it."

"It's hard not to listen. And that's coming from an almost deaf girl."

"I'm glad you can *laugh* at cruelty. You'll go far with that attitude."

As he handed her the paper, something fell from his desk.

Shawna studied the fallen object. A flyer. Not just any advertisement but one for the homecoming show her mother had mentioned that morning. Angie, in a sexy dress, stared up at her. The event of a lifetime, the ad copy promised. She begged to differ. She'd had enough of her sister to last *several* lifetimes.

"Where'd you get that?" she said, lifting the flyer.

"Found it on my desk this morning. From the sound of it, so did every other teacher in the building. Maintenance and the cafeteria too. They're really pushing her, aren't they? At this rate, she's going to burn out."

"Good." She gritted her teeth. "I hope she burns in *hell*."

"I didn't mean to touch a nerve." He handed her the slip of paper, several poetry journals listed.

She took it without thanking him and crumpled the flyer with her other hand, tossing it into the trash bucket on her way out.

It landed crookedly, bouncing off the rim and unfolding so that Angie's eyes were exposed.

♪

Esmeralda was explaining the poster behind her counter—the pentagram of elements—to a customer when the hooded men stepped into the store.

The bells above the door were enough to make her wince. She'd been meaning to replace them but it had fallen further and further down her list of priorities.

The customer, a large man with an undersized, generic Salem shirt, eyed the three men and stopped talking mid-sentence. She could practically see the beads of sweat forming along his upper lip. Without another word, he stumbled out of the shop, tripping on the incense display on his way out.

The bells jangled once more, giving way to silence aside from Esmeralda's heavy breathing. The extra-large breakfast burrito threatened to exit the way it had entered that morning. She belched under her breath.

"What's this about?" she said when none of the men offered any explanation.

Their cloaks were long and dark, trailing onto the floor. They stood in a line, the one in the middle closest to her. Their skin seemed too smooth, without any hint of blemish or facial hair. Everything above their noses lay in shadows, hoods obscuring eyes. That felt like both a blessing and curse.

"I don't mind if you guys come in here dressed up but you can't go around scaring customers away. If you're not going to buy anything, I suggest you leave." Her voice croaked and any ounce of authority was lost.

It was nothing new to have costumed customers but normally they dressed as witches and vampires. This seemed ... different somehow.

Like they weren't wearing costumes to begin with.

She eyed the door but that fantasy was shattered when she saw a fourth robed figure outside, blocking the exit, turning away potential customers.

Potential *rescuers.*

Don't be so silly. These are just some weirdos who take Halloween a little too seriously.

She tried a different approach. "Enjoying your stay?"

Nothing.

"First time in Salem?"

Nothing.

"I love your costumes."

Nothing, aside from the closest figure stepping forward.

Salem was relatively safe, even in the city center, but she kept a pocketknife and a can of pepper spray in the top left drawer of the counter. Her hand gravitated that way.

The robed man stood inches away from her face now. He smelled both foul and sweet, fruit left to rot. Though she couldn't see his eyes, she could *feel* them.

She pulled open the drawer, grabbed the pepper spray, and pointed.

"If you're going to give me trouble, think twice." With her free hand, she grabbed her cell phone, dialed 911, and hovered her thumb over the green call button.

He lifted his gloved hands, latched onto his hood.

Esmeralda prepared for the worst. Whatever was under there, it surely wasn't human. No normal man could make her feel such fear. Her pulse grew uneven. Was that the atrial fibrillation the doctors had mentioned or was she having a full-fledged heart attack? She held her chest, held her breath.

And cocked her head when the man revealed his true form.

No fangs or scales. Instead: a plain, non-descript face. He could have been thirty or forty, nothing to distinguish him from anyone else. The man smiled, revealing normal-sized, pearly white teeth. He removed one of his gloves and offered his hand. "You must be Ms. Hopkins."

She breathed, fought waves of nausea. "Yes, that would be me."

"You own this establishment?" His voice was smooth and she couldn't decipher its accent. Wherever he was from, it wasn't Boston. "I'm sorry if we scared you. My colleagues and I are merely getting into the spirit. I'm sure you've seen scarier costumes in your time."

"Yes," she lied. "And no need to apologize. I've just been on edge is all." An understatement. She'd barely slept the night before. Not since the encounter with the figure outside and the flyer.

And now that she thought about it, hadn't that figure been wearing a robe? It had been too dark to know for sure but—

The man set down a piece of paper onto the counter. For a moment, she was certain it was another advertisement for Angie's homecoming show but as she read its contents, she realized it was much worse.

A contract of some sort.

"Ms. Everstein wishes to hold a meet and greet at your shop."

"I'm sorry?"

"She speaks highly of you. I understand she used to frequent this shop as a girl."

"A long time ago." She recalled their conversations, though she'd tried countless times to forget.

I want to learn an evocation spell.

Why's that?

Because I'm trying to evoke something.

Magic isn't anything to be taken lightly, Angie.

I'm not taking it lightly.

What are you trying to evoke?

"If you don't mind," the man said, pulling her out of the past, "I'll have you sign here and initial here."

She shook her head. "I'm afraid not. It's a busy time of year and I can't afford to hold an event like that. Maybe next time." That was it. Blame it on the season.

"The owner of the property has already given us permission. Technically, we don't need your approval."

"That's not possible."

"I can put him on the phone if you'd like. This is simply a formality. A courtesy, if you will, since Ms. Everstein is so fond of you."

She gritted her teeth. "Tell Ms. Everstein she can forget it. This is my shop and I call the shots."

He tapped the contract. "Regardless, we'll see you this weekend and we'll be in touch with further details. We hope we're able to bring in plenty of customers."

She opened her mouth but the words died in her throat as she noticed the other men. She'd all but forgotten them. They still hadn't removed their hoods and something told her that was for the best. While the man closest to her had a face, she suspected the others did not. Irrational, of course, but so was the contract on her counter.

"I didn't catch your name," she said to the leader of the group, not taking her eyes off the other two.

"No," he said, pulling his own hood back up, "you didn't."

He turned toward the door and exited. The others followed.

The bells gave one last ear-piercing jingle that reminded her of screams.

CHAPTER FOUR
BAR TALK PART I

A DRINK WAS IN ORDER.

Make that five.

The bar did laps around Josh. McMurphy's Pub was everything you'd expect: dim lighting, sticky stools, and a jukebox that hadn't been updated since Y2K. The speakers blared a dance tune from the early nineties. He couldn't remember the artist, couldn't discern the words, but anything—*anything*—was preferable to the song that had been drifting through his mind all day.

Forever with You.

He shook his head and hoped that wasn't the case.

Downing the rest of his beer, he signaled Jimmy and lifted his empty glass. One more to close out the night. Aside from the six-pack in his fridge he'd finish off when he got home. What else was there to do in a studio apartment the size of a sardine can? He felt closed in just thinking of it. It was all he could afford, recent events considered, and he couldn't find another place until the divorce was finalized and the condo was sold.

Jimmy set another Miller Lite onto the bar and closed Josh's tab without asking. The bartender wasn't the original owner but he faked an Irish accent just fine when college girls ordered from him.

The place was tucked back in an alley between a laundromat and convenience store. Even though it was October, the crowd had thinned considerably. It was the only bar without a line out front during the holiday season.

"Who died?" Jimmy said, wiping down the counter.

"Sorry?" Josh shook his head.

"You look like you just came from a funeral. Someone stop breathing on you?"

"Just my marriage."

They shared a laugh, though the moment passed quickly. Jimmy found a group of girls farther down the bar. His accent came out in record time.

The woman sitting next to Josh stood, left a two-dollar tip, and stumbled out the front doors. A cool draft blew through the bar. Josh shivered but his skin went from frigid to boiling when he spotted the man two seats down.

Don't start anything, he thought. *He's not worth it.*

He being Dan Peterson, one of the men who'd fucked Melissa. They'd gone to high school together. Not friends exactly, though they hung in the same circles. Dan worked construction for the city. His skin was covered in grime that defined the contours of his muscular arms. His hard hat lay on the counter beside two shot glasses. When Dan caught him staring, Josh was certain the guy would mock him.

But instead of a cocky grin, Dan Peterson offered a vacant stare. It was, Josh supposed, not unlike how he himself looked that very moment.

Preoccupied.

Scared as hell.

"I don't want any trouble," Dan finally said. His words slurred badly. He sounded as drunk as Josh felt. "I just want to finish my drinks and forget about my day. That okay with you?"

Josh's anger subsided. "Yeah. Fine by me."

After a few awkward moments, Dan slid over one seat and leaned in close. "Look, I know you're not my biggest fan but I need to ask you something. You didn't order it, did you?"

"Order what?" He sipped his beer, throat suddenly dry.

"That cardboard cutout. Not exactly aimed at your target audience. Which got me thinking: I bet it just showed up on your doorstep."

Josh wiped his mouth and set the glass back down. "Not my doorstep. That thing was *inside my store*. None of my employees know where it came from. Not to mention they didn't see anyone bring it in."

Dan ran a hand through his oily hair. For a moment he was no longer the bully that screwed Melissa. For a moment he was human again. "Had a feeling."

"What's that supposed to mean?"

Dan looked around as if they were being watched. "Between you and me, there's something going on in this city. Something big. Something *wrong*."

Josh wanted to say Dan was being foolish, that the cutout was an elaborate prank. Instead he nodded. Because Dan was right. There *was* something wrong.

"They're building a stage," Dan said before downing the first of two shots.

"Who is?"

"Technically I am. The city, I mean. But the city isn't who's behind it. The city just okayed it. *They're* behind it."

"I'm not sure I follow." He took another sip. Not because he wanted to get any drunker but because his hands fidgeted.

Dan nodded as if Josh was on the same page. "It's being built in the woods up on Gallows Hill. Not like the ones they put up for the bands downtown on Halloween night. Those things only take a few hours. Can barely fit four guys on them. This one's the real deal. City cut down a shit ton of trees to make way for it. Can't be legal. That place is conservation land. I asked around but no one will give me a straight answer."

He's nuts, Josh thought. Except he knew that wasn't the truth. The guy had a buzz going but his words made sense even if Josh didn't grasp their meaning. "What's the stage for?"

Dan downed shot number two. "What do you think?"

Josh shook his head. "I hope you're not talking about—"

Dan cut him off, held a finger up to his mouth like they'd been bugged. "Damn straight. She's coming home, Josh. Coming back to Salem. Hell, from what I've heard, she's already here."

Josh shrugged, pretended his balls weren't shriveling that very moment. "So what? Girl wins a reality show, blows up overnight, and has a homecoming concert. What's so strange about that?"

"It's not a concert," Dan said, his words barely audible over the jukebox.

"What?"

"I said it's not a concert. There's something else going on. Something that isn't *normal*. And it's happening on Halloween night. Don't they say that's when the barrier is at its thinnest or some shit?"

"What barrier?"

He slammed a twenty-dollar bill onto the bar and stood up too quickly, grabbing onto the sticky wood to regain his balance. "The barrier between the living and the dead. Listen, if I were you, I'd make myself scarce that night."

"I'd have to be crazy. The shop is already failing. I'll make a third of my year's earnings that evening. I can't just skip town if that's what you're saying."

"That's exactly what I'm saying. And what I'm *doing*. I'll finish building the damn thing. Ain't much choice in that department. I signed a contract and from what I heard they don't like it when you violate the terms."

"The city, you mean?"

He shook his head, blood-shot eyes framed by raccoon lids. "No, the city's not in charge. They just gave the go-ahead."

"Then who *is* in charge?"

"I gotta go. Long day tomorrow. That girl and her managers or agents or whoever the hell they are—they're trouble. Remember what I said. Think about taking a vacation."

Dan left without another word. More cool air infiltrated the bar before the door slammed shut.

Josh tried to make sense of the conversation but found he was too drunk and too exhausted to come up with any answers.

But he did manage to form one coherent thought that stuck with him.

Like him or not, Dan Peterson and Josh Meyers actually agreed on something.

Angie Everstein was bad news.

From the corner, the jukebox changed tunes. For a moment, he thought it was *the song*. He could practically hear it pulsing within his ears. But it turned out to be some hip-hop tune about drinking champagne.

He left in a hurry, thought about walking instead of driving, on account of his buzz that was more of a hangover in progress.

But the endless alleyways and dark corners swam with movement. He swore the shadows breathed and the fog chattered.

He waved down the nearest taxi and dove in before it came to a full stop.

CHAPTER FIVE
CHICKEN TETRAZZINI AND BOTTOMLESS PITS

"SHAWNA, SUPPER'S READY."

She winced, huddled in her room. Lights off. Computer glare washing her face in strange shades of blue. She'd been stalking Mia's Facebook for nearly an hour. A pile of geometry homework stood on her bedside table, all of it unfinished.

Whenever Shawna looked through Mia's photos, she saw fewer images of herself. Even though they'd broken up only months ago, it felt more like years, another life altogether. She could see the evolution of Mia's new personality, which in turn showed the de-evolution of their relationship.

Not for the first time, she wondered what had caused such a drastic change. And so quickly, nonetheless. The more she thought about it, the more unnatural it felt. Like there was something else at play. Something she couldn't quite fathom.

"Shawna? Come eat. It'll get cold."

Her mother, signaling the only thing worse than the morning bell. Dinnertime.

They hadn't eaten together this much as a family since Angie had been accepted to *Harmony Club*. Since then, on the rare occasion her sister had been home in between episodes and concert dates, they'd gone *out* to eat. Angie had treated them to four-star restaurants in Boston, where the prices were astronomical and the portions miniscule. While Angie had been on the road, dinner was served with remaining daughter and mother eating separately. Kristen on the couch, watching her soaps, and Shawna alone in her room.

"Shawna, come on, will you?"

Should she pretend? Blame it on her hearing aids? It wasn't the first time she'd taken advantage of her condition. Fate had played her a shitty hand and she didn't feel the least bit guilty flipping it off now and then.

A knock at her door.

Soft, barely touching the wood, but it sent every inch of Shawna's skin into a fit. She didn't need to hear the voice to know who stood on the other side.

"Hey, Sis. You want to eat or what?" Angie said. "Mom's not gonna wait all night. You know how she gets."

Shawna nodded without answering, forgetting for a moment that Angie couldn't see her. It certainly *felt* like she could. Shawna flipped on the light. She closed her laptop, set it on her desk, studied her face in the mirror and pretended to fix her hair. These were normal actions, actions people took when they weren't scared out of their mind. She almost fooled herself.

"Be right down."

"See you soon. Can't wait to catch up."

She listened as Angie stepped soundlessly down the hall and down the steps. She'd always been great at sneaking out in the middle of the night. Her footfalls were so quiet it was uncanny.

That's because she's not human. Not in the traditional sense, at least.

She shivered, the creeping things from her past crawling back into her memories. If she allowed them to invade, the fear would be too much. She'd have a panic attack and then her mother and sister would be up here, treating her like someone who needed a couple rounds of shock therapy.

She closed her eyes, steadied her breathing, and, most importantly, pushed away the thoughts. At least for the moment.

Then she opened her door and made her way to the kitchen, telling herself it would just be a normal dinner. There was nothing sinister about chicken tetrazzini.

But as she stepped through the doorway and saw the way Angie glared at her—dark eyes hiding awful secrets—the smell of cream and meat made her gag.

"Have a seat," her mother said, pulling out the closest chair. Just like that morning, Kristen Everstein was in a chipper mood. How could she *not* be? Her famous daughter was rolling in enough dough to reverse all the debt she'd accrued. Bye-bye, maxed-out credit cards. Hello, new lavish lifestyle.

Shawna wondered if they'd get a new house, some mansion far from Salem. Or maybe they'd downsize so Kristen could spend more money on purses and jewelry.

Her mother set down a plate of tetrazzini a little too hard. The table shook along with Shawna's nerves. She did not look across the table, for that would mean looking into her sister's eyes. If she kept her mind occupied, stared at the mountain of white mush on the plate before her, she just might keep from choking on nothing.

"Shawna, dear," her mother said, "would you mind passing me the salt?" As if her meal didn't already have a day's worth of sodium. Shawna reached across the table for the shaker and—

And almost gasped when her hand touched not cool glass but cool *flesh*. Her sister's fingers. Angie had reached at the same time, perhaps trying to outdo Shawna, like she hadn't already won that battle a thousand times over. Their hands stayed like that for a long time, Shawna's insides recoiling in response.

Angie smiled. It was the first time Shawna had seen her this close since her triumphant return.

"I got it," Angie handed it to Kristen, who looked so proud.

"How is it?" their mother said.

"I'm not hungry." Shawna drank from her glass and cringed when she realized it was milk. It tasted warm. "Can I be excused?"

Kristen put a hand onto Shawna's forehead. "Are you coming down with something?" As if she cared.

Shawna shrugged. "Maybe."

Kristen shook her head. "Well, you best eat up. It's still early in the semester and you can't afford to miss any days."

"I'm a senior. They don't care."

"*I* care."

"Since when?"

She could sense the fight looming but Angie's voice, so soft and soothing when she wanted it to be, eased the tension. "She's probably just exhausted. Senior year is tough on all of us." Another staged smile.

All of us? You got your pick of boys and friends all because of those tits and that face and that fucking voice of yours.

Angie continued. "Anyway, I wanted to talk to you about the

homecoming show, since it's almost Halloween."

"What about it?" Shawna forced herself to eat a heaping spoonful of creamed chicken, not breathing through her nose until she'd swallowed the salty mess.

"I want to make sure you have a good spot. Things are going to be . . . crazy that night." Shawna sensed there was more to her words than she was letting on. "It's general admission but there's a spot roped off for VIPs. And you, Sis, are the biggest VIP of them all. Aside from Mom, of course."

Kristen smiled and winked.

"Do I have to go?" Shawna said.

"Of course you have to go," Kristen said. "Your sister needs our support. She's been working her butt off for all this success. Would it kill you to watch her sing for one night?"

She gulped. *It just might.*

"It's okay, Mom." Angie fake-pouted. "I get it. She's embarrassed. It must be tough for her, with school and all. I bet she's getting a lot of unwanted attention. Where's Mia, by the way? Haven't seen her around."

Shawna's blood boiled. Her eyes grew misty.

I will not cry. I will not cry.

"She's been busy." Shawna wasn't sure why she lied. Maybe because saying the truth aloud—that her best friend and ex-lover had exited her life—was too painful. Maybe if she internalized it for all eternity, she could delay the inevitable nervous breakdown coming her way.

"I hope she can come too," Angie said. "It's going to be such a special night."

Shawna stood. "I have homework to do."

"Sit back down," Kristen said, mouth half full of her soggy concoction.

"Good night." Shawna stormed out of the kitchen but froze for a moment in the doorway.

"*Forever with You.*"

Her joints froze in place. She'd done her best to avoid hearing that damn song, though it was impossible. It played everywhere you went, crept into your mind when you least expected. "What?" She didn't dare look back.

"That's what I'm opening with that night. 'Forever with You'. Did I ever tell you what the song's about? It's about you, Sis. It's always been about you."

Shawna took the steps two at a time and made it to the bathroom just in time to lose what little she'd eaten.

♪

Dan Peterson's phone rang.

He gasped, waking suddenly from a horrid dream. He couldn't remember the details but he knew he'd been falling. Some bottomless pit. He heard screams all around him. The hole was scorching and his skin melted quickly, like candle wax, revealing bones within.

He wiped away cool sweat and looked at the clock on his bedside table.

One-fifteen in the morning.

Who the hell was calling so early?

His cell was within reaching distance but for some odd reason the thought of touching it made him feel sickly. His bowels felt ready to give way.

The phone kept ringing, the vibrations almost sending it over the table's edge. Chalking his fear up to post-nightmare blues and a whopper of a hangover, he grabbed the cell and answered the call.

And gasped at the voice on the other end.

"You're wanted at the job site."

Dan did not speak for a long time. Not because he was exhausted but because he'd developed sudden onset lockjaw.

"Mr. Peterson, did you hear me? Please come to Gallows Hill."

He nodded, forgetting the man wasn't in the room with him and feeling blessed that wasn't the case. He imagined the hooded figure stepping through his door, sitting on the edge of his bed, and removing the fabric that hid his face.

Or maybe he was in the closet this very moment. The darkness in his room was obscene. He could barely see past the table, let alone beneath the closet door. Was that cloth peeking out from underneath the extra space?

Dan rubbed his bloodshot eyes. "This better be urgent." He tried to sound brave instead of scared shitless. *Tried* being the key word. "Is everything okay?"

"Get here as quickly as you can. We've run into some . . . complications."

"What kind of complications? I'm not due on the site for another three hours. You've already got us working twelve-hour days. Can't this wait until later?"

The line went dead.

He got out of bed, took a quick piss, a quick shower, and a hundred other quick activities to delay arriving before the sun was up.

When the coffee finished brewing, he poured it into his oversized thermos. His ex-wife Sheila had bought the thing. Kept liquid hot for up to twenty hours. She would recite that fact in her radio voice and they'd both giggle. It was a longstanding joke until she left his ass. She'd been smart to do so. He was angry when drunk and even angrier when sober.

Separation made him think of Josh Meyers. Poor bastard. His wife was becoming the town whore and he'd sat back and let it happen. Surely the guy had known of Melissa's lovers on the side all along. Even now Dan couldn't bring himself to feel bad about the whole thing. There was something about Josh, some woe-is-me air, that begged for a punch in the face. He'd always been that way and Dan couldn't see him changing anytime soon. At least the two were finally getting divorced.

He thought about his time with Melissa Meyers, how she'd moved her hips quicker than he'd thought possible, and his cock stiffened to half-mast before he recalled where he was heading. He grew limp again within a half second.

He grabbed his keys and stepped outside, got into his truck, backed out of the driveway. Stalled for a moment, trying to remember if he'd left any lights on. Every window was dark. Maybe the faucet then. Had he locked the doors? Sometimes they stuck.

Stop being such a pussy and get to work.

Easier said than done when you took into account where he was headed.

It only took fifteen minutes, door to stage, but he avoided short cuts at all costs. The moon was hidden behind clouds, the landscape so dark it was hard to imagine daylight ever coming to Salem. The wind picked up, not strong enough to sway his truck but enough to form cyclones of dead leaves.

He turned up the hill eighteen minutes later and parked at the foot of the park. The first thing he noticed was the empty lot. No other cars for as far as he could see.

Had it gotten colder? He flipped up his collar, shivered against the wind. Though he couldn't see anyone, he heard something. Voices. Hypnotizing, joining like a chorus before splitting up again, chant-like.

In the distance, behind the trees, he sensed movement. Shapes danced about. The spotlights the crew had set up were ablaze. It was blinding, like staring into the sun, and when his eyes adjusted he nearly dropped his coffee.

He didn't see a single crewmember. Tom and Gabe were usually the first ones on the site, followed by Bart and Andrew, but none of them were present. Not unless they had taken to wearing robes.

When he'd first been assigned the job, he knew something wasn't right. They were breaking a thousand different zoning laws. Gallows Hill was part of the historic district after all, and making any alterations required countless legal loopholes. Gary Williams, the city planner, hadn't offered any explanation.

"How are they allowing this?" Dan had said. "Those trees have stood since before this town was founded."

"I understand how strange this all seems. I thought so at first too. But you'll understand come Halloween. When the people gather and Angie sings, you'll understand."

"What the hell is that supposed to mean?"

No answer. Just the back of Gary's head as he stared at something out the window of his office toward the cobblestoned street. He began to hum a melody. Dan's skin prickled when he placed the tune.

He felt that same fear now, staring at the stage he'd helped build.

The robed figures up ahead hummed the song in unison.

He wasn't sure who they were. Only that they were in charge of the construction, had somehow convinced the city it was a good idea. They visited often, checking to make sure everything was going according to plan. They never spoke for long and their faces were usually obscured by their hoods. He'd never seen this many in one place.

They danced and frolicked as they sang. Some of them grunted and growled, the sounds distinctly animal-like. He got the sense, without fully understanding, that they were performing a ritual of some sort. It seemed silly yet it fit perfectly.

He backed away. It didn't matter that he'd been called in. The foreman could go fuck himself if he thought Dan was going to stick around for whatever this was. The prick could keep his money so long as Dan didn't have to spend another day near that monstrosity.

For it seemed more like a living, breathing *thing* now. Not a stage but an *entity*. He didn't like where his thoughts were headed. Didn't like the way his gut screamed for him to get the hell out of there. He was inclined to agree.

Except when he turned around, there was a shadow blocking the way.

One of the robed figures had broken away from the group.

Or perhaps they'd been there the entire time. Watching. Waiting. Humming.

"What took so long?" The voice was calm and calculated yet there was anger beneath its words.

"I came as soon as I could," he lied.

"I find that hard to believe."

Behind the figure, Dan's truck called to him, a beacon of hope in a world of darkness. "You want to tell me what this is all about?"

The figure stepped forward. Its face was hidden.

It? When had it become *it?*

"May I remind you of the non-disclosure clause you signed when agreeing to this project?"

He nodded. "Sure. I remember it. But don't you think everyone within walking distance knows about this thing?"

The hood rustled. Whoever (*what*ever) lay beneath nodded. "Yes, of course. We are not concerned with the stage itself. This is a matter of the plans *behind* the stage."

"I haven't said anything about that to anyone."

"Are you certain of that?" Another step closer.

He opened his mouth to respond but shut it quickly. He'd been right to keep his voice down at the bar earlier, during his conversation with Josh, but he apparently hadn't been discreet enough. They'd heard him somehow. No surprise there. They heard everything. "You were listening in on me."

Another rustle. Another nod.

"That's illegal."

"It's all quite legal. You'd know that if you read the contract. Something tells me you also skipped the section about punishment."

He swallowed. "I think I skimmed that part."

"We are allowed to take action as we see fit for any leaks regarding this project."

"But I barely said anything."

Another step. Face to face now, though the darkness beneath the hood was still absolute. "You implied something other than a concert, did you not?" He didn't give Dan the chance to respond. "This is your first and last warning, Mr. Peterson."

Dan prepared a response, his last bit of bravery. He'd worked construction since he was nineteen, was an asset to the city. If need be, he'd go above all of their robed heads. But his speech never made it out.

The figure pulled down its hood and offered him a clear view of the face that lay beneath. Although *face* was a strong word. There was a nose and a mouth and there were eyes—piercing green eyes like toxic waste in contaminated rivers—but it wasn't like any face he'd seen. Not in his waking life, at least. It looked better fit for the endless pit from his nightmare.

He blinked and the creature was just a middle-aged man with deep wrinkles.

"Do we have an understanding, Mr. Peterson?"

He nodded, pissed his pants, and ran to his truck when the figure stepped aside.

He did not bother slowing for the stop sign at the bottom of Gallows Hill, nor at the one on Washington. Did not stop until he was back home and every single light was turned on.

CHAPTER SIX
GOING VIRAL

ESMERALDA RENTED HER SHOP FROM a man named Arnold Goldman. He was short, ancient, and reminded her of the grandfather she'd never had. Both of hers had died years before she was born. Heart attack on her mother's side, diabetes on her father's.

And now you're heading down both roads, she thought as she sipped a large iced coffee (extra cream, extra sugar) and finished her third breakfast burrito.

She wasn't parked outside Arnold's home to reminisce about family members. She was here to find out what the hell was going on. Though she didn't own the property, she operated her business honestly and wasn't about to bend over while that pop princess signed autographs for her mindless followers.

She's not just a pop princess.

She's pure evil.

Esmeralda turned up the heat and turned down the volume of her radio, an ad for a local no-kill shelter urging her to adopt a kitten today. She couldn't risk hearing a certain song by a certain someone that always seemed to play when she least expected it.

When the lyrics started to creep into her head, she focused her attention on the fourth and final burrito. The cheese had hardened and the bacon was slimy but it calmed her some. Her car was a disaster zone. Discarded soda bottles and crumpled fast food wrappers lined every surface. These were the signs of her declining health. At home, in her refrigerator, was a shelf dedicated to fruits and vegetables. All of them had rotted. She'd bought them weeks ago, during her newest I'm-going-to-lose-weight period, which had lasted precisely one night, when she'd eaten low fat macaroni and cheese to which she'd added a stick of butter for good measure. She was aware of her habits, aware that she was slowly killing herself, but she was also aware that eating made her feel good. McDonald's was her safe zone, Burger King her therapist's office. Everyone had their vice. Eating soothed her worries.

And right now she had worries aplenty.

She stepped outside and made her way up Arnold's driveway. She'd called several times earlier and was met with a prehistoric answering machine until Arnold finally answered, heard her voice, and hung up immediately.

She knocked on the door loud enough to wake the neighbors. From behind the curtain she could see faint light and movement. Arnold was home and she wasn't leaving until he gave her an explanation. Finally, after another round of knocking, the knob turned and the door opened.

The man who stood before her looked less like a grandfather and more like a corpse. Arnold Goldman had seen better days. His eyes were dark circles and it was evident he hadn't slept in a long time. His dentures were as uneven as his glasses. "Esmeralda. I didn't expect to see you here."

"I called you five times."

"I've been busy."

She covered a belch with her hand, blew the breakfast fumes out through her nose. "We need to talk."

"Can't it wait?"

"I'm afraid it can't. It's about the shop."

"What about it?" He tried to close the door but she placed her foot in the way.

"What *about* it? You let Angie set up a signing without so much as *asking* me. I ought to tear you a new one. In fact, I'm not sure that's even legal. I should get a lawyer."

He shook his head, sighed. "It won't matter."

"Oh, it'll matter when I sue your ass."

"No, I mean even if you *win*, it won't matter. In the end, none of this will matter."

She raised an eyebrow. The longer she looked at Arnold, the more she suspected he wasn't just exhausted. Perhaps the man had finally lost his mind, old age sabotaging his brain cells. "You want to tell me what you're talking about?"

He stuck his head from the crack in the door, looked around the neighborhood as if they were being watched. Come to think of it, that's exactly how it *felt*. Esmeralda sensed someone nearby, unseen eyes peering at the two of them in the early morning. Suddenly the world was too quiet. She coughed. Not to clear her throat but to break the silence.

"They didn't give me any choice," he said.

"Who didn't?"

"*Them*. Her managers. They kept calling and I kept ignoring but they're persistent, those bastards. They started following me, *taunting* me. Threatening me."

"Jesus, Arnold. *Threatening* you?"

He nodded. "And my family."

She grabbed his arm, could feel the brittle bones beneath his sleeve. "Come on. We're going to the police station. You don't have to stand for this. I'm sorry if I was a bitch. I had no idea."

He batted her away, fell onto his backside. He winced in pain, sucked air through his teeth. "Like I said. It won't matter in the end."

"The end? What *end*?"

He managed to pull himself up, declining her help. "Whatever you do, don't resist them. Maybe they'll leave you out of this." He laughed, though it was the least funny gesture she'd ever seen. "If that's even possible. Once that thing's built . . ."

"You mean the stage? The one up on Gallows Hill?" She wasn't sure why her mind automatically traveled in that direction but once it set sail, she couldn't reverse its path. She'd taken a drive up the hill just to confirm it was there. Every inch of her skin had buzzed when it came into view. Now it did so again.

"Just let them have the signing and stay out of their way. And please, whatever you do, don't tell them you came here. I'm begging you. My daughters . . ." His bottom lip trembled and a single tear made its way out of his left eye before he slammed the door in her face.

"Good morning to you too," she said, fixing her dress and walking back to the car.

Before sliding into the driver's seat she flipped Arnold's house off, hoping it would make her feel powerful, as if she had some semblance of control over the situation. If anything, she felt more exposed, more attractive to the hidden eyes she was certain lay nearby.

Back inside the car, she locked the doors once, twice, three times before driving away from the curb too fast. On the passenger seat lay a forgotten hash brown. Though the smell churned her stomach, she ate it in two large bites.

Her worries remained.

♪

Sitting in homeroom, minding her business as usual, Shawna heard Derek Sorrentino snicker. He whispered something and his little fan club giggled in response. It was no secret that Derek's father liked to drink and *loved* to smack his boy. Shawna often wondered if that was the source of his tormenting. Didn't they say all bullies had some unresolved issue causing their behavior?

Or maybe he was just an asshole.

Mr. Fuller looked up from his desk, eyes narrow, went back to grading papers when the snickering stopped.

She considered removing her hearing aids, basking in the silence, when there came a tap on her shoulder.

"Check this out," Derek said.

She tried to ignore him, hands caught halfway between her desk and her ears.

Before she could make a move, someone set a phone onto her desk. There was an image on the screen. A naked girl. Eighteen or nineteen, she wore only a pair of barely-there panties. Her breasts were perky and even, nothing like her own. Despite her annoyance, the picture *excited* her. Skin pleasantly tingled in response, the way it used to when Mia would send her pictures, but the moment passed quickly. She recognized the girl's face.

It was Angie.

Derek and his friend laughed in response. "That's right," he said. "Everyone's seen it. You're never going to live this one down. You thought you had it bad before?" He grinned, yellow teeth churning her stomach. "You ain't seen nothing."

She fought back hysteria. Her eyes burned with the threat of tears.

How could her sister do this? She'd ruined Shawna's life a thousand times over. First, the talent and the spotlight and the fame, but now *this*. Sometimes, Shawna daydreamed Angie turned out to be a one-hit wonder, her number one single fading into obscurity. Her albums would collect dust in bargain bins. But thus far, the opposite was proving to be true. And with the spotlight shining even brighter on her, Shawna, too, received more attention. Only not the same kind.

And you had to go and take a picture of yourself topless.

Who had it been intended for? She had no boyfriend as far as Shawna knew. Had she done it on purpose? Had she giggled while snapping the photo, thinking how much worse her twin sister's life would be once the image went viral?

She looked around the classroom. Though there were a few outliers pretending not to overhear, it felt like every set of eyes bored into her. Every index finger pointed. Every tongue stuck out.

"When's the sex tape come out?" Derek said, taking back his cell. "She'd look good with a pearl necklace."

More laughs. More taunts. More insults.

"That's enough." Mr. Fuller stepped into the crowd, slammed his fist onto Derek's desk. Derek finally stopped laughing, the rest of the class following suit.

"Hey," Derek said, "you can't do that."

Mr. Fuller brought his hand down a second time. "I beg to differ. If there's one thing I won't tolerate, it's bullying. So do me a favor— do us *all* a favor—and cut the shit. Leave Ms. Everstein and her sister alone or you won't be able to count the number of detentions on both hands. Does that sound like a plan, Mr. Matheson?"

Derek nodded slowly. He didn't look defeated exactly, though his trademark grin had faded to something like a half-frown. She'd take it.

The bell rang. The class grabbed their bags and books and hurried into the hall, staring at Shawna as they went. Derek was the last to leave. He said something under his breath, some threat or warning. The only words she made out were *fuck* and *cunt*. How charming.

"I've never heard you swear before," Shawna said when she and Mr. Fuller were alone.

"That won't be the last time." He fixed his hair, straightened his collar. "Not if this shit keeps up." He stopped pacing. "Sorry."

"No need to apologize. But what shit do you mean? The bullying? Thank you, by the way."

"No swearing. Do as I say and all that." He forced a smile. "It's not just the bullying. And it's not just the kids. The whole school has been acting strangely. The whole town, for that matter."

"Strangely how?"

"They seem to have forgotten about things like manners and morals and everything else that makes them civilized human beings. It's like they're . . . like they're—"

"Changing," Shawna said, not quite knowing what it meant but certain just the same.

He nodded, eyes wide like he'd just received terrible news. "Exactly. I know it sounds crazy but this all started when . . . never mind." He waved away the rest of his sentence, though she knew exactly where his thoughts were headed.

Angie. It all started with Angie.

She stood up too quickly, the room spinning. "I have to go."

He said something else but it was obscured by the second bell.

♪

Shawna stepped through her front door and slammed it shut. There were voices in the kitchen. Her mother was talking to someone. She faked a laugh, her signature move whenever a stranger was in her presence.

Shawna stormed into the kitchen, ready to tell her mother she'd had enough. Angie could not stay under the same roof. Not after what she'd done. The semester was still in its infancy and the school year was bound to get worse now. She imagined the image of Angie floating around the Internet, downloaded countless times. Someone was probably jerking off to it this very moment.

And the drawings—oh, the drawings. They'd be on her locker every day. Cartoonish tits, nipples like googly eyes, and more stick figure drawings of the ugly Everstein sister.

"You'll never guess what your daughter did." She stopped short when she saw the visitor. A woman with a clipboard stood by the table, sipping what appeared to be a Frappucino through a straw. Behind her stood two men, one holding a camera, the other a boom mic. "What the hell?"

The woman groaned, signaled to the men. "Cut." She set the clipboard on the table.

Kristen apologized on behalf of her daughter. "Shawna, sweetie, I think you just ruined the take."

Sweetie? It sounded almost convincing. Her mother should've taken up acting.

The woman held out her hand and Shawna shook it. Her skin felt cold and rough, almost reptilian. "I've heard a lot about you. Your mother is proud." She spoke too loudly. Whoever she was, she must've been briefed on Shawna's hearing problem, though not properly. "We're filming a documentary on behalf of your sister. For her homecoming. To show her family and home life."

Shawna let go of the sandpaper hand, turned toward her mother. "When were you going to tell me about this?"

"I could've sworn I did, honey." Another fake smile.

Shawna shook her head. "No, you didn't. Just like you didn't tell me she was coming home so soon."

"The date was pushed up," the woman said. "We wanted to hold the concert in time for Halloween. It seemed fitting, considering your sister's hometown."

"I'm sorry, who are you?" Shawna studied the woman's eyes and wished she hadn't. There was something distinctly wrong with them. The irises were shaped incorrectly, more octagonal than circular, and the pupils were far too large. They reminded her of Angie's eyes.

"My name is Glenda. I'm Angie's manager." She pointed to the two men behind her. "This is Tim, our camera man, and William, our audio engineer." The men grunted in unison. Glenda looked at her watch, an expensive model that likely had Kristen salivating. "We're almost done with your mother's interview and then we can get started on yours."

Shawna shook her head, stepped back. "No way."

"Dear," Kristen said through gritted teeth, the concerned mother veneer beginning to crack. "These people are guests in our home."

"Our home? This place hasn't felt like our home since Dad got smart and left."

Kristen apologized for the second time, though Glenda did not seem fazed. Her eyes stared, unblinking. "Not a problem, Ms. Everstein. We can come back later."

"That won't be necessary. I'm sure she'd love to be interviewed. She's just tired is all." She turned her head. "Isn't that right, Shawna?"

"Yeah, I'm tired. Tired of you and tired of Angie. Do you know what your little angel did, Mom? Your daughter's tits are all over the Internet."

"That was unfortunate," Glenda said. "But these things happen to most artists her age. It will pass in time. Besides, you know the old saying about publicity."

"She's right," Kristen said. "It's really not a big deal." She pulled out a chair. "Now sit and let them ask you a few questions, okay?"

Shawna's mouth hung open. "Not a big deal? I don't know why

you bothered having kids. You don't have a motherly bone in your body."

Glenda and Kristen exchanged a few words, discussed whether or not they ought to reschedule the interview. Neither of them consulted Shawna. Neither of them seemed aware of how fucked this all was.

That's because they're all in on it.

Her heart stopped at the thought.

Mr. Fuller had been right. There was something strange going on in Salem, something that kept pointing back to the same source.

She left the kitchen. Her mother called her name but she ignored her. On her way out something caught her eye. A pile of clothes lay on the living room couch. At first she thought they were sweatshirts but the fabric seemed different somehow. Unnatural. She picked up the closest and studied it. It was not a hoodie, though it did have a hood. The material was worn by time. Heavy and rough, not unlike Glenda's hands.

Robes. There were three robes and three strangers in her home.

Had the crew showed up dressed in these? It was broad daylight. The temperature, though chilly, did not call for such garb. The clothing seemed better fit for trick-or-treating.

"Beautiful, aren't they?"

Shawna nearly screamed at Glenda's voice. She did not dare to turn around, lest she catch another glimpse of her eyes. "I could give you one if you'd like."

She dropped the robe and it fluttered to the floor, landing in front of her feet.

"Are you sure you don't want to join us for an interview?" Shawna sensed the woman moving closer. Her feet clattered along the hardwood, sounding more like hooves than shoes.

"Positive." Shawna stepped toward the front door, her only escape route.

"That's a shame. We'll get you to join in the fun eventually. If you haven't noticed, your sister is quite persistent. Angie doesn't take no for an answer."

Shawna left without another word. She took slow, deliberate steps down the drive, showing that she wasn't afraid.

But at the corner of her street, when she was no longer visible from the living room windows, she broke into a run.

CHAPTER SEVEN
AN AUTOGRAPH, A KIDNAPPING

THERE WAS A CROWD GATHERED on Derby Street and, for a moment, Josh thought they were lined up to enter his store. Had there been a sale he'd forgotten about? Not out of the question, considering how exhausted he was, but these didn't look like his normal clientele. Missing were the leather jackets, the band logo patches, the ripped jeans. Instead there were jeggings, spandex, and worst of all, what he referred to as the herpes of the fashion world: glitter. The tiny dots sparkled in the sunlight, almost blinding.

"Not for us, boss."

Josh nearly screamed at Trish's voice. He held his chest. "Jesus, you scared me."

"What's the matter? Up too late?" She smirked as she took a drag off her cigarette.

"Something like that." He thought of his conversation with Dan and tried not to shiver. "I thought we talked about you not smoking out here. Pushes customers away."

She rolled her eyes. "Because crust punks are so squeaky clean. And besides," she pointed toward the mass gathering, "we don't *have* any customers to push away."

"No sales today?"

"Not a one. These glitter critters are scaring them off."

"Glitter . . ."

"Critters. That's what they call her fans."

"Whose fans?"

"Angie Everstein. Who else?" The tip of her cigarette fell to the cobblestone, the ash taken away by the breeze. It landed in a teenage girl's hair, though she didn't seem to notice. She was staring toward the front of the line, complaining about how long she'd been waiting.

Josh's throat constricted. "You mean she's nearby?"

"Over in the magic shop."

"Esmeralda's? No way in hell would she agree to something like that."

Trish shrugged. "I don't know what to tell you. All I know is what I heard. And what I heard is our little pop princess is signing autographs by the potions aisle." Josh admired how she kept her cool. Not for the first time he wished she looked at him the way she looked at some of their customers—when they *had* customers. She liked her men rough around the edges. While Josh might've been a metal head himself, he was, in every sense of the word, a glorified nerd. He had an encyclopedic knowledge of his favorite bands, could recite all of their lyrics and album catalogues in chronological order. But despite that, he wasn't her type. He ought to give up any thought of them ever being anything other than boss and employee.

Assuming the shop didn't close its doors before year's end.

"More of them," Trish said.

Josh shook his head, rubbed his eyes. "What?"

"I said there are more of them. The CDs, I mean. Even got a shipment of vinyl."

"Tell me you're joking."

"Do I look like I'm joking?" She did not smile. She never smiled. But the longer he stared at her features, the more he began to suspect she wasn't as relaxed as she let on. He wasn't sure what to make of the revelation but it was there nonetheless. Her hands fidgeted, nearly dropping the cigarette, and her feet tapped.

Almost as if she was anxious to go somewhere.

Anxious to step in line.

He pushed the thought aside. Trish? Go meet the queen of everything she hated most? Fat chance of that.

"Watch the store," he said. "I'm going to talk to Esmeralda."

"Gonna grab yourself an autograph?" Did she sound jealous?

"No, I'm going to see if we can get the line away from our front door."

The crowd shouted with excitement, singing a cappella versions of Angie's songs that made Josh's scalp tingle. From his backpack he retrieved his headphones. The lyrics vanished as he turned on his iPod. "Forever with You" was replaced by Helmet.

Now that he could think clearly, he studied the line more closely. At first he'd only noticed the teenage girls. The closer he got, the more out of place some of the attendees became. A small group of bikers smiled as if riding through Laconia. Their leather jackets displayed skulls and American eagles, yet they held in their hands posters and CDs of a teenage pop star. Josh was all for listening to whatever you wanted. Hell, he'd been criticized over his musical tastes (mostly by Melissa) for years, but the bikers seemed . . . wrong somehow.

In front of them stood two postal workers, older men with graying hair and deep wrinkles. Then there were waste removal workers, what looked like surgeons, and perhaps the strangest of all: a police officer. Josh thought the man was working security but as the line inched forward and the officer stepped up, it was clear he was just a fan.

Josh followed the line around the corner and stopped suddenly in front of Esmeralda's Ye Olde Magic Shoppe.

Two robed figures stood on either side of the front door. The sight should not have bothered him. This was Salem after all. And it was Halloween season. There were costumed street performers everywhere you went. But these two didn't seem like performers. They seemed as though they took their jobs quite seriously.

The figure on the right held up a hand, hidden beneath fabric. "Back of the line."

"I just need to talk to Esmeralda. We're old friends." Not exactly true. The two knew each other from working on the same block. They occasionally talked business, she asking him why he'd thought a metal music store would work, and he asking her how she managed to stay in business for so long.

The robed figure studied him for a long time, facial features mostly obscured, before allowing Josh to pass.

The closest members of the line, two middle-aged women with perms gone bad, protested. "Get back here," they said in unison. "Who the fuck do you think you are?"

For a moment, the surrounding crowd joined in the insults and Josh imagined them growing not just impatient but violent. Aside from the off-duty officer in line, there didn't seem to be any security. If things took a turn for the worse, who would control the crowd?

Josh stepped inside and was met with Esmeralda's huge form as she nearly knocked him over on her way to the counter. "You can't do this," she said to no one in particular—or perhaps everyone. "This is my store. I won't let you take it over like this."

"I'm guessing this wasn't your idea?" Josh said as he took off his headphones.

"Of course not. And please tell me you're not here for an autograph."

"Not unless she wants to sign my forearm. I forgot my poster."

She snickered. "She just might. Two girls have already had their tits signed."

"What is this? A Mötley Crüe show?"

"I wish it were so simple. I might've actually agreed to that."

"Then if you didn't agree . . ."

"Apparently her little management team—those creepy bastards in the robes—went above my head and got permission from the property owner."

"Is that legal?"

"I don't think so but that girl has reach now that she's a millionaire. Not to mention she has a way of . . . getting people to do what she wants. Getting in your head."

Don't think of the lyrics. Don't think of the lyrics.

"I understand completely."

A few fans left with signed merchandise and a few more entered, giddy with excitement. They walked past the potions and entered the farthest curtained room, reserved for tarot cards and fortune telling. It seemed dark in there. Infinitely dark. He could not see Angie Everstein and for that he was thankful.

"I came to see about moving that crowd away from my store but I'm guessing that's out of your hands too."

She nodded, eyes glued toward the curtained room. Two more robed figures guarded the entrance.

"If it were up to me, I'd have these people arrested for trespassing. You know how much business I'm losing today?"

"No one's buying these on their way out?" He lifted a vanity magnet with a cartoonish image of a witch.

Esmeralda shook her head. "Not one sale. It's like these people don't see anything other than the Angie sign out front."

"Well, if you need more CDs for her to sign, come find me."

"How do you mean?"

"It's the weirdest thing. Driving me crazy. They keep showing up in the shop. Not to mention records and a cardboard cutout. Thought it was a joke at first."

"That's quite an elaborate joke."

He thought about the cardboard clone of Angie, how her static eyes never seemed all that static. "I don't think it's anyone that works for me, though."

"Then who?"

He shrugged, mostly because he didn't want to speculate.

Esmeralda lowered her voice. "If I were you, I'd get rid of it. *All* of it. You don't want that shit in your store, Josh. It'll only draw *them* in."

"Them?"

She nodded. "The glitter—"

"Critters."

"That's right. Her fans are very loyal. Just take a look out there."

The crowd had grown more disorderly. One of the perms tried to cut in line but the police officer elbowed her in the face. She held her nose as blood streamed from between her fingers.

"You can't do that," someone in the line said from behind him.

"Says who?"

No one answered.

Esmeralda sighed. "Like I said. Get rid of her merchandise. You don't want to draw those . . . critters into your place."

"Yeah," Josh said, watching the bleeding woman. She didn't seem to notice the pain anymore. Instead she stared into the front doors, intent on meeting her idol while her nose gushed. "Maybe you're right."

♪

The stage was bigger now.

Much bigger.

Shawna climbed Gallows Hill, winded from her trek, and took a seat on the stone wall. She kept her hearing aids in, listened for birds, though she didn't hear any. Nor crickets or squirrels. Perhaps her condition was worsening with age like the doctors had warned. The aids were more of a Band-Aid than a cure. Eventually they might not help anymore. Then she'd hear nothing at all.

But that was the least of her worries.

She checked Facebook on her phone. Several new comments and she had been tagged in four posts. All of them mentioned the photos of her sister. Some speculated if Shawna's own breasts were as nicely shaped, ugly face aside. Twitter was just as bad, let alone Instagram.

She shut her phone off and stared at the stage. It had seemed deeper within the forest the last time. Now, she could've sworn it was closer, like the construction crew had lifted and repositioned the behemoth. Lights had been set up along with what looked like pyrotechnic equipment.

She did not want to picture her sister up there, shaking to the beat of her synthetic songs. And those lyrics. She'd never liked pop music but there was something in particular about her sister's words that made her stomach tie itself into knots.

What was it her sister had said yesterday?

It's about you, Sis. It's always been about you.

Her mind traveled dark pathways. The creeping things invaded her memories.

Suddenly the stage was something living. Something breathing. Something with more eyes than there were people in the world. You could run but its reach was far. It would find you one way or another.

Her once peaceful spot, the place she went when the world was too much, had turned into a nightmare. She couldn't come here anymore. It didn't feel safe.

Her heart hammered. She made to spin around but something grabbed her from behind, rough hands securing her throat and squeezing.

"I'm not going to hurt you," a voice said.

She tried to kick, to bite, to scream, but her mouth was covered. She smelled chemicals, stinging her nose and eyes and then stinging no more as Gallows Hill and the stage with a million eyes faded into nothingness.

♪

For a long time there was only darkness.

Slowly, sounds crept toward her. Shawna supposed she was dead. Otherwise the voice that spoke couldn't have been so clear, like she'd never suffered hearing loss to begin with. It wasn't the same as whoever had restrained and maybe killed her. This was softer, calmer, yet it was the least soothing thing she'd ever heard.

"She wants to play," Angie said.

"Who does?" It was Shawna's voice except she wasn't the one speaking. This was a much younger version of herself, a memory she'd tried desperately to forget. Did the dead dream?

"You know who, silly. *Her.*"

"I don't know what you're talking about."

"Don't play dumb, Sis."

"I'm going to tell Mom."

"Do it and she'll find out how much you've been swearing."

"I don't swear that much."

"And I'm a good liar. Ethel wants to play."

Though Shawna couldn't see her sister or her younger self, she could picture it just fine. They'd been in their room. Nearby lay a SpongeBob SquarePants blanket and a pile of stuffed animals. Moments before, the items had been under Angie's bed. Not just being stored but covering up the symbol that had been drawn months before.

"Would you like to say hi to her, Sis? She's been dying to see you again."

Present day Shawna opened her mouth to scream but nothing came out.

Angie grabbed onto Shawna's sleeve, pulled her under the bed. Pulled her toward the symbol and everything it promised.

Pulled her toward hell.

She opened her eyes.

Someone paced in front of her, stopping suddenly now that she was awake. "Finally. Thought you'd be out for the rest of the day." A man. The man who'd restrained her.

She sat on a cold metal chair, hands and feet zip-tied. Her mouth was not covered. She started to scream but the man moved forward, inches from her face. His cheeks were covered with black and gray stubble. His hair was an oily mess, strands pointing in every direction. "No one's going to hear you out here. Plus I've got a bitch of a headache." From his pocket he pulled out a bottle of Advil and dry swallowed three pills.

"What do you want?"

"You. At least I think I do. Please tell me you're Shawna Everstein. I checked your pockets. No ID of any kind."

She shrugged. "I don't drive yet."

"But you are her, then?"

"Are you going to kill me?"

"Far from it. You might be my only hope."

She wasn't sure what he was talking about. Not to mention he looked crazy. "Are you kidnapping me?"

"Not exactly." He walked toward a workbench, ruffled through pages of some sort. The bench was littered with folders and crumpled documents. Along the wall were corkboards and pictures. Arrows had been drawn, dots connecting to dots. Chaotic and calculated at once.

Finding what he'd been looking for, he turned and held an image in front of her face. A head shot of Angie, taken during the final week of the competition. "This is your sister, correct?"

She did not answer. She looked around for an exit but there were only walls. From behind she felt a cool draft and realized where she was. A storage unit. She was in a maniac's storage unit and would likely be chopped to pieces.

He caught her looking at the walls. "I know this seems . . ."

"Crazy?"

"Yeah, crazy. Sometimes it seems crazy to *me*. I wish I was just losing my marbles. Things would be easier that way."

"Why are you looking for my sister? Are you a stalker or something?"

He rubbed his eyes, both bloodshot. "No, I'm a police officer. At least I was."

"Please let me go."

"Soon. Now just tell me. You're her sister, right? You're Shawna?"

She nodded, unsure if she'd just prolonged or shortened her life. "Now tell me what you want."

He studied the image of Angie, ripped it in two, tossed it to the floor. "I want her dead."

"You and me both."

He gave a sad smirk and looked at the mess of information on the wall. They weren't all pictures of Angie. Many were strangers, each positioned above newspaper clippings. "She's clever, your sister. She makes you think she's an angel but it's quite the opposite. She's even better at killing than she is at singing."

Shawna wiggled her hands but the zip-ties were too tight. They dug into her skin, cut off the circulation. "What are you saying? That Angie killed all those people on your little collage? My sister is a cunt. I'll give you that much. But she's not a murderer."

"Maybe not in the normal sense. But trust me, she killed these people and plenty more will die if we don't do something about it."

"Who are you?"

He stopped pacing. "My name is Mike Mallory and I'm here to stop the apocalypse."

CHAPTER EIGHT
SOMETHING UNDER THE SURFACE

CLOSING TIME.

Esmeralda usually ended her day around five. She ought to stay open later, especially around Halloween, but she made enough during peak business hours to keep the lights on and pay her rent. Now, though, it was pushing seven and those robed figures were just now ushering the last of the fans onto the sidewalk.

She'd made three sales today: a bottle of water, a broomstick key chain, and a book about the Salem witch trials. The rest of her customers had been too consumed with the signing.

She wondered how much money she'd lost but her thoughts were quickly replaced as the last fan stepped outside.

The doors closed.

And locked.

There were four Robes in the shop now. Two at the entrance, two near the tarot booth. The curtains were still closed. Strange thing was, she hadn't once seen Angie. Hadn't even caught her entering the shop. Her managers—if that's what they were—had probably let her in through the back before Esmeralda even got in this morning. But that begged the million-dollar question.

Where had they gotten keys?

From Arnold, she supposed. She thought of his haunting face, the way he'd looked ready to scream at any moment. He didn't seem like the type to back down but perhaps he really had been threatened.

"Okay," Esmeralda said. "I let you have your signing. Now it's time to get out of here."

No one answered. The Robes stood still. *Everything* stood still.

Aside from the curtain. It fluttered from a breeze that wasn't there. There were no windows in the rear of the shop.

She cleared her throat. "You got what you wanted. Now please leave."

"Not yet."

The voice did not come from any of the Robes, nor from the tarot booth. It came from her left, and when she turned, her heart worked overtime.

Angie Everstein stood mere feet away.

"Been a long time," she said.

Esmeralda gulped. Her throat was a desert. An extra-large Mountain Dew stood on the counter. She licked her lips yet she couldn't bring herself to move.

"Thirsty?" Angie smiled.

"What's this all about? I asked you nicely to—"

"To leave. Yes. I heard you the first time. And the fifth. I just wanted to say how much I appreciate all this. You don't know how much you've helped, Esmeralda. Not just this but with . . . everything."

She was talking about the spells, of course. The spells that a younger, slightly less evil version of Angie had been so eager to learn. Spells that even experienced witches shied away from. Witchcraft was, for the most part, misunderstood. The movies would have you think it was all curses and conjuring. But in reality, it was more about nature than demons. Still, there *was* a dark side, a subsection of spells reserved only for those brave enough to learn them.

Esmeralda recalled how she'd helped the girl find the right books and ingredients, taught her the correct words. It had seemed harmless at the time. Surely nothing malicious would come from it. All fun and games. Stiff as a board and all that.

How wrong she'd been.

"What did you do?" Esmeralda said, throat drying by the minute. "What did *I* do? I should've never taught you."

"Maybe it *is* your fault. Or maybe I would've figured it out eventually. You're tired, Esmeralda. I can tell by looking at you. Your heart can't keep going like this."

Esmeralda's pulse struggled to keep up. Dehydrated now. Food half digested, midsection flaring with pain. Maybe she'd skip dinner tonight. Maybe tomorrow was the day she stuck to her diet for good.

Except now that she thought about it, she *was* hungry. Just as hungry as she was thirsty. *Famished.* She imagined her favorite artery-clogging meals. Burgers and fries and milkshakes and bacon. Yes, those heavenly strips of pork fat she so enjoyed. She could actually smell them. Could actually hear them sizzling.

Her stomach gurgled. Despite the pain she *wanted* to eat. Wanted to eat for the rest of her life until she could eat no more. Until the food blocked her esophagus and her airway. Until it stretched her gut so far the flesh tore. And still she would chew and eat, chew and eat. She would never stop. Not until her *heart* stopped.

She opened her mouth, tongue salivating. She breathed in the salty aroma.

"Here," Angie said. "I want to give this to you."

Esmeralda opened her eyes. She was back in the store. The scent was gone. The discomfort in her midsection returned. As did her fear.

Angie held a ticket.

"A VIP pass," she said. "For the concert. It's open to the public but we think there will be quite the crowd. It would be a shame if you didn't have a good view of the stage. Especially after all the work that's gone into it."

"I'm busy that night."

Angie pretended to pout. "I understand. It's Halloween, after all. But I'm extending the offer anyway. Believe me, you won't want to miss it." She set the ticket down on the counter, next to the Mountain Dew calling Esmeralda's name. "Just think about it, okay?"

Esmeralda nodded. She would think about it, all right. She would also think about packing her bags and heading down to Florida.

"I wouldn't if I were you," Angie said.

"What?" And that's when Esmeralda knew for sure. The girl was not just a girl anymore. God knew what she'd been playing around with, what she'd managed to invoke.

Angie smiled. For a split second, so quickly it seemed a mirage, her teeth were more like fangs, jagged and long and uneven. And were those drops of blood along the tips? And were her eyes green? Reptilian? Inhuman?

The moment passed and she was the world's most famous pop star again, though Esmeralda knew it was just a charade.

"Do you smell bacon or is it my imagination?" Angie wrinkled her perfect eyebrows. She studied a watch encrusted with diamonds. It sparkled even in the dim light of the shop. "It's getting late."

The Robes moved in unison, marched toward the door and unlocked it.

"Good to see you again." Angie touched Esmeralda's arm and her pulse tripled. Every strand of hair stood to attention in response.

She strutted out of the shop, followed by her team.

The silence that followed was heavier than Esmeralda herself. She grabbed her keys and thought about sipping her soda. But it seemed too close to the curtained tarot room. The darkness over there swayed on its own accord and even though she was alone in the shop, it didn't feel that way. It felt like a million things watched her.

A million things with sharp teeth.

♪

"Apocalypse?"

The man—Mike Mallory, apparently—nodded and began his pacing routine all over again. "Don't tell me you haven't noticed that your sister's songs have . . . a certain effect on people."

She shrugged. "I guess she has a lot of fans if that's what you mean."

"Cut the bullshit. You know exactly what I mean."

She thought back to every time she'd heard "Forever with You" and how it made her feel. She'd attributed it to headaches and heartburn and sibling rivalry. That and she hated pop music. But there was *something*, some undefined feeling that surged through her body whenever Angie's voice spilled from speakers. Which is why she'd avoided the single at all costs. Not to mention she had a secret view into the life of its creator. She knew what Angie was capable of.

"Who's Ethel?" Mike said.

"What?"

"You said something about Ethel while you were out. She your friend or something?"

She shook her head. "I don't have many friends these days." She wondered if things would be different if Mia were still around, if she hadn't changed her entire personality right around the time that . . .

She tensed in the chair, zip-ties digging further into her wrists and ankles. "Holy shit."

"Believe me now?"

"Maybe. I don't know. I have this friend and she changed, you know? But not like a *normal* change. Not the kind that happens in high school. It was instant. One day she was like me and the next she started wearing glitter like it was perfume. Her skin always shimmering in the light. She was blinding. And that was right around the time that—"

"That Angie won the competition."

She nodded.

"You want to know where I was that night? I was responding to a domestic dispute. Only it wasn't a dispute at all. It was a double homicide. A little girl killed both her parents then gouged out her own eyes. She came at me. And I . . ." He covered his own eyes for a moment. "I got to thinking. There was something wrong with that girl. The girl on TV. The girl that turned out to be your sister."

"Where was the murder?"

"Indiana."

"So you think my sister killed two people through the television?"

"Yes. As crazy as it sounds, I do. It was her voice or her lyrics or something else I haven't figured out. And it wasn't just the one murder. There have been numerous deaths connected with that song." He pointed again at the makeshift diorama on the storage unit's far wall. She thought of every stereotypical detective in every stereotypical detective movie. Breaking out on his own to solve a case. Losing his marbles in the process. Mike fit the bill perfectly.

Only, in those movies, the cops were the good guys. She still wasn't sure about Officer Mallory. He seemed to be on Shawna's side but she wasn't counting anything out just yet. After all, she was the one tied up.

His index finger landed on a picture of a woman. Red hair, smoker's lines, and eyes that looked slightly off center. "Renee Walters. Forty-eight years old. Meter maid. Retired early because of rheumatoid arthritis. She moved to Georgia from Michigan because her doctor said the heat would help the pain. She was found dead in her living room, a shotgun in her right hand, most of her brain in her left. Before she killed herself, she went next door and murdered an entire family, as well as their two cats and a puppy."

He moved his hand toward a teenage boy with a chiseled jaw and shaved head. "Billy Lockheart. Dropped out of school at sixteen. Started as a bag boy at a local grocery store in Wisconsin. Worked his way up to the register, then assistant front-end supervisor. Officials found him after responding to a noise complaint. He was in the back room, hanging from a noose with rope he'd bought at the hardware store across the parking lot. He didn't kill anyone but there was a sizeable hit list near his body."

Next: a curvy college girl with deep dimples in her cheeks. "Karen Lopes. Found—you guessed it—dead in the bathroom of her local mall in Arizona. She'd busted one of the mirrors and slit her throat but not before dragging Timothy Girard into the stall with her and stabbing him in the face thirteen times. He was six. Are you beginning to see a pattern?"

"I'm seeing a bunch of dead people who lost their minds."

He nodded. "And what ties them all together?"

"I'm guessing they were all fans of my sister."

"Not necessarily. But her music was playing during the crimes in every single instance when police officials arrived, whether it was on their phones or the store speakers or car radios. Like I said: your sister's music has an effect on people. And it's spreading."

He stepped toward a poster she hadn't noticed until now: a map of the United States. There were perhaps one hundred thumbtacks, some red, others blue, scattered along the country. At least one in every state. "The blue ones are attempted murders. You'll notice there are more red ones. Those are the successes."

The storage unit grew cold, though she was almost certain it was weather controlled. A strong breeze blew against the walls, rattling the metal like something outside wanted in. "Okay, that's a lot of people. But why doesn't it happen to everyone? Why hasn't everyone killed themselves and everybody around them? Angie is the biggest star in the world right now. We should all be dead."

He studied the map without blinking. "That's the part I can't figure out. The part that's driving me nuts. Remember the sixties? When they said the Beatles were putting subliminal messages into their songs? And then again in the eighties. A bunch of conservative pricks said Iron Maiden and Judas Priest were doing the same thing."

"I'm eighteen."

"It's like that but real this time. There's something . . . under the surface of her music. Something that affects us all but not at the same time."

She thought of her sister's lyrics, that robotic yet perfect voice crawling through her mind. She thought of what the words might make her do. She thought of the world slowly slipping into madness. Of Mia, her deadbeat mother and her bullies. Of Ethel. She thought a thousand horrible thoughts and wanted to gag. Mike Mallory may have been a few singles short of a pop album but his argument was beginning to make sense.

"And besides," he said, "I haven't listened to the song enough to actually study it. And I don't plan on it. All I know is that she has to be stopped before it's too late. Before they finish that stage."

"You think something's going to happen during the show."

"Yes."

"Like what?"

He changed the subject. "I know someone. A professor. He's an expert in this area."

"What area?"

"Subliminal psychology. Real smart guy if a bit eccentric. We've been in touch since the world started going to hell. He tends to agree with me when it comes to your sister. I think he can help us."

"Us? Does that mean you're not going to kill me?"

He stepped toward her, pulled out a long and sharp knife.

She closed her eyes, stopped breathing, stopped thinking.

And gasped a sigh of relief when he cut the zip-ties. Her wrists and ankles flooded with pins and needles. She rubbed them and stood, dizzy.

"Go home," Mike said. "Sleep on it. Think about what I said and let me know if you're going to help me."

"How will I find you?" She wasn't sure if she planned on going back to him or going straight to the cops.

"I'll find *you*. Thank you for listening to me tonight."

"You didn't give me much of a choice."

They stood in silence for a moment, save for the wind picking up outside. In the distance, something—a trash bucket or recycling bin—was blown along the street. It sounded like a scream.

She left without saying anything else and despite how badly she wanted to stay away from home, she jogged back, breathless as she stepped through the front door.

The rooms were too dark. Like her sister or something worse—if there was such a thing—waited just beyond her periphery. She did not stop until she was in her bed, door closed and locked behind her.

She lay awake until morning.

CHAPTER NINE
PROGRESS

THE STAGE WAS NEARLY COMPLETE.

Many of the surrounding trees had been removed to allow for construction. The previous spring, a real estate developer had proposed erecting two oversized condo complexes. Hundreds of protestors had proudly held makeshift signs warning of the environmental effects of such a thing. The project was called off shortly after. But *this* project had either escaped their notice or they were too busy to care.

If you walked through Gallows Hill and the construction site tonight, you would notice certain trees deep within the woods. *New* trees that had not been there weeks or even days before. The scenery, it would seem, shifted by the moment. Even the roots beneath the ground twisted and turned like worms just before rainfall.

Wildlife mostly kept away from the area. Last summer, there had been a gypsy moth outbreak. Hundreds if not thousands of caterpillars climbed the bark, feasting on the wood before their bodies went into hibernation. Weeks later they bloomed as pests.

But the park was nearly silent now. No signs of squirrels or birds or raccoons. No signs of beetles or ants or earwigs. From the outside it was a dead zone, though that wasn't exactly true.

A stray cat made its way up the hill, oblivious of the stage and the historical significance of the area. It knew nothing of witches and black magic. It knew only hunger. Its owners had abandoned it two weeks prior, moving out of their apartment complex in a hurry. It had once been overweight, gluttonous, but fourteen days of living in filth had transformed its body. Ribs poked through patchy fur. Its belly ached. It would kill for food.

Its nametag read *Whiskers*.

Whiskers turned the corner, jumped onto the stone wall, and peered into the forest where the stage lay. It cocked its head, listened. Nothing. No chirping or howling or breathing. No sounds of any kind. On an instinctual level, it knew something was wrong but hunger overpowered these internal warnings. If it had known who Angie Everstein was, been able to interpret the message beneath her lyrics, it would turn around and sprint back the way it had come.

Instead it jumped from the wall and walked slowly toward the stage.

Though the day had been warm, the New England weather about as predictable as the future, the night was near freezing. A dense fog resulted, moving in from the ocean like a wall of smoke. It obscured the forest so the stage was more of a suggestion. As were the trees and the bushes and the—

And the shapes that could've been human or something else.

Whiskers stopped suddenly when the forms came into view. Its periphery swam with movement. Shadows danced and swayed. It heard something like music in the distance.

It hissed as the shapes moved closer, looked in every direction for escape, but it was surrounded now. The only way out was to climb the stage. It did so with ease. Though it was exhausted, fight or flight took precedence. The metal platform was cool beneath its paws.

The shapes ascended the steps and soon its chances of escaping lessened with each moment. It located the closest tree, prepared to jump.

Something reached out of the darkness, grabbed onto its tail, pulled it backward.

Whiskers hissed again, opened its mouth and bared its teeth, the movement more dog-like than feline. It sunk its teeth into flesh, heard the figure moan in response. Whiskers dove for the tree, claws locking onto ancient bark, and climbed to the closest branch. From its perch it watched the shapes gather. The music grew louder. They sounded like humans, like its former owners before they abandoned it. *Those* humans used to hum songs under their breath while they cleaned. This was similar but lacked melody. More archaic. Whiskers did not understand, yet it knew the song was wrong. Its patchy hair grew stiff. Its skin grew taut.

The cat did not stay long enough to see the ceremony nor the ritual. It climbed farther, tight-roped across a brittle branch, and dove to a neighboring tree. It repeated this process until it was finally out of Gallows Hill. Though its stomach still ached with emptiness, it was preferable to whatever it had just witnessed.

Back on the hill, with Whiskers gone, the robed figures sang and danced and prepared for their princess to bring forth the new era.

The soil warmed.

The temperature lowered.

And the days until the concert lessened.

CHAPTER TEN
NEW ADDITIONS

THE NEXT MORNING JOSH HEARD Angie's voice in a dream.

It was early, the sun too dim to filter through the curtains of his one-room apartment. The lack of natural light was normally a blessing. He liked to sleep in when he could, though he rarely slept at all these days.

Now, though, he begged to wake up.

Across from his bed, leaning against the kitchen counter, stood Angie. She wore nothing at all. Her skin shimmered even in the darkness and her eyes were two dark storm clouds.

"Do you want to fuck me?" she said.

He *wanted* to shake his head. She was too young for him, not to mention there was something . . . wrong with her. Something he hadn't yet figured out. But instead he nodded against his will.

"I bet you do. I bet you'd like to stick that cock of yours right up inside me. It's so tight, Josh. Tighter than that ex-whore of yours. Just say the word and I'm yours."

He opened his mouth to say *no*. "Yes."

She smiled and sang that song that had taken over the world. Every inch of Josh's skin tingled as it had that day in the shop, when he'd first heard the chorus. He'd known then something was wrong. Talk about an understatement.

Her voice grew louder and her belly, smooth and flat a moment before, expanded exponentially. Something beneath the skin rippled and swayed. Something that wanted out.

She's pregnant, he thought.

As if to confirm this revelation, the skin shredded and something made its way onto the floor. Something misshapen and ancient and ugly beyond description.

He woke screaming.

His alarm clock read nine. It was a CD player combo that played the same song each morning, an old Black Flag B-side, but today it had somehow triggered the radio, which had in turn triggered the world's most popular single.

"Forever with You."

He turned it off and got out of bed. The apartment swam around him and his mind felt capsized. He couldn't remember the night before, wasn't sure if he'd gone out to drink or stayed home. The crushed cans near the recycling bin solved the riddle for him. There were twelve in all. Cheap stuff he hadn't drank since college. Melissa had told him he was becoming an alcoholic near the end of their marriage. Maybe she'd been on to something. He didn't like to give her credit but the proof was in the pudding, or in this case, the hangover.

He opened the cabinet and retrieved his beloved bottle of aspirin, washed down two capsules with tap water.

In the bathroom he disrobed and stepped into the shower. Normally he bathed quickly but this morning he allowed himself some indulgence, basking in the heat of the spray. Flashes of his dream steamrolled into his mind. His stomach churned and his bowels protested but, despite his body's disgust, his lower half didn't get the message.

He was far from flaccid as he recalled Angie's dream face. Never mind that her body had been a vessel for something else. Something more nightmarish than the nightmare itself. His balls tingled and he began stroking himself like a reflex. He would've stayed that way had he not remembered he needed to meet with Melissa and the realtor she'd chosen without his input.

His erection shriveled in mere seconds after that.

In the kitchen he made coffee and dry toast. The thought of food was repulsive. His stomach gurgled as he forced it down.

Running late, he sped outside and into his car. Even now, when they were separated, when he let Melissa stay in the home he'd bought, he still let her run his life. Pathetic wasn't a strong enough word.

The CD in his stereo, an old thrash band called Nuclear Assault, skipped badly. He took it out and examined its bottom surface. No scratches. He tried again with the same result. Finally, he gave up and backed out of the driveway, wincing at the glare from the sun.

At the end of his street he turned left, stopped at the red light, and hung his mouth open as he saw the billboard. The night before it had been an advertisement for a local mechanic and an offer for the cheapest oil change in town. He'd gone to the place plenty of times, admired the way they ran such an honest business. Today, though, there was nothing resembling their logo or their money-back guarantee.

This morning it was an advertisement for the new Angie Everstein CD, named after its title track.

She smiled, teeth glowing a preternatural shade of white. The image seemed three-dimensional, like the mouth could open and close without a moment's notice. Her eyes were a sickly shade of green. He swore they followed him, no longer poster material but gooey flesh. If he stayed there long enough, studying her features, those eyes would blink. He was sure of it.

The car behind him honked its horn, the driver flipping him off. The light had turned green. Thankfully, it was a *different* shade of green.

Josh sped off. His ears rang, the headache sharpening despite the pills. He pinched the bridge of his nose and, against his better judgment, turned the radio on.

Part of him was not surprised to hear Angie's robotic voice shouting at him.

Forever with you. I'll never leave your side.

He turned the dial. The next channel played Angie as well. He turned it again with the same result. And again.

He switched over to AM and found a distorted broadcast of a religious talk show. The host was yelling and rambling, barely breathing between words. For a moment it was actually soothing.

Until he focused on the subject matter.

"She's evil," the deep and raspy voice preached. "I can tell you that much with absolute certainty. I can practically see some of you out there rolling your eyes but I say to you: she is unholy. Believe the rumors. She has made a pact with the devil. We must reach out to her fans before it's too late."

He changed the channel. A local news program.

"That was today's sports. Now to today's top story." Another man's voice, much higher in pitch and speaking instead of yelling. "A teenaged girl in Worcester was found dead last night of an apparent suicide. We received reports that the girl cut out her tongue and removed her teeth with pliers before jumping from her bedroom window. A note left behind cited Angie Everstein, stating that the popular singer was inside her thoughts."

"Terrible," the female co-anchor said. "Just awful. In related news, Angie will be playing on Gallows Hill in Salem on Halloween night. Admission is free but local authorities expect a large crowd. They're urging attendees to arrive as early as possible. Her fans are expected to number in the thousands. Personally, I'm not surprised. Her songs do have a way of getting stuck in your head."

"They certainly do," the man said, laughing.

♪

The bathroom mirror was fogged over. Shawna wiped away some of the condensation, revealing her distorted reflection. She did not like what she saw. Eyes a bit lopsided. Teeth a bit crooked. Skin that seemed oily no matter how often she washed. She brushed her hair, considered wearing it in a ponytail the way Mia used to like it. That would only draw attention, and today of all days, she wanted to blend in.

She peered outside. The bathroom window overlooked her street. There were no white vans with tinted windows but she suspected Mike Mallory would not be so obvious. He'd assured her he'd be watching. Had he been lying?

Rubbing her wrists, she winced at the leftover pain from the zipties.

She finished dressing, put in her hearing aids, and opened the door.

And stopped suddenly when she saw the shape standing there.

"Good morning," the woman said.

Not just any woman. The one from yesterday. Angie's manager. This close, Shawna took in her features. Glenda's skin was just past its prime. The woman had been attractive in her day but age was taking effect. Her face was unnatural in a way that made Shawna's scalp tingle.

"Morning," Shawna said, looking at the floor.

"How would you like to take the day off from school? We can

film your interview. I'll make sure you're pretty if that's what you're worried about. We have a professional makeup crew in the trailer. After we're done, you'll look just like your sister."

"I don't want to look *anything* like her. Now, excuse me. I'm going to be late."

Glenda did not move. "She said you might resist. You really should reconsider. All you have to do is sit down and answer a few questions."

Shawna tossed her hair towel onto the floor. She'd hoped the movement would make her seem defiant but, if anything, she felt childish. "What could you possibly want to ask about her that you don't already know? I'm not exactly going to bring in the ratings. I hate my sister, in case you hadn't figured it out. I'm not going to look into that camera and pretend everything is peachy. She's made my life a living hell."

"And she can make it much worse if you don't cooperate."

Shawna froze. "What did you just say?"

"Your sister's homecoming isn't just about publicity. It's so much more than that."

"Listen, lady. I don't know what you're talking about but I do know you're going to get out of my way or I'll call the cops. This is my house, not yours."

"Don't be foolish. Take the day off. Do the interview."

Shawna went into her room without answering and grabbed her backpack.

She spun back around, ready to tell Glenda off once more, but the woman was gone. The hallway was empty. She did not hear creaking steps or a closing door, nothing to indicate where she'd retreated. She was just light on her feet, that was all. Nothing more to it.

Who are you kidding? There's something wrong with her and the crew and this whole business.

She took the stairs two at a time. Her mother was in the kitchen, humming, happy as could be. Probably picturing her debt disappearing. Shawna could practically see the fantasies. Excesses that had long been out of her budget. Diamond jewelry and a new convertible. Flat screen TVs and a patio ten times too large. "That you, Shawna?" There was a package of Pop-Tarts on the kitchen table. Angie must have been out somewhere, signing autographs or being interviewed. No fancy spreads today.

Shawna's stomach grumbled. She hadn't eaten the night before on account of being kidnapped and the thought of food made her mouth water. Even the cardboard pastry seemed like an indulgence. But it felt like surrendering somehow, acknowledging how little she meant to this family. She would not give her mother the satisfaction.

She ignored the Pop-Tarts and Kristen Everstein, slamming the door on her way out.

At the foot of the driveway she saw the trailer Glenda had mentioned. The camera crew talked amongst themselves, looking up and down the street, perhaps planning their next shot.

Before she turned the corner, she took one last look at her home. It seemed foreign now, the house of a stranger. Hard to believe she'd lived there her entire life. But that wasn't what made her stomach switch from hunger to repulsion.

Glenda stood in the bay windows.

She waved.

♪

"You've got to be shitting me," Shawna said twenty minutes later when she showed up to school. Her skin was covered with sweat and any hopes of catching her breath were dashed as she saw the banner hanging over the front doors.

It read: *Welcome Home, Angie!*

It was not a shabby flag picked up at the local party store. This was an expensive job. The lettering seemed professional. Weren't Mr. Fuller and his close colleagues always complaining of budgets being slashed? She'd heard rumors of a teachers' strike in the near future, yet the school had chosen to spend their money on *this*?

Someone elbowed her arm. She lost grip of her books and phone. The former were fine, landing on the grass. The latter fell a little too far to the right, hitting the concrete, screen side down. She heard the undeniable crack of glass.

"Sorry about that."

She looked up to see Derek smirking. He did not offer to help her pick up the mess. "Guess I didn't see you there." He stopped just in front of the steps. "You'll never guess what's inside. You're going to love it."

"What the hell is that supposed to mean?"

He stepped through the entrance without answering.

She picked up her books, shoved them into her bag, and flipped over her phone. The screen was shattered, as she'd expected. Her home page, a picture of her and Mia from seven months ago, was sliced into a hundred tiny sections. She knew she ought to change the background, had tried plenty, but each time her thumb froze. It seemed final. Like changing the wallpaper meant accepting the truth. The truth being that Mia was gone, changed somehow. And the rest of the school—the rest of the *town*—seemed to be following in her footsteps.

She shoved the phone into her pocket, careful not to damage it further, and hurried inside just as the first bell was sounding.

Late students filtered in, bumping into her, paying her no notice. To be fair, she was asking for it, standing mannequin-like in the middle of the crowd. She understood Derek's choice of words now, although he'd been wrong in his assessment. She did not love what she saw. Quite the opposite.

The front display case that housed awards and pictures of star athletes had been torn out. In its place hung several large paintings of her sister, each expertly framed. Shawna walked toward the closest, touched the wooden frame. It felt cool and clammy and made her mouth run dry. There were small etchings along the edges. Not just designs but renditions of things she'd rather not see. Tiny creatures and a list of other atrocities.

The paintings themselves appeared old-fashioned, something from a museum. All the pictures showed her sister in crude positions. Naked, of course. Just like the photo leaked online the day before. Angie's perfect breasts and body on display for all to see.

Beneath each painting was a plaque and written on each plaque were lyrics to her songs.

The surrounding crowd surprised her. Some snickered as Derek had but for the most part they did not bat an eye at the new additions. They walked toward homerooms, spoke of weekend plans and crushes and normal high school subjects while Shawna Everstein tried to process what the hell was happening in Salem, Massachusetts.

Mr. Fuller, she thought. He would know what to do. He would help her through this.

She hurried along, putting the paintings in her periphery, but stopped only a few steps into her trek.

There was movement back there. Not of the crowd or the cleaning crew that swept and mopped nearby. The movement came from the paintings themselves. It conjured images of old haunted house films. Black-and-white and, more often than not, cheesy as hell. Wasn't that one of the clichés in such movies? The painting with the eyes that followed your every step? It was comical on a screen but here, in reality, Shawna did not find anything particularly funny.

She did not turn around to test her theory, did not turn around until she rounded the corner and the paintings could no longer be seen.

CHAPTER ELEVEN
REAL ESTATE IS A DANGEROUS BUSINESS

ESMERALDA'S CHEST HURT. SHE HAD not followed her doctor's orders from her last office visit. Her blood pressure and cholesterol were through the roof and, her physician had warned her several times, if she did not make a change, she was headed for trouble.

But trouble had found her.

It was hard to think about diet and exercise when she had other things on her mind. Last night, she wasn't able to shake the feeling that someone stood outside her front door. Watching. Waiting. But for what? Her mind offered no answers but it was certain of one thing.

She was in danger.

It was all connected to Angie and her team. The longer Esmeralda stuck around, the worse things would get. If an event could be held at her own store against her will, the place she'd owned and operated for nearly twenty years, how far was their reach? It was time to throw in the towel. She was going to die young. Part of her knew she'd reached the point of no return with her weight. She could eat all the salads in the world but Esmeralda was still heading for heart failure followed by cardiac arrest.

So why not spend her final years—however many were left—doing something she liked? Her savings account was nothing to laugh at, though it wouldn't afford her many luxuries. It *would* allow her to live within her means, though. Especially somewhere that offered cheap land.

Like Florida.

Her laptop lay open on her kitchen counter, screen alive with images of the ocean, next to a nearly empty bag of doughnuts. Grease leaked through the bottom, turning the paper soggy. She wondered what it did to her insides.

After she'd given up on sleep, she'd made a pot of coffee and compared condominium prices. Most of those within her range were part of giant complexes, more like hotels than homes. Her own apartment, the third floor of a Victorian house, was spacious and had character aplenty. The appliances may have been outdated but the place oozed a certain charm only found in New England. She would miss this place but most of her family had died young or fallen out of touch. There was nothing keeping her here.

Her mind was made. She would contact a realtor from the list she'd created and start packing. Her rent was month to month, both at home and at work. Once she found something, she could leave with little notice.

The sooner, the better.

Her phone rang. Not her cell but the landline. Her skin crawled at the sound. She hadn't heard that tone in months, only owned the thing to save money on her cable bill as part of a package deal. It was probably a telemarketer and she wasn't in the mood. She let it go to voicemail.

Except once the recording played and the beep sounded, no one left a message. Not of the normal variety at least. There was only what sounded like heavy breathing. In the background was whispering of some sort. She considered answering just to hang up but the telemarketer beat her to it. The message ended.

She threw away the remnants of her breakfast, lunch already on her mind, and thought of all the fun to be had in Florida. Her college friend, Jeanie Rogers, had moved there ages ago. It really was a blast, she insisted. The temperature was perfect and the cocktails were unparalleled. Not to mention the food and the—

The phone rang again.

She dropped the bag, greasy doughnut rolling onto the floor.

Don't answer it.

But she'd put up with enough bullshit to last a lifetime these last few days. She walked across the kitchen and lifted the phone. "This better be good," she said. "I don't have time for anything other than an emergency."

A pause. Then breathing. Then whispering. Then a voice. "This *is* an emergency, I'm afraid. Is this Harriet Hopkins?" Female. Indeterminate age. Neither young nor old.

It was strange hearing her real name. Good news never followed those words. "Yes, speaking."

"I'm sorry to bother you at home but I wanted to catch you before you left for the day."

"What's this about?" *And how do you know my schedule?*

"It's about Arnold Goldman."

"What about him?" She rolled her eyes, thinking he'd gotten himself into trouble. She knew her shop's owner had a bit of a gambling problem but if that were the case, surely his family would be notified.

"He had an accident last night. He fell down the stairs."

She covered her mouth. "Oh my god. Is he okay?"

"I'm afraid not, Ms. Hopkins. He died early this morning."

She did not speak for a moment. Not because she mourned the man. Arnold had been nice enough, had been a pleasure to rent from, but there was something else that caused her reaction. Something more primal.

Fear.

She recalled their last meeting, how he'd looked exhausted, eyes darting as if someone watched them both at his doorstep. What was it he'd said?

They started following me, started taunting me. Started threatening me.

Her chest tightened. She could feel the blood protest as it moved through her body, thick like sludge from a lifetime of fats and sweets.

Not just threats after all, she thought.

"Ms. Hopkins? Are you there?"

She shook her head. "Yes, I'm sorry."

"I understand this is a lot to take in but I do want to talk about next steps with you if you're able."

"Next steps? How do you mean?"

"I'm speaking about your business, Esmeralda. I want to make this transition as smooth as possible."

"Pardon me, but who am I speaking with again?"

"Pardon *me*. How rude. I haven't even introduced myself. My name is Glenda and I'm Angie Everstein's manager. I purchased the property from Mr. Goldman just prior to his death."

She went on but Esmeralda stopped listening. She turned her

attention toward her front door. For the second time in twelve hours, she was certain someone stood just outside. And even if she turned the knob to find her front yard empty, the suspicion would not dwindle.

♪

The realtor's name was Roberta Jenkins. Her skin was dark orange, the poster child for spray tanning. Her hair was fried from a lifetime of do-it-yourself dying kits. She stood outside Josh's door, holding up her phone as he climbed the stairs. "I was just calling you."

"What's wrong?" Josh said.

"I've been knocking for twenty minutes. No answer."

"She ought to be home." He checked his watch. It was ten o'clock and Melissa rarely left the house. As far as he knew she'd stopped going to yoga class and aside from the occasional visit to her Aunt Marie—the only relative with whom she still spoke—his soon-to-be ex-wife was a shut-in.

That's not quite true. She frequents plenty of bars, doesn't she? That's where she met her suitors. That's where they picked her up before they fucked her brains out while you were trying to start your business.

"I'll let us in," he said, removing his keys from his pocket. It had been three days since he'd last been inside the condominium, stopping by to grab a bin of records he'd forgotten. The place seemed less and less familiar with each visit. Just a shell he'd once shared with the love of his life.

"You've got twenty minutes," Roberta said. "I have a showing." This said with an air of annoyance, like Josh was an inconvenience.

"Will that be long enough?" He slid his key into the door.

"It'll have to be." She tapped her foot as he turned the knob.

He tried the light but nothing happened. The kitchen and living room remained dark. *Too* dark. Every window and curtain was closed. As if night had never left. He squinted and made out piles of trash: cups and bowls overflowing in the sink, a stack of pizza boxes, something that could've once been a sandwich.

Next, he noticed the smell. It hit his nostrils and stomach simultaneously. His eyes watered. His throat tightened. "I'm sorry about the mess."

She turned up her nose. "I can come back if you'd like."

He shook his head. He'd rather get this over with, needed to sell the place. They would make a sizeable return on their (his) investment but this wasn't about the money. This was about moving on.

Otherwise he'd be stuck like this, in limbo, pining over a woman who no longer loved him.

A small swarm of flies took flight from the kitchen garbage bucket and flew into the living room. They landed on something. A shape of some sort on the couch. What he first thought to be a pillow moved on its own accord. For some odd reason, he imagined the lump was not human. It was something else. Something not meant for the light of day. Hence the darkness.

But it was not a monster.

It was Melissa.

And she was in bad shape.

She wore a pair of headphones, an oversized Red Sox t-shirt, and not much else.

"Melissa?" he said. "Are you okay?"

Her mouth opened but her voice was much too soft.

He stepped farther inside, despite his pulse warning him, and flipped up the closest shade.

And wished he'd slept in that morning. The migraine and hangover and the inexplicable erection were all preferable to what he saw before him.

"I didn't pay the electric bill," Melissa said too loudly, perhaps forgetting about the headphones. "The lights. That's why they don't work." Her eyes were bloodshot. The irises were too large and they'd changed shape somehow. "I know that's my responsibility but I couldn't pay it. Not this time. It wasn't my fault, Josh. I swear."

There were several adult coloring books open on her criss-crossed knees. He used to tell her the things were just a marketing ploy but she insisted they helped with her anxiety and depression. She'd been good at them too. A natural artist. He'd suggested she take up drawing or painting classes. It would get her out of the house more often, make her feel productive.

Today she'd done plenty of coloring, though not with markers or crayons.

With blood.

He covered his mouth at the revelation. Both of Melissa's wrists had been crudely sliced. The horizontal incisions bled freely. The pages of the top coloring book were soaked through. Another lay open on the floor, a rendition of a skyscraper obscured by red smears.

"I couldn't remember," she went on. "She wouldn't let me."

"Honey, what are you talking about?" He hadn't called her that in a long time. The word seemed foreign now.

"Angie. There isn't time for things like bills anymore. She stepped inside my head and she showed me things. She showed me what's coming. And it's beautiful. Fucking gorgeous. She said a lot of people are going to die and some will say she's bad but she's *not* bad. She's exactly what we've been waiting for. She said the end of the world is really just the beginning."

From behind, Josh heard Roberta gasp. Either she hadn't seen the blood until now or shock had delayed her reaction. "Call the police," he said without turning around. "Call an ambulance. Call *someone*. And make it quick." He tried his best to sound calm, talking to Melissa like she was a would-be jumper.

But his calm vanished when he noticed the knife.

Stainless steel. A wedding gift from her parents before they'd disowned her. Melissa hadn't had the easiest life. Her family was . . . difficult to say the least. And she hadn't asked for her depression. Though he wouldn't admit it out loud, he often thought she used her condition as an excuse, a means to treat her husband like shit, but now he saw just how sick she truly was.

This isn't from depression, though.

As if on cue, he noticed the music for the first time. Low and muffled but present nonetheless. The headphones. Melissa took them off and set them on the side of the couch. He backed away as the sounds grew louder. He eyed the tiny speakers like snakes.

Forever with you, Angie sang.

From within his jeans, his cock stiffened. Like the shower that morning, his entire body tingled with pleasure. He imagined Angie slipping out of her clothes and into his bed. He'd make Melissa watch. Tie her up. Pin her eyelids open so she couldn't blink. He'd stuff a sock into her mouth to keep her from screaming. And then he, alongside the world's most famous singer, would cut her many more times.

He blinked and he was back from wherever he'd traveled. He wasn't sure if it was a daydream or a delusion but one thing was certain.

Those thoughts had not been his own.

"She talks to you too, doesn't she?" Melissa brushed away a loose strand of hair, leaving behind a drop of blood on her forehead. "She said you were next. Said you were important in all this. You're a fighter, Josh, but she's stronger."

She licked the blade clean and dropped it onto the floor, giggling and bleeding.

Josh grabbed the headphones, pulled them out of her iPod, and tossed them across the room. They landed with a thud against the bathroom door. The music played for a moment longer and he wasn't certain if it was a delay or his subconscious picking up where the song left off.

Then the melody was replaced with another sound.

Sirens.

CHAPTER TWELVE
SHE'S ALREADY HERE

SHAWNA DID NOT ATTEND ENGLISH class. She couldn't afford to miss any more time and her grades were plummeting, but grades were the furthest thing from her mind. Let the school call her mother.

Her heart skipped. No, she didn't want that. Didn't want to be grounded, at home alone in her room while *you know who* roamed the halls. She imagined two rectangular shadows, her sister's feet, beneath her bedroom door. In no rush as she waited for Shawna to come out.

Her sister was patient.

And also evil.

That much was evident in Salem High this morning. Homeroom had been strange, her fellow students barely speaking. Most of them wore headphones and the few that did mutter words did so quietly. It felt as if she'd entered some bizarre church mid-ritual.

Now, standing outside that same room, watching Mr. Fuller silently address the class, she knew she'd been smart to skip.

There were only two empty desks: her own and Mia's. Mr. Fuller paced back and forth, speaking with his hands. She wasn't sure what they were covering today. The last *real* assignment had been three days ago: a literary analysis for *On the Road*. She'd forgotten to pass hers in, though Fuller hadn't called her out. He'd been acting as if something was on his mind. She'd thought at the time it was more budget cuts but now she saw it was nothing so simple.

On the board behind him were thousands of chicken-scratch words. They looked as though they'd been written with urgency. She imagined Fuller threatening a student with detention if they didn't cover the board with text of his choosing. Only it wasn't anything funny or witty or disciplinary.

It was, unsurprisingly, her sister's lyrics.

Not just the single either. There were plenty of *Forever with You*'s but there were other lines too. Lines from deeper cuts that seemed innocent at first. But stare at them long enough and they grew sinister.

No matter how far you are, I will always find you.

We aren't over yet cuz I'll never stop following.

And perhaps the worst line, the one that made her blood curdle:

The end is just the beginning.

This close to the door's window, her breath fogged the glass, obscuring the room, which felt like a blessing. Mr. Fuller looked angry and happy at once, if that was possible. A large, almost synthetic smile stretched across his face, distorting his features so his eyes looked . . . deformed somehow. Even from here she could tell they'd changed shape, the green and blue irises now more square-like.

"Skipping again, huh?"

Shawna's bladder threatened to burst at the sound of the voice. She spun around and held a hand to her chest.

Mia smirked. "Is the left one still smaller? Or did they finally even out?" She nodded toward her breasts.

Shawna dropped her hand. She felt exposed, looked left and right but the hall was empty. And even if there had been onlookers, who was to say they'd be on her side?

On her *side*?

She didn't like her own choice of words. They implied a line was being drawn. A line that separated good from evil.

"You scared the shit out of me. How long have you been standing there?"

"Long enough." Another smirk. Mia's braces were gone. Her teeth were perfect aside from a stubborn incisor that still poked out. They used to call it her vampire tooth, back when they were together. She wore sequins and skin-tight leggings, a ghost of what she'd once been. "You're better off giving in."

"What?"

"How long do you think you can fight it? Look how far things have come. Give it another month and she'll be everywhere."

Shawna gulped. "Who?" She knew the answer.

"You know, I'm actually jealous of you? In a weird way, I look *up* to you. But it pisses me off too. You're her *sister*. You can talk to her anytime you want but you don't take advantage of it. No, you keep going around like Angie isn't the world's most important creature."

Shawna noted the last word. It hung in the air for much too long.

Mia took a step closer. "We can sense it, you know. That you're not a fan. You might want to change that. I'm only telling you because of what we had. I don't owe you anything after this."

"What are you talking about? What's happening?"

She sighed, closed her eyes. "Can't you feel it? It's in the air. Like the feeling just before a hurricane. Something's coming. *Angie's* coming. No—" she cut herself off. "She's already here."

She opened her eyes as if for the first time. They were different now. Just like Mr. Fuller's. Whatever change had taken place affected her too. It wasn't just a shift in personality and fashion sense. It was deeper than that. This wasn't Mia. Not anymore.

"I loved you," Shawna said. "Still do. And maybe it's just puppy love or a crush but you were more than just a girlfriend. You were my *best* friend. You kept the bullies away because we were in it together. Us against the world. I don't get what's happening but I know it has to do with my sister and her songs. I'm going to figure it out. And I'm going to save you."

Another step forward. One more and Shawna would be pinned against the door. Then it would be painfully easy for Mia to reach for the knob. She imagined the class moving in on her. A horde of mindless cannibals, singing pop lyrics as they dined on her innards.

"You're too late," Mia said. "I've already been saved."

As she took that final step, Shawna dodged and jogged down the hall. She did not stop until she was outside. The temperature was too cold for this time of year but she welcomed the bitter breeze.

An RV pulled up to the curb: black exterior with cheesy graphics of ghosts and ghouls and text. A generic haunted walking tour of Salem. The windows were tinted. The driver's side was rolled down.

Mike Mallory wore sunglasses that hid his exhausted eyes. "I need an answer."

She ran down the steps, opened the passenger door, and dove in.

"Yes," she said.

♪

Esmeralda had gone to the same bank since she'd cashed her first check at age fourteen. It was illegal in Massachusetts to work prior to sixteen unless you got yourself a work permit. That's all she'd asked for for her birthday that year.

"Why do you want to work so badly?" her mother had asked, pausing between breaths. Three years shy of her first heart attack.

Two hundred pounds lighter, Esmeralda had shrugged. "I just do." What she'd really meant was *I want to make something of myself because I don't want to be like you and Dad.*

Her parents had been massively obese. They worked as little as possible. She grew up in her father's childhood home across town. The mortgage was paid off and the place was falling apart. There were countless promises to fix it up but he never followed through. She watched them die a slow death while they ate themselves into oblivion. They weren't bad parents but they weren't exactly role models either.

And now look at you, she thought as she walked up to the revolving door of Salem National Bank. *You followed their footsteps to a T.*

The bank had not changed much in all the time she'd been visiting. Same carpet. Same lights and desks. Same everything aside from the employees. Normally, she took comfort in this. It was like stepping into a time capsule. But today she wasn't in the mood for reminiscing. She wanted to get her money and get the hell out of town.

She waited in line for an eternity. Her feet ached and swelled within her shoes. Another early sign of heart failure, her doctor had warned. She needed to lay off salt immediately. She had. For precisely one week after her last visit. Then she'd traded vegetables for chips and cheese curls. And burgers. You couldn't forget the burgers.

This morning, though, she'd barely been able to think about food after the phone call. Maybe that was the answer. Maybe fear was the ultimate diet.

She wasn't certain what the woman—Glenda—had been implying about the shift in ownership and she didn't intend to find out. Once Esmeralda reached Florida, she could sort out the details. Once she was sipping something fruity under the sun, she'd call Glenda back and let her know she'd abandoned the business.

The line moved up and she finally reached the closest teller.

The girl smiled too eagerly. New to the job. "Can I help you?"

Esmeralda nodded. "Yes, I'd like to withdraw my savings account." She told her the account number.

"Of course. How much will you be withdrawing?"

"All of it."

The girl frowned. "Okay. Let's take a look." She typed for what seemed like eons.

Esmeralda looked around. She didn't spot anyone that seemed out of place but that did her nerves no favors.

The girl cleared her throat and made a noise under her breath.

"Is everything okay?" Esmeralda said.

"Yes. I . . . it looks like there's been a hold on your account."

"A hold?"

The girl nodded. "It says here it went into effect this morning at 8:47 AM."

Esmeralda did not need a mathematician to know that was the exact moment of the phone call. "That's impossible."

The girl shrugged. "I'm sorry. There's nothing I can do."

"Why would there be a hold?"

"It doesn't say. I'm sorry," she said again, on the verge of tears now.

"I'd like to speak with your supervisor."

"Of course. I'll go get him."

She walked into the back room, head down, eyes to the floor. Her fellow tellers watched as if she was on her way to get fired or worse. Esmeralda felt a moment of guilt. Obviously the girl had nothing to do with this error. And obviously that was the correct term for this: *error*. Because Esmeralda had always been good with her money. She hadn't withdrawn from her savings since three winters ago, when her brakes had finally rotted away on her Ford Taurus. The same car she'd be driving to Florida. It had been on its last legs *then*, was on borrowed time. What if she broke down on the side of the highway? What if it broke down *before* she left town?

A man cleared his throat. She looked up, blinking away her thoughts. According to his nametag, the front-end supervisor's name was Gregory Charles. A formal sounding name for a grumpy looking person. He scowled at her. She could practically hear his inner voice judging her weight. He should've spoken aloud. She'd heard it all before.

Fat ass.

Tub of lard.

Heffer.

And her personal favorite: *tower of diabetes*. At least that had been original.

"You've made a mistake," she said.

He looked at the screen and shook his head. "It says here there's a hold on the account."

"Yes, thanks. She already told me that much."

The girl stood behind him, nibbling a nail that already looked nibbled. She said nothing.

"Then what is the mistake you mention?" Gregory said.

"The mistake is that there can't *be* a hold. I deposit money into that account every week. I check it religiously. Why in God's name would there be an issue?"

"I'm not sure. We'll need to contact the administration department." He said the words as if they were obvious, as if he were schooling her. Not unlike doctors giving dieting tips.

"How long will that take?"

He looked at his watch. "I'd guess we could get you in by noon."

She slammed her hand onto the counter. "That won't do. I'm in a hurry."

The line behind her murmured under their collective breaths. She wondered how crazy she looked. "Isn't there anything else you can do?"

He shrugged and she could've punched him in the throat if it weren't for the thing in her periphery. The thing that had not been there a moment before. Through the closest windows, something dark and fluid shimmered across the street. No, not a thing, despite what her imagination insisted. A human. A human wearing a robe, the material swaying in the wind.

"Miss?" Gregory said. "Is everything okay?"

She belched up the taste of partially digested doughnuts. "Do you have a back exit?"

Gregory raised an eyebrow. "Are you sure you're okay? Would you like to sit down?"

Her stinging chest agreed with him. She *did* need to sit down. A nap didn't sound bad either. But the man across the street—the man who worked for that little she-demon—disagreed. He had something other than rest on his mind.

"Answer the fucking question. Is there another way out?"

"Near the bathrooms," the girl said, pointing in the opposite direction. She sounded on the verge of tears now. Esmeralda knew the feeling well.

She left without thanking either of them, without meeting the stares of her onlookers. She marched down the hall, past the bathrooms, and through the rear exit.

The breeze stole her breath for a moment. And in that moment, she knew two things.

She knew Angie Everstein had somehow put a hold on her savings account.

And she knew she wouldn't be allowed to get out of Salem without a fight.

What she didn't know was how much of a fight she had in her.

CHAPTER THIRTEEN
CREEPING THINGS

"WHERE ARE WE GOING?" SHAWNA said.

"To meet my colleague." Mike Mallory did not look away from the road. He wore sunglasses despite the tinted windows and his face could have been a mask.

"Yes, but where? You said he was a professor, right? Are we going to his school or something?"

Mike shook his head. "He said it's not safe there."

"Not safe?"

"Said his coworkers couldn't be trusted with what we'll be discussing."

"You mean my sister's music and how it makes people go crazy?" She thought it *sounded* crazy but she couldn't say she disagreed with the theory. Not with the way Mr. Fuller and Mia and just about everyone else in the world was acting.

"Yes," he said. "Among other things."

"Such as?"

He stopped at a red light, turned right without answering the question.

"I had you pegged as a talker the other night," Shawna said. "You know, when you kidnapped me?"

"I didn't kidnap you." Eyes on the road. Hands clenching the wheel until the knuckles turned white.

"Then what would you call it?"

He slammed a fist onto the wheel, blaring the horn in the process. An old woman on the sidewalk looked up. She'd been checking her mail but the envelopes fell to the ground as she watched them pass. "I let you go, didn't I?"

She shrugged. "Barely."

"Look, I'll explain more when we meet Professor Foster. Gary Foster."

"This Gary guy—you think he can actually help us?"

"I hope so."

They grew silent. She stole glances at him every so often. Not an ugly man by any means, though she wasn't exactly an expert, but he wasn't Ryan Gosling either. It was clear he'd been better looking before his job had gotten the best of him. Wrinkles bordered his eyes and lips, making him look ten years older. His eight o'clock shadow was turning gray by the minute.

"Where are we meeting him?" she said to break the silence. Normally she didn't mind the quiet on account of her condition, but lately she cherished background noise. Because lately she had a certain song stuck in her head.

"A recording studio."

"Say what?"

He nodded. "His friend is a producer. Helps him out with his experiments."

"Experiments."

Mike sighed. "Look, enough questions, okay? Usually, I'm the one doing the asking."

She rolled her eyes. "Fine. Ask away."

"What happened to your sister?"

"How do you mean?" She knew exactly what he meant. She just didn't want to think about it. She'd fought so hard to forget about certain things. Certain *creeping* things. Some days were easier than others. Today was not one of those days.

"I mean something must have *happened* when you guys were younger. She couldn't have always been like this. Who the hell taught her to sing?"

Shawna rubbed her eyes. She couldn't remember the last time she'd slept. "Do we have to talk about this?"

"Sooner or later. Might as well make it sooner."

She closed her eyes. "Okay, but you're going to think I'm crazy."

"Do you remember how many pictures of dead people I had

hanging on that wall?" Outside, the wind picked up as they headed closer to the studio, wherever it was. "Try me."

♪

She called them the creeping things but in reality they were stubborn memories that refused to become repressed. She'd managed to keep them in the background, stored in some distant chamber of her mind, but they were always *there*.

And if, by some miracle, she went a few days or, rarely, a whole week without thinking of the creeping things, that's when the nightmares came around. Only the nightmares couldn't match what had happened in reality. Nothing could match that.

It had been harmless at first. Before the spells and the thing under the bed, etched into the floor, it had just been them and an invisible woman named Ethel. Their mother had thought it was cute. Two girls and their imaginary friend. Except the longer the game went on, the more Shawna suspected Ethel may not have been all that imaginary.

"She's real," Angie had insisted on so many nights, huddled under their comforter, flashlight under her chin like she was about to tell the world's scariest story.

"She can't be," Shawna would insist.

"Why not?"

"Because she's just make-believe."

"Ghosts aren't make-believe."

Most of the ghosts she'd been exposed to were of the friendly variety. Scooby-Doo and Casper. Innocent apparitions that wanted to be your friend or, at the most, cause mischief.

Shawna couldn't remember their first encounter with Ethel. It was probably a combination of things: too many late nights sneaking glances into the living room while their mother and father (before he left) watched horror movies.

There seemed to be no transition about it. One moment it was Shawna and Angie, twin sisters and best friends, and the next there was a wedge driven between them. A wedge by the name of Ethel.

♪

"Why's her name so ugly?" Shawna said about a month after their friend appeared, though Angie had been the only one to see her.

Angie rolled her eyes. "She didn't get to pick it. That's just what it is. Why's your name Shawna?"

"Because that was our great grandmother's name."

"Okay, so maybe that was Ethel's great grandmother's name too.

And don't say it's ugly. She doesn't like that."

It was Shawna's turn to roll her eyes. "How do you know that?"

"Because she told me." There was a knock at the door then, probably Kristen checking they were in bed.

Except their mother's voice did not come. No voice at all in fact. Just slow, steady breathing.

"What was that?" Shawna said, tears forming in her eyes.

"That was Ethel. *Now* do you believe me? She's as real as your stuffed animals. And she wants to be our friend, okay? So stop calling her ugly."

♪

Shawna didn't bring up their supposed friend for a few days after that. They were at the school playground, playing hopscotch, surrounded by their real and tangible classmates.

Shawna pulled Angie away from the group. "What did you mean the other night?"

"About what?"

"When you said Ethel wants to be our friend." She winced at the name.

"She says she wants to cross over. And she needs our help."

"Cross over? You mean, like, into our world or something?"

Angie nodded, a hint of a smile contorting her face. It was much more human-like back then. "We have to help her, Shawna. Please."

"Why does she want to come to our world so bad?"

Angie didn't answer. Not at first. Not even as they helped Ethel cross over. Not until the spell was complete. And by then the answer was pretty damned obvious.

Vengeance.

It was all about vengeance, though at the time, Shawna hadn't understood the word's definition.

♪

The night they invoked Ethel, their parents had gone to a Christmas party. It seemed absurd, dabbling in amateur witchcraft while light snow fell outside their window, the sounds of *Frosty the Snowman* drifting upstairs from the living room television. Their babysitter, Anne Marie, sat on the couch making out with her boyfriend. She had only one rule: don't tattle on her and she'd hold them to the same standard. In hindsight, Shawna wished Anne Marie had tattled instead of getting to second base.

Angie had taken a trip to Esmeralda's Ye Olde Magic Shoppe

earlier that day. Though it was only a few blocks from their home, Kristen had warned them never to go. "I don't like that place," she'd said on more than one occasion.

"It's cool," the girls would counter in unison. "None of that stuff is real. It's just potions and powders. They're like toys."

Shawna had her headphones on, lying on the bed the way young girls do: stomach down, feet in the air. She flipped through a *J-14* magazine that didn't hold her interest. Boy bands and divas, something her sister would eventually become, were boring as hell. She much preferred the rock and roll bands her father listened to. Her head bopped along to Guns N' Roses. The kids at school had given her grief when they learned of her musical tastes but she didn't care. Besides, the doctors had warned her hearing would eventually worsen. Why not enjoy the music she actually liked while she still could?

Halfway through the CD she heard something like a creaking door over the music. Then there was a hand on her shoulder. She spun around and nearly screamed.

Angie held up a brown paper bag. "I got the stuff."

"What stuff?"

"The stuff we talked about. For the spell that will bring Ethel to us."

"You mean provoking?"

"*In*voking. At least that's what Esmeralda called it."

"The fat lady at the witch store?"

Angie nodded. "She's nice. And I think she actually knows what she's talking about." She turned her attention toward her bed across the room. "You wanna try?"

"How's it work?"

Angie's face contorted with a smile that was more like a snarl. For a moment, Shawna swore her teeth were all wrong. Jagged and uneven. Like a vampire or something. Probably just her imagination. "I'll show you. Help me with the bed."

"What's under there?"

Angie didn't answer. She grabbed one of the posts while Shawna grabbed another. They struggled and pulled until the bed was at a perpendicular angle.

Downstairs, the television muted. They could hear the sounds of wet lips before they stopped suddenly. Anne Marie's boyfriend groaned in frustration. "What're you guys doing up there?"

"Just playing." Angie grabbed the blanket that had been laid over the floor.

"Keep it down, will you?"

The television returned, Frosty's husky voice once again filling the house.

"What's under there?"

Angie pulled the blanket and revealed a symbol of some sort. At first Shawna thought her sister had used a Sharpie to draw it but the longer she looked, she realized it had been scratched into the floorboards themselves. A circle and star in one, except the star seemed wrong. "You drew it upside down."

Angie shook her head. "That's how it's supposed to be."

"Mom and Dad are going to kill you."

"Us."

"Huh?"

"They're going to kill *us*. And only if they find out. We keep it between *us*."

"What do you mean? I wasn't even here when you did this."

"They don't know that." From the paper bag she pulled out several candles and a lighter of the cheap plastic variety. There was a generic graphic along its edge: a sexy witch, breasts practically bursting out of a low-cut top.

"What're you doing?" Shawna didn't like the idea of playing with fire, though she didn't yet know that was the least of her worries.

"You'll see." Angie lit the candles and placed one on each point of the star. Next she grabbed a jar of pink powder from the bag and spread it along the outer circle.

"You're making a mess," Shawna said.

Angie ignored her. She pulled the last remaining item from the bag—a small, leather-bound book that reminded Shawna of the bible her parents kept in the cupboard downstairs. But when her sister flipped through the pages, she saw it couldn't have been more different. There were pictures of monsters and demons and things meant for nightmares.

"A spell book," Shawna said.

Angie nodded.

Downstairs, Frosty giggled, as if in response.

Angie settled on a page and wrinkled her brow. "Seems more complicated than when Esmeralda explained it but I think we can figure it out. Hold my hand."

"What?"

"The spell, silly. We need to hold hands in order for it to work."

"I'm hungry. Are you hungry? Maybe we should make some nachos and watch the rest of the movie."

"You mean watch Anne Marie's boyfriend touch her boobs? Gross. Stop being a wuss and grab my hand."

She did as her sister asked. Angie's hands were not cold and clammy like her own.

Angie began to read the spell but Shawna cut her off. "What if it's not her?"

"Not who?"

"Ethel. What if it's something that's just *pretending* to be her?" The thought appeared from nowhere. She'd been thinking of their imaginary friend for days now but hadn't formulated the theory until that moment. She didn't like her choice of words. Some*thing* instead of someone.

"And why would something pretend to be an old woman named Ethel?"

Shawna shrugged and posed another question. "What if it *is* her but she's not nice?"

"She's been nice the whole time."

"But what if she's just faking it so we'll help her? What if she's secretly a bitch like Mrs. Fielding? Or worse." Diana Fielding, their fifth-grade teacher, was the epitome of pure evil in their eyes. She gave every Disney villain a run for their money.

"Are you going to help me or what?" Angie said. "This stuff cost me a week's allowance and we're almost done. Those candles aren't going to last all night."

"But—"

"But nothing. You can either sit here and hold my hand while we say the spell or you can go listen to Air Smith."

"Aero."

"Whatever. You can listen to old people music while I summon our friend. What do you think Samantha and Jill will say at school on Monday? You think they won't make fun of you when they hear that you chickened out?"

Shawna gulped instead of answering. Her sister had her at a standstill. The only option was to go on with the spell.

She closed her eyes while Angie read the words aloud. Her pronunciation seemed off, though the phrases themselves were strangely put together. More Pig Latin than English. Or maybe just *Latin* Latin.

"Repeat after me," Angie said.

Shawna wanted to run but her sister's grip tightened. The sooner she got this over with, the sooner she could head downstairs and pretend to be interested in the cartoon.

Angie's speech grew faster. Louder. And . . . different somehow. As if she wasn't the only one speaking anymore. Her mind did the math against her will.

There were three voices now.

A cool breeze blew through the room even though the windows were shut.

"It worked," Angie said some time later. Shawna wasn't sure how long. She'd kept her eyes closed so hard they felt glued.

"What do you mean?" A single tear tried to crawl out of her eye.

"Open your eyes and take a look, silly."

Shawna could practically see the grin on her sister's face even in the blackness. That same grin from earlier that didn't seem all that human.

She opened her right eye, too frightened to see the whole scene. That stubborn tear made its way out just fine, trickling down her cheek. It was followed by more when she saw not one but two individuals sitting on the floor before her.

"It worked," Angie said again.

"We're almost there," Mike said.

Shawna expected him to laugh or sneer. Instead, he scratched at the stubble along his jawbone, perhaps in thought. Perhaps trying to decide if he ought to drop her off at the corner and tell her to find the nearest insane asylum.

"That isn't the whole story," she said. "There's plenty more."

"There'll be time for that later."

She hadn't realized how long she'd been talking. According to the clock, an hour had passed. They were no longer in the suburbs. Skyscrapers lay in the distance. They'd reached Boston.

Mike pulled off the highway and soon there were brick buildings for as far as she could see. An industrial part of town. "Where are we?"

He pulled into a nondescript parking lot. The building in front of them had tinted windows that matched those of the RV. The brick was crumbling in several places and she wondered if the place hadn't been condemned. "We're here."

She had one last, panicked thought about Officer Mallory. What if this was all some elaborate plan? Make her think he was on her side but really he just wanted to isolate her so no one would hear her scream.

He started to get out of the car. "Wait," she said.

"What?"

"Aren't you going to say anything?"

"About what?"

She unbuckled her seat belt. "I just told you about how we conjured a dead woman and you have nothing to say?"

"I have plenty to say but I'll let the professor take it from here. Whatever your sister is, we're going to put an end to her."

He stepped outside and entered the closest door. A dark hallway awaited. He'd left the keys in the ignition. She didn't have her license, couldn't afford driving lessons on account of her mother's crippling debt, but she was a fast learner.

But where would she go? Back to Salem, where everyone seemed to be losing their minds? Her hometown didn't feel safe anymore. *Nowhere* felt safe. Sitting in the RV with the tinted windows, in the nondescript parking lot, she felt hundreds of eyes on her.

The dark hallway didn't seem all that sinister anymore.

CHAPTER FOURTEEN
MORE ANSWERS AND MORE QUESTIONS

JOSH SPENT MOST OF THE day at the hospital. It was two hours before he was given an update. Both he and his ass had fallen asleep in the emergency room. The chairs were hellish, made from plastic that felt more like concrete. In the upper corner of the wall, a muted television played news stories about suicide bombers and school shootings. During every commercial break there'd been at least two advertisements for Angie Everstein's debut album, featuring the titular track.

The closed captions had been turned on. Though he couldn't hear her voice, his skin still tingled at the sight of her lyrics scrolling across the screen. He crossed his legs to hide his excitement. What the hell was happening to him? And while he was on the subject: what the hell was happening to the *world*?

The questions spiraled from there, bringing on a migraine that bordered on unbearable. He closed his eyes, nodded off, and found peace for the first time in a long time.

Until a short doctor wearing a long white lab coat shook him awake. The headache was still there, resting just under his left eye. If anything, it had worsened. He wanted to ask for some painkillers but feared he'd come across as a junkie. He made to stand and almost tripped, held the wall for support.

"Mr. Meyers?" the man said. "Are you okay?"

He nodded, held out his hand. They shook.

"I'm Dr. Girard. I've been taking care of your wife."

He winced at that word. *Wife*. They'd been separated for a year, yet they were, legally speaking, still married. He'd hoped to speed up the process by selling their condo. Maybe then she'd come around to the divorce. He wasn't sure why she kept delaying. Perhaps some part of her still loved him. More likely, she was just lazy.

"How is she?"

Dr. Girard's voice transitioned from empathetic to the robotic tone reserved for healthcare professionals. "I'm afraid she's lost a lot of blood. We have her under observation. After forty-eight hours, we suggest she be transferred to a psychiatric facility for further evaluation. There are several local options we can discuss."

"She's never done anything like this. I didn't even think she was capable."

"Of course." He did not sound all that convinced

Nor did Josh. The way Melissa had been acting these last few years, the way she'd spent more and more time indoors with the lights off, the way she'd taken on so many lovers instead of job interviews—was this really that far off?

Yes, he thought. Because *this* wasn't just her depression. *This* was something else. It had to do with the song she'd been listening to. The song that silently played on the floating television as they spoke.

"Can I see her?" he said, though he wasn't sure if he meant it.

"We'd like to run some more tests. Perhaps you could come back tomorrow?"

Josh nodded. "That would be fine. You'll call me if anything happens?"

"Yes, of course. We'll be in touch with any developments."

"Thank you." He opened his mouth to ask about those painkillers after all but Dr. Girard was already navigating the maze-like hallways behind the nurse's station. His lab coat fluttered behind him like a persistent ghost.

Josh left in a hurry, braved the tourist traffic, and parked a half-mile away from the shop. He would've been better off walking from his apartment but it was a moot point as he made his way through the front doors. Trish wasn't behind the counter.

The speakers played something horrid: a combination of feedback and ambient noise that did his headache no favors. "What the hell is that?" he said, covering his ears.

When no one answered, he stepped toward the stereo and turned the volume down. His ears rang in protest of the sudden silence. "Trish? You here?"

"Out back," she said. "That you, boss?"

"Who else would it be? When's the last time you saw a customer in here?"

She didn't answer but his question hadn't been entirely rhetorical. Despite the Halloween season, business was less than booming. If their sales didn't spike soon, he'd be forced to close up shop for good. And then what? Go back to his insufferable office job? Become a barista? He didn't want to go down that road. His store was still open. The proverbial fat lady remained quiet for the time being.

Though he wondered when she'd speak up as he surveyed the store.

It came as no surprise that more of his inventory had been replaced with Angie memorabilia. Her face was at the front of each rack, covering up death and black metal albums. There were two cardboard cutouts now, one for each back corner. He had to convince himself their paper eyes wouldn't blink at any moment.

"That's it." He grabbed the closest box of CDs that hadn't yet been unpacked, searched for a label. Why hadn't he thought of such a simple solution before? Except it *wasn't* a solution.

Every box was void of information. No writing or markings of any kind.

"It's gotta be Jeff or Tommy. I can't remember if they gave their keys back."

"You're wrong," Trish said from behind.

He spun around, hand to his chest, unsure how many more scared-shitless moments his heart could take. "Jesus, will you stop sneaking up on me like that?"

"Jeff and Tommy didn't do this."

"How can you know for sure?"

She evaded the question and waved him toward the front counter. She set down a pile of CDs onto the counter, none of them Angie's. From her pocket she pulled out a cigarette and lit it like a reflex.

"How many times have I told you not to smoke in here?"

She dodged that question too. He didn't find cigarettes attractive but there was something endearing with her. He could not deny the crush he'd developed but even if he did manage to ask her out—and that was a big *if*—he could see it ending the same way as his marriage. She would control him, call every shot, while he sat back and obeyed like a good little boyfriend.

The static noise appeared again. He covered his ears and winced. "What is that? Turn it off, will you?"

"That's just it. I can't. Not really, at least."

"What do you mean?"

She stopped smoking for a moment and retrieved a Pig Destroyer CD from one of the clamshell cases. On the cover was an image of a bloody corpse that seemed much more innocent than the shop's new inventory. She put the disc into the stereo and pressed play.

And the noise reappeared, even worse this time.

"There's something wrong with the stereo now too? We don't have the money for a new one."

"The problem isn't the stereo. Check this out," she said, cigarette dangling from her mouth. She swapped the CD out for one of Angie's and her voice spewed from the speakers, singing lyrics about loving you for all eternity and other such nonsense.

Josh's blood rushed below his beltline. He leaned forward to hide his erection and told her to shut it off. "What's your point?"

"My point is that the only CDs that work are hers. I've tried about fifty others. Same goes for the records."

"That's not possible."

"I didn't think so either but it's the truth."

He didn't speak for a long time. Outside, tourists passed by in droves, though none of them visited the shop. It didn't make any sense. If half of their inventory was now the most popular album in the world, why in God's name were their sales dwindling?

The answer came to him. So simple. So *alarming*.

Because everyone already has *her album*.

"I think I know where all of the merch has been coming from," Trish said.

He was barely listening. "Huh?"

"The merch. I think it's coming from the pop princess herself."

"What makes you say that?" His mouth went dry.

"Because when I came in this morning, I saw someone out back. They caught me looking and ran off. At first I thought they were just dressed up for Halloween. Not all that out of the ordinary. But then I realized I'd seen that same costume around town. They were wearing this long robe. Reminded me of a druid or something. I think they're part of her team. And I think they're the ones dropping the shit off. Not to mention breaking in and setting it up."

Ludicrous. Just a conspiracy theory. He looked into Trish's eyes for a hint of her trademark sarcasm but her face was deadpan. She was telling the truth. "Why?" he said. "Why are they doing this?"

She shrugged, blew another cloud of smoke that momentarily clouded his vision.

And in that moment, his periphery played a trick on him.

He saw yet another cardboard cutout of Angie Everstein, standing just behind Trish. The cardboard winked, just as he'd predicted, and held up a stiff hand, waving him toward her. He almost screamed but the vision—if that's what it was—passed. He blinked and she was gone altogether.

"Come on," Josh said, grabbing his keys and hurrying toward the exit. "We're closing early tonight."

CHAPTER FIFTEEN
BENEATH THE SURFACE

"IT'S JUST UP HERE," MIKE Mallory said. He climbed two sets of stairs and turned the corner toward yet another hall. There were small windows along the way, offering views of Boston Harbor. Shawna wondered how many of Angie's fans were in the city this very moment. No, not just fans. What was the term they used?

Glitter Critters.

She didn't like the moniker. It brought to mind other things aside from fanatics. Aberrations that defied every law of the physical world. Joints with too many angles that housed limbs with too many claws.

By the time she climbed the second set of stairs she was sweating and not just from the exercise. A cold sweat. A *fear* sweat.

On the right lay a doorway. She caught the back of Mike's feet as he stepped inside. Music filtered into the hall. Hip-hop of some sort. She peeked her head in and saw what looked like a small recording studio. A console with infinite knobs and switches and faders. Two laptops sat nearby, sound waves flickering on the screens.

Behind the console was a window overlooking an even smaller room. The walls were lined with mesh foam. Sound-proofing. Two strangers occupied the studio. The first was a man of perhaps twenty-five. His body was covered in tattoos, many crudely done. A dollar-bill sign rested under his right eye, like he cried money.

The second stranger was perhaps twenty years older. His beard and wavy hair had gone prematurely gray and his glasses were much too big for his sunken face. The professor, she assumed.

Mike whispered something into the older man's ear and he nodded, held his hand out. "Gary Foster. Nice to meet you."

She studied his fingers before shaking them. Her gut insisted this was a safe space but she wasn't counting anything out. "Hey."

"You're her sister?" Gary studied her, probably shocked at just how different twins could be.

"In the flesh."

"I'm glad you're here. Come in and shut the door. We have a lot to talk about and a short time to do it."

Mike beat her to it, closing the door and locking it.

"Would you like some coffee?" Gary adjusted his glasses as they began to droop down his nose.

"I'm fine," she said, though her eyelids told a different story. They felt plastered to her pupils, shutting on their own accord. It had been a long, sleepless few days.

"I'll grab you a cup anyway," he said. "Just in case. I suspect we won't be getting any rest for a long time."

Before she could ask what he meant, he turned toward the man sitting down. "Curtis? Three coffees if you don't mind."

"Am I your servant now?" The man—Curtis—stood. He touched the nearest fader and turned the music down.

"We don't have time to argue. Just get it, will you?"

Curtis adjusted his backwards Red Sox hat and walked through a side door she hadn't noticed until now. He made a show of it for the professor, let him know he wasn't happy.

"I apologize for him," Gary said, keeping his voice down. "He's a talented producer and engineer, one of the best I've ever worked with. But he's got a chip on his shoulder. And he's on edge. All of us are, I suppose."

"You can say that again." Mike rubbed his eyes and scratched his stubble.

A few moments later Curtis returned with three cups of coffee. He handed them out. The paper cup was thin and burned her skin but the strong aroma calmed her some.

"We're out of cream and sugar, I'm afraid," Gary said.

"That's fine," she said. "I drink it black sometimes." A lie. She drank it with enough cream and sugar to constitute a milkshake. She'd never had a cup in her life until Mia introduced her. Now if she didn't drink at least two a day, she developed a caffeine headache. A gift from their time together. A scar in a weird sort of way.

"What is this place?"

Mike looked too exhausted to explain and the professor, supposedly an expert on whatever subject they were here to discuss, wasn't the world's most social person. He radiated an awkwardness he'd likely had since childhood.

"This is my studio," Curtis said. "Built the place myself. Big G just wrapped up his newest mix tape here. Ever heard him? Gonna be big. Mark my words."

Foster smiled apologetically. "Curtis is right. This is a recording studio but more importantly it's an under*ground* one. Lesser known, if you will."

"The hell's that supposed to mean?" Curtis said.

"What I mean is that this place—it's not on certain individuals' radars."

"You mean my sister."

He nodded. "And I'd like to keep it that way. Our experiments have proved crucial."

"What kind of experiments?"

Foster took two large sips of his coffee. A few drops clung to his upper lip but he didn't notice. He set the cup town, walked toward the console, and asked Curtis to switch the song. "I apologize in advance," Foster said, looking at both Shawna and Mike, the latter of which covered his ears.

Before Shawna could ask what he meant, the hip-hop song ended abruptly. A new song replaced it. No, not a *new* song. She'd managed to hear it plenty in the last six months. No matter how hard she tried to avoid the melody, it always seemed to slither into her life. Just like the creeping things. She'd be at a store or on the bus and the soft, haunting voice of Angie would appear from nowhere.

"Forever with You" played through the speakers.

The room halved in size. She hadn't noticed the lack of windows until now. Behind her, the locked door was miles away. She made to remove her hearing aids but Mike uncovered one of his ears and held her arm.

"It's okay," he said.

"How do you feel?" Foster said. He wore headphones, yelling a bit too loud.

"Horrible," she said. "I feel horrible."

"Be more specific. Tell me exactly what's going through your mind."

"Nothing really. Except I want to scream. I want to reach over there and rip out every wire until they're sparking. And when the song's done I want to take those wires and wrap them around—"

Foster nodded for her to go on but the song was too much. Her heart threatened to stop beating if it didn't burst first. The room shrank again until she was inside of a grave. No light. No air. Nothing but darkness. She swayed, nearly fainted, but Mike caught her.

"That's enough," he said.

"Very well. Curtis, turn it off, will you?"

"Yes, Master."

The song faded, though Shawna swore she heard it a few extra moments longer.

"It's still there, isn't it?" Foster said. "In your head, I mean."

She nodded, mouth hanging open. "How'd you know that?"

"Because I've been studying your sister's music and the effect it has on people since she won that little talent show. And the effect, I'm sorry to say, is not good." He turned toward Mike. "Officer Mallory first brought it to my attention. The murders, I mean. They seemed unconnected, given how far apart they occurred, but there was one common thread that eventually could not be ignored."

He took another gulp of coffee, finishing the cup and crumpling it. "Her music stimulates the amygdala, the aggressive portion of our brains, the fight or flight response. Only in this case, the listeners almost always choose fight."

"So like a subliminal message?"

"Yes and no. The song itself is harmless. The lyrics are average and dull and the melody is nothing we haven't heard a thousand times over. It's what's beneath the surface that causes the effect." He turned toward Curtis. "Show her the isolated track."

Curtis, for all his defiance and tough-guy attitude, looked childish in that moment. He tried to play it off as annoyance. He failed. "Do we have to?"

"Yes, unfortunately."

Curtis sighed and played with more of the knobs. On the computer screen, several of the sound waves vanished until only one remained. The song was still paused and the line was jagged, not unlike fangs.

"Ms. Everstein, what you're about to hear is . . . quite disturbing. I won't play it for long but you need to see what we're dealing with.

Are you ready?"

"Yes," she lied.

"Very well." He nodded toward Curtis, and everyone, Shawna included, took a deep breath.

The noise played over the speakers. For that's what it was: a noise. There was no music or cadence to be found. It reminded her of a radio signal gone bad. Something you heard late at night in between channels, when stations went off the air. It was harsh, a bit like white noise, except it wasn't entirely random. There was something inside the chaos, something like screaming. Yes, that was it. Screaming. Hundreds upon thousands of shouts so distorted, so high-pitched and shriek-like, she couldn't help but reach for her ears.

Except her arms froze. She didn't *want* to stop. The revelation came suddenly. She felt both euphoric and disgusted. She thought of those wires again, how easy they'd be to wrap around each of the others' necks. She had little to no upper body strength but she was certain she could kill at least one of them.

Her upper lip felt warm and she tasted salt. She wiped her nose and the back of her hand grew dark red with blood. The sight of the fluid angered her and she longed for those wires—her potential weapons—even more.

Her sight vanished. As did every other sense save for her hearing. How ironic. The one thing that was guaranteed to fail her now kept her in this state or trance or whatever the hell it was.

A hand on her shoulder. And a voice. Not Angie's but a man's. A man calling for her from eons away. Telling her to open her eyes.

She did so.

And was back in the recording studio.

Mike and Foster hovered over her. Curtis held what looked like a rag. He tossed it to her and she held it against her nose. The bleeding died down some but it was replaced with a dull headache in the back of her eyes.

"What the hell was that?"

"That," Foster said, "was the hidden track. There's one within all of your sister's songs. It's made in such a way that it disappears when coupled with the instruments and vocals. But it's there nonetheless. Working its magic, so to speak. As you may have noticed, it has quite the effect."

She managed to lift her head and prop herself up with her elbows. "I noticed."

"Good," Foster said. "Now that we've identified the problem, we can move onto the next step."

"Which is?"

"Solving it."

He let the sentence hang in the air but Foster's proposed plan was simple, in a sense. It was, she supposed, the same solution Mike had theorized. What did you do when a song you loathed came on the radio?

You shut it off.

♪

It took three tries for Esmeralda to dial Jeannie Rogers on her cell phone. She kept second-guessing herself, hanging up just before sending the call. They had, admittedly, not been the best of friends these last few years.

More like a decade, she thought as the dial tone pierced her ears. She winced at the sound, feeling anxious. Not just from reaching out to Jeannie after radio silence.

It was the sign across the street. The sign above the front doors of her shop.

Only it wasn't her shop anymore, was it? That much was evident from the newly erected words, the neon light flickering in obscure patterns.

She read them again, hoping in some stupid section of her mind that she was just dreaming, that she'd suffered a heart attack and the surgeons were unclogging her arteries this very moment.

Fat chance of that, she thought. She could've laughed if she wasn't so scared.

The words read: *Angie Everstein's Ye Olde Magic Shoppe.*

"Hello?"

Esmeralda gasped at Jeannie's voice. She'd all but forgotten about the call.

"Hello?" her old friend said again.

Esmeralda paused. She didn't want to be a bother. Jeannie probably had better plans than to talk with an overweight phony witch that had fallen out of touch.

"Jeannie." Her throat constricted. She wasn't sure how long she'd been crying.

"Who's this?"

"It's Esmeralda."

A gasp. "Is it really you?"

She nodded. "Sure is. All four hundred pounds of me."

Jeannie snorted. What came from her mouth during moments of joy was more like the sound of a pig at a trough than a laugh. In their younger years, Esmeralda would tell jokes every chance she got. She bought comedy books, memorized punch lines just to hear that squeal.

"How the hell have you been?" Jeannie said. "God, I can't even remember the last time we talked."

"That's my fault." She wiped her eyes but fresh tears replaced the old ones.

"Don't be silly. I didn't mean it like that."

"I did. I honestly don't remember the last time I gave you a call. I blamed it on being busy but the truth is that I haven't been busy in a long time. I work and come home and hate myself a little more each day."

"Honey . . . are you okay? You sound like you're crying."

"Me? Cry? We really have fallen out of touch."

Another joke they'd shared. During the four years they'd roomed together, Jeannie had never seen Esmeralda shed a tear. Not from the stress of college, nor from her break up with Dylan, one of two serious boyfriends she'd ever had—not even when Esmeralda had learned her cousin Lisa had been killed by a drunk driver. Tears, it seemed, refused to pay her a visit.

How things had changed.

"Are you sure you're alright?"

"How is it down there?" Esmeralda said. "In Florida, I mean."

"Same as always. Sunny and warm, if not a little boring."

"Sounds glorious."

"What about up there? How's Salem?"

Dangerous, she almost said. "Flooded with tourists per usual."

"How is your shop doing?"

Her bottom lip quivered at the question. "Look, I was thinking—have been for a while—what if I moved down there? To your neck of the woods. You think you could point me in the right direction? I looked into condos and apartments but there're too many to count. It's overwhelming."

She could sense the smile from thousands of miles away. Jeannie was moments away from her signature snort. "You kidding me? I've been waiting years for this call."

In college, they'd vowed to head to the sunshine state the moment they graduated. Jeannie had gotten a job as a dental hygienist, made good money and benefits. Esmeralda had stayed back and worked a series of part-time, in-between jobs. She just needed some extra months to save money. Except extra months turned to years. Her parents got older and sicker, hearts failing with each passing day. So her dreams of Florida had grown distant until it seemed less like a state and more like some exotic country. After her parents died, just shy of six months apart, she'd started her business, thinking she could swindle tourists out of money. It worked. But with it, came the death of her dream.

"Esmeralda? You there?"

"Yeah, I'm here and that's the problem. Look, if I were to head down there in the near future, you think I could stay at your place for a while? Just until I got on my feet."

Esmeralda was certain she'd overstepped her boundaries. She hadn't so much as called her best friend in a year, maybe longer, and here she was asking to be taken in indefinitely. She ought to hang up. She ought to accept defeat.

"Of course," Jeannie said.

"Really?" She almost convinced herself those were happy tears in her eyes.

"I'd love to have you. I have a guest room I've been meaning to clean out. This will be the perfect excuse. I should be thanking you."

"I think it's the other way around. I can't thank you enough. It means the world."

"When are you leaving?"

Another glance at the sign. Her eyes were growing blurry but she could still make out the words just fine. "As soon as possible. I just need to get some things in order."

"I can't wait, Ez. I think you're going to love it down here."

"I think you're right."

They spoke for another few minutes, small talk at first, though the conversation turned to inside jokes and reminiscing about better times. When it came time to hang up, Esmeralda couldn't help but feel she was saying goodbye for the final time.

Don't think that way.

Across the street, shapes moved inside what had been her shop twenty-four hours ago. The woman on the phone—Glenda—had said Esmeralda could continue to operate her business with a few changes in place.

It was dark outside but the streetlight cast enough glow to see inside. The shop's lights were turned off yet whoever lay within walked through the shadows as if they had night vision. She couldn't make out details aside from their robes. They moved swiftly, quickly, and Esmeralda thanked the stars she hadn't gone into work today.

She backed away, swallowed by the darkness of the neighboring alley. Her feet nearly slipped on several cobblestones but she did not dare turn away from the windows. It didn't feel safe having her back to the shop.

Not until she reached the next block did she finally turn around and walk back to her apartment to gather what little belongings she planned on keeping.

Her chest heaved and her pulse protested. She wondered if she could run if the need arose.

And something told her it *would* arise.

CHAPTER SIXTEEN
BAR TALK PART II

"WHAT'RE YOU WORKING ON?" JIMMY said, sliding another beer across the bar. A small drop of foam spilled onto one of the several pieces of paper spread out in front of Josh.

"My finances," Josh said. "My *future*. Or lack thereof." There were hundreds of numbers scrawled in his chicken scratch. He'd added and subtracted and subtracted again. Math had never been his strong suit but the answer to this equation was simple.

If something didn't change, he'd be bankrupt come the first of November. The store had never brought in an excess of cash but it allowed him to pay his mortgage and keep the lights on. Now he was paying for *two* homes, one he'd let his estranged wife destroy, and another he'd littered with empty beer cans. If he didn't sell the condo soon—and it was looking grave after Melissa's incident—he couldn't afford to keep his business.

"Tough times, huh?" Jimmy wiped at an invisible stain on the bar.

"The toughest," Josh took a sip of his beer. Then another. Until it was nearly drained. Jimmy gave him a refill without asking. Josh was a quiet drunk, didn't make a scene like some of the other regulars. He was rewarded with never being cut off or asked to leave. At least he was good at something.

He crunched more numbers, started a new list of solutions but nothing stuck. By the time he'd nearly finished his next beer, it was clear he was, for lack of a better term, fucked.

A group of college girls erupted with laughter at the corner of the bar as one of their friends fell from their stool. Jimmy walked over to clean up the mess, flirting with a blonde wearing sunglasses despite the dim lighting.

Josh was so caught up in the scene he didn't notice the man sit next to him and whisper into his ear. "Don't say anything. Don't even turn to look at me. Keep doing your homework and pretend I'm a stranger." Dan Peterson set his glass on the counter a little too hard.

"I'm really not in the mood tonight," Josh said, staring at the liquor bottles ahead. Though Dan had grown on him during their last conversation, he was still one of the men who'd fucked Melissa. Not to mention he'd sounded off his rocker.

But so much had happened since then. He thought of his store and the cardboard cutouts and his wife's bleeding wrists as she did a poor job coloring within the lines.

Maybe he hadn't been off his rocker after all.

"I'm only telling you this because I feel bad, okay?" Dan stared at his sopping napkin, took a sip of what smelled like whiskey. "I shouldn't have did what I did. You're a good guy. A pushover, sure. But you're not an asshole. That's rare these days."

Josh set his pencil down and arranged his papers into one stack. "Look, whatever it is, I don't want to hear it. I've had a hell of a day."

"You're not the only one." He lowered his voice, as if anyone in the bar could hear them over the college girls and the blaring music. "I have to be quick. They're watching us. They're always watching."

"Who's *they*?"

"Haven't you figured it out by now?"

"Enlighten me." Only Josh didn't *want* to know.

"Her team, man. Don't tell me you haven't seen them. They follow her around like a fucking cult. In fact, I think that's exactly what they are."

"Is this about the stage again?" He hadn't visited Gallows Hill this Halloween season. Work and life had gotten in the way but also he hadn't *wanted* to visit. It felt safer not seeing the stage with his own eyes.

"It's just about done now. Should be finished up in another day or two. Just in time for the big night."

"You mean Halloween."

Dan nodded in Josh's periphery. "You need to pack up and leave town. Tonight, if possible. I already told my parents and my sister. I don't know if they believed me."

"Believed you about what? Look, Dan, I'm tired and you're ruining my buzz."

"It's the concert. Something's going to happen at the concert."

"What?" He took another sip of beer and gagged. It tasted sour.

Dan slid his stool over so his breath grazed Josh's ear. "They do things out there, in the woods. They dance and they sing and sometimes, if it's quiet enough, you hear something singing back."

"You're not making any sense."

"I'm telling you what I've seen and heard. You can do what you want with that information. Something rotten—bad with a capital B—is going down during that show. And when it does, you don't want to be anywhere near this place."

Josh did not respond. His insides curdled. The music and the patrons and everything else vanished. He was alone with his thoughts and he didn't like where they led.

Maybe this guy's crazy but he does make a terrible sort of sense. Look around. This town is going to hell. People are acting strange, as in slitting-their-wrists strange. Not to mention what's going on below your belt lately. And it all comes back to Little Miss Everstein.

He couldn't help but picture her perfect body. The way her skin seemed to glow a shade of white that reminded him of bone. The way her breasts jutted. The way her eyes—

The way her eyes were cold and dark and not the least bit inviting, though you couldn't look away even if you wanted because once she had you, once she wrapped her elegant little fingers around you, there was no going back.

He shook his head and saw that Dan had left. The bar stool was empty and a woman with pink hair, skin dabbed with what looked like glitter, moved in to fill the vacant spot, ordering a martini—extra dirty.

"You're a fan," she said, catching his stare. "Aren't you?"

Josh stood up. "What did you just say?"

"You're a critter. I can tell. You love our queen and savior."

Josh slipped two twenty-dollar bills onto the bar, much more than he needed to pay, though his finances had suddenly become less important. He kept his papers on the counter and left without saying anything else.

Outside, the breeze touched him like probing fingers.

CHAPTER SEVENTEEN
HUMMING WHILE KILLING

IT WAS ALMOST MIDNIGHT WHEN Mike dropped Shawna off at her house. The documentary crew's trailer was still parked across the street, windows tinted so they matched the night. She couldn't tell if anyone watched. Maybe it was better that way.

The drive back had been quiet, her mind replaying the conversation with Professor Foster.

"This has to be a dream, right? I'm in a nightmare and if I scream loud enough I'll wake up."

"It's a nightmare, sure, but it's all real. And it's only going to get worse."

"What you're asking me—it seems impossible. I can't kill my sister. I'm not a murderer."

"Even after everything you've learned about her?"

She looked toward her house and tried to recall the good times, before Angie was a pop star, before her father hit the road, before her mother had decided to spend their life away. The memories were light years away. She did not feel at home in her own home. Mike was right. This *was* a nightmare. "How would I . . . you know . . . do it?"

He shrugged, looking into the rearview mirror, then studying the trailer. She hadn't seen him blink once since they'd met. "Let me figure that part out."

For a moment, she saw through the tough guy façade and Mike Mallory seemed just as scared as she felt. "Her songs, they really made that girl kill her family like you said?"

His eyes went out of focus and she could practically hear the screams, smell the blood. "They prepare you for the worst. The force, I mean. You might see a murder or a car accident. Might witness someone bleed out in front of you, hold a civilian while they breathe their last breath. What I saw in that house was nothing like that. You can't prepare for that. And it stays with me. I've seen five shrinks and they all come to the same conclusion. I'm a nice, easy diagnosis. PTSD with flashbacks and anxiety. Nothing fancy. With enough therapy and pills, they tell me, the visions will fade. But let me tell you: they've only gotten worse. Because she's still out there. She's still killing without lifting a finger. I don't want to see any more little girls lose their eyes."

"I never told you the rest of my story. About Ethel."

"Does it really matter?"

"Yes," she said. "It does." Her throat grew several sizes too large as the creeping things crawled into her mind. "She was a witch."

"A what?"

"Ethel told us her entire life story. We thought it was a joke, just an old, cruel, dead woman playing games, but we did some research, talked to some librarians who pointed us in the right direction. A couple of kid detectives. You would've been proud. She was a witch and they burned her right here in Salem. Except she was the real deal. Used to torture animals and perform ceremonies in the woods. She didn't bother the settlers and they left her alone. Until she stole a baby from its crib." A sob threatened to burst from her mouth. Ethel had imitated the baby's cry one night, cackling as she did so. And they'd *helped* her back into this world. Shawna was partly to blame for everything that had happened.

That poor girl would still have her eyes if she hadn't let Angie perform her spell.

"I don't get it," Mike said. "Even if you did conjure a ghost or a witch or whatever she was, what does that have to do with your sister's music?"

"Ethel wasn't just good at rituals and killing. She had the prettiest voice in all of Salem. You could hear her singing in the woods while she did her dirty work. So they said, at least. Imagine that? Humming while you kill. She taught Angie how to perfect her voice, how to hit high notes no eleven-year-old should be able to hit. She created a star."

"And what happened to this Ethel?"

She shrugged. "One day she just kind of faded away. I didn't see her anymore, which was fine by me. And if Angie did, she kept it quiet. Maybe she's still there, in my room, waiting for the right moment to show herself."

The room in question lay in the upper left corner of her house. The window was not so much pitch black as it was dim gray, hall light filtering in through a partially closed door. She did not see any unaccounted for shapes, though that did nothing for her nerves.

"You ought to get some rest," Mike said. "The next couple of days are going to be busy."

"I'm guessing you'll find me and not the other way around?"

"I'll be close by even if you can't see me."

She should've felt safe but it would take an army to soothe her worries. She wished him a good night and jogged up the walkway, opening the front door and closing it gently behind her.

The house was silent. No creaking steps or hushed television. Nothing but the faint hum of the refrigerator. She took a deep breath and made her way toward the stairs.

"Where the hell have you been?"

Shawna held a hand to her chest and turned toward the kitchen entryway. Her mother sat at the table, a cup of coffee in one hand, a cigarette in the other.

"You scared the shit out of me." Her heart jackhammered.

"What did I say about swearing? And you didn't answer my question."

"I was . . . out." The stairs seemed so close. Just another few steps.

"This late on a school night? With who? It sure wasn't Mia. I haven't seen her around in months."

"Don't give me that concerned mother act again. You can drop the charade, okay? Your favorite daughter isn't listening in." She shocked herself by taking a step closer to Kristen. "Or maybe she is. It's not like I get a moment of privacy when she's home."

"She *isn't* home. She flew to New York for a talk show. And she was very upset with you."

"About what? She mad that I don't wanna go to her stupid show?"

Kristen stood. The coffee cup shook in her hand, a few drops spilling onto a new bathrobe. Expensive by the looks of it. "As a matter of fact, yes. And Glenda let us know you wouldn't do the interview."

"Of course I won't do the interview. It's a waste of my time and hers. I don't have anything good to *say* about Angie. Leave me out of it. Pretend she's an only child. Isn't that what you've been doing all along?"

"That's enough. You need to start treating me like your mother and not some stranger."

Another step closer, heart beating faster. "Then start acting like one."

Smoke poured from Kristen's nostrils in two shallow streams. "You think you know everything. You think you have your mother figured out. I'm just a dead-beat bitch with a spending problem. And maybe you're half right. But you're only eighteen, hardly old enough to know how it feels when life beats you down."

"Oh really?" She had two constant reminders of just how bad life could get, two hunks of plastic lodged in her ear canals this very moment.

Her mother nodded. "You think I don't miss your father? I miss him with every ounce of my body. But he's never coming back. And I know I have a problem. But it's hard being a single mother. Harder than you could imagine."

For a moment, Shawna actually felt bad for her. Then the anger returned. "When was the last time you had a job for more than six months?"

"It's . . . complicated."

Shawna shook her head. "No, it's not. Let me break it down for you. You have been waiting for Angie to make it big and now your dream has come true."

Her mother stared for a long time. Shawna could feel the tension floating through the air. Kristen had never hit her but Shawna wasn't counting it out. Finally, she set the coffee cup onto the table and dropped her cigarette into the remnants. It sizzled out quickly. "That's where you're wrong." She sniffled instead of screaming. Her bottom lip quivered. Were those tears in her eyes?

"What're you talking about?"

"Your sister promised to help me with the mortgage and the bills, at least until I got back on my feet. And yeah, I thought about taking advantage of the situation, if you want the truth. But it doesn't matter because she might not give me *any* money. She doesn't have to. She's eighteen, after all. And she's pissed at both of us, wants us to be a family again."

"A family? I find that hard to believe. Sounds like she's blackmailing you."

Kristen dabbed her eyes with her fancy new robe. "Maybe she is. But the ball is in her court and no matter how stupid you think that interview is, I'm begging you. Smile for the camera and pretend everything is okay. Just this once."

Shawna's mind spun in a thousand different directions. She could not recall ever seeing her mother cry, not even the day Dad left. She needed sleep and she needed it quick. She turned around.

"Where are you going?" Kristen said.

"To bed."

"You'll think about what I said, right? Just tell me you'll consider it."

Shawna paused at the first step. "I'll think about it," she said without knowing if it was the truth.

She took the stairs two at a time, shut her bedroom door tightly. Her sister may have been out of the state but her followers—they were everywhere. She pulled her ottoman in front of the door and lay on her bed, staring at the ceiling and willing sleep to come.

It did not.

CHAPTER EIGHTEEN
JUST LET HER IN

SUZIE COLLINS DID NOT LIKE the woman in 3B. There was something about the way she stared at the television like it was a miracle, like god himself had appeared before her, that made Suzie's bowels run cold. She ran through her list as quickly as possible, checking vitals and portioning out pills.

The television's volume was too loud for this time of night. Some talk show where Joey Fallon, or whatever the hell his name was, welcomed his guest. A blond bimbo by the name of Angie Everstein.

Why did that name sound familiar?

The crowd cheered and stood and the studio lights made their skin glisten. At first she thought it was sweat, but as the cameras zoomed in, she saw it was *glitter*. Their arms and legs and faces—every bit of exposed skin—were covered with glitter.

The shot panned back to the girl and Suzie finally recognized her. She sang that song that played all over the radio. "Forever into You" or something. Suzie didn't listen to the radio all that much—or to music in general for that matter. She spent most of her time working as many shifts as her health would allow, flat feet be damned. All this for a teenaged son named Bruce that wanted to be called Jax (his middle name as chosen by his father, wherever he was) who rarely gave her the time of day. Some nights, when exhaustion took hold, she dreamed of leaving. The guilt from such fantasies hurt, sure, but not as much as her feet.

"Thirsty."

Suzie shook her head. She'd almost forgotten all about the woman in 3B. "I'm sorry?"

"I'm thirsty."

Suzie pointed to the cup of lukewarm ginger ale on the bedside table. The woman's wrists were still bandaged, would have to be cleaned the following morning. The guards hadn't restrained her, which bothered Suzie Collins in a way she couldn't vocalize. Not that she wanted to vocalize anything to the woman (Melissa, she thought her name was). She *wanted* it to be midnight so she could head home and grab a few measly hours of sleep. She *wanted* to run into Matt Damon on the street and fuck his brains out. But, if she was being honest, she'd settle for Joey Fallon—if that was his name.

"I'm not thirsty for that," Melissa said.

Suzie sighed. She wasn't in the mood. "What do you want? Water? Apple juice? Too late for coffee. And as a matter of fact, too late for television. You ought to get some rest." She lifted the remote.

"Don't," Melissa said.

Suzie's hand froze. There was something in the woman's voice now, some timbre that made her seem less human. You could blame it on the drugs or the suicide attempt but neither theory rang true.

"Fine but at least turn it down."

Melissa did not react, nor did she say anything else about her thirst. She lifted the cup in question and took several loud sips that made Suzie's gag reflex work overtime.

Joey Fallon asked Angie a few generic questions and then she was on a teeny-tiny stage. Her skirt was comically short but the audience didn't seem to mind. They screamed and whooed at the first notes of her song. That one from the radio.

Suzie's mind switched back to her fantasy of running away, except this time it was different. This time she did not rush past Bruce's room. Instead she opened the door, grabbed the pillow he'd left on the floor for days, and covered his ungrateful little face. He so resembled his father she couldn't help but hate the little shit. He struggled, even managed a scream or two, but the pillow did a good job at muffling his voice.

"Beautiful, isn't it?"

Melissa's voice again. Back in 3B with the woman who gave her the creeps.

Suzie shrugged, pretended she wasn't scared. "It's okay, I guess.

Sounds like every other song out there."

"That's where you're wrong." Melissa stood and stretched.

"You shouldn't do that." Suzie eyed the hallway. The nurse's station was four doors to the left. A skeleton crew tonight. Amelia would be outside smoking and Suzie could hear Tanya's snores from the utility closet. She was, technically speaking, alone.

"You're not alone," Melissa said, cracking her neck. She seemed to be in a great mood for someone who'd sliced their wrists earlier that day.

"What did you just say?" Angie's song still played. The crowd still cheered.

"I said you're not alone. You'll never be alone again. We're a very accepting bunch, us glitter critters."

"Glitter what?"

"All you have to do is open your heart and let her in. We're a happy family and we're always growing. We need all the help we can get. Our time is almost here. Our queen will rise."

"Is this a joke or something?" Suzie had heard about the Halloween concert. Everyone had. The city was taking extra security precautions and that was saying something. There were enough cops on the street to wage a war if the crowd turned bad tomorrow night.

"It's no prank. Come with me. All you have to do is say yes."

"*Forever with you, always by your side . . .*" Had the volume been turned up?

Yes, because the remote was still in her hand and her thumb pressed the button down. The little blue bars on the screen reached their highest peak. Still not loud enough. She needed more.

Melissa stepped closer. "What do you say? Isn't it time you have a *new* family? One that actually appreciates you? We can make that little daydream of yours come true. Let's take a stroll to your house."

"How do you know about that?"

"We know everything because *she* knows everything."

Suzie's mouth ran dry and her blood ran cold and she had a strange buzzing sensation along the base of her skull. She was aware of Melissa holding her by the hand, leading her out of room 3B, down the hall and past the abandoned nursing station. She was also aware, yet oddly not surprised, that her feet had stopped hurting. Not an ounce of pain or sorrow or anxiety. Only that buzzing that spread through her entire body.

"That's it," Melissa said. They were on the first floor now, leaving through the front doors. "Angie is going to be so happy. All you have to do is let her in and she'll be with you forever."

"Just like the song." Suzie's lips felt numb. Her brain too.

"Yes," Melissa said. "Just like the song."

"Where are we going?" It was cold outside. Her jacket was back in her locker, yet she didn't mind the temperature.

"I told you already. Home. To teach Bruce a lesson in manners."

Suzie nodded. "Home."

"Then I'll show you your new family. Introduce you to *her.*"

"I'd like that." A block away from the hospital now. The only thing she cherished about her job. The commute was less than five minutes. Ten if you walked. So close.

"Let her into your heart and soul," Melissa said. Her gown fluttered in the wind. It reminded Suzie of a robe for some reason. A long, black robe. "Give yourself over to her."

And Suzie did. Just before they stepped through her front door that she didn't remember opening. Just before they crept up the stairs and down the hall and into Bruce's room. Just before Melissa grabbed one of his lacrosse trophies from his shelf and handed it to Suzie. Not a pillow but it would do.

Just before she stood over the bed and raised the hunk of metal.

Just before she brought it down on her sleeping son's face.

♪

"The cause of death appears to be blunt force trauma," the news anchor said. "Someone entered the home of Suzie Collins in the middle of the night and crushed her son's head with a heavy object. The murder weapon has not been found. The boy's mother is also missing." The speaker was blond, non-descript, could've been thirty or forty-five. She'd had some work done, preventing her face from seeming all that worried but something told Shawna even if she could show concern, she wouldn't have.

The camera zoomed out and revealed her co-host. The man's salt-and-pepper hair was gelled and spiked, nothing like his usual comb-over. Gone were his suit jacket and button-down shirt. He wore a sparkly t-shirt with words that made Shawna cover her mouth.

We Love You, Angie.

She turned the television off. From downstairs, she could hear the crew, Glenda barking orders.

Things were getting bad out there, just as Mike had predicted. The murders may have been scattered but they had arrived in Salem. The boy wasn't alone. She'd flipped through four local news programs. Each described a different scene and while none of them mentioned her sister, the connection was obvious.

She looked outside. Was Mike nearby? Maybe he'd been followed last night. Maybe he, too, had been beat to death with a heavy object.

Shawna would play it cool. March down there and eat whatever her mother had concocted. Bacon and eggs if she was in a good mood, Pop-Tarts if not. Then she would sit down with Glenda and smile for the camera. She had to sell it, make them think she gave a damn about Angie. But she couldn't overdue it, either.

"You can do this," she told her reflection. The mirror did not seem convinced.

After that, she would skip school, hope they didn't call home, and find Mike, assuming he didn't find her first.

She took a deep breath and then five more. Her foot caught on her bureau and moved it to the left a few inches. It scraped the floor and she wondered if the crew heard her. But that wasn't what made her bladder nearly burst.

It was still there. The symbol Angie had drawn all those years ago. A creeping thing in and of itself.

Moving the bureau back into place, she opened her door, headed downstairs, and entered the living room. The crew stopped speaking. All eyes turned toward her.

"There you are," Glenda said, clipboard in hand. "We were worried you'd never wake up." A faint smile. Something like a threat.

"I'm a teenager," Shawna said. "Sleeping in is what we do." That was good. Give them some attitude. Make them think you weren't scared shitless.

"We adults do it from time to time as well." Glenda held the clipboard out and one of her assistants took it without being asked. "Your mother tells us you've had a change of heart. About the interview."

Kristen stood in the kitchen, holding a cup of coffee with an unsteady hand. The first floor smelled pungent. Cigarettes and Febreze.

She cleared her throat, steadied her pulse as best she could. "That's right. But it's got to be quick. I'm already running late."

"We can write you a note."

"No," Shawna said a little too quickly. *Calm down or you'll blow what little cover you have left.* "I already left early once this week."

Glenda nodded. "A regular old teacher's pet."

She thought of Mr. Fuller, how his eyes had turned just as hollow as the rest of them. Brainwashed by subliminal pop music. "Something like that."

"Well, we'd better hurry." Glenda turned toward anyone who would listen, which turned out to be everyone. "Can I get makeup here quick?"

The crew erupted into contained chaos. Moments later the trailer door outside opened. The interior was dark, though she could make out the shapes of several other people. Her skin went prickly, thinking about how small it must be in there, how easy it would be to become trapped if Glenda ordered one of her servants to restrain Shawna.

The front door opened and a woman with purple hair stepped into her home.

Her v-neck was dangerously low and just above her breasts was a single word tattooed into her flesh. It looked recent. And mildly infected.

Angie.

She powdered Shawna's face and applied eye shadow. Afterward, she held up a mirror and Shawna managed a faint smile. She didn't look half bad. Her acne was well hidden. No more oily forehead. A consolation prize for having to pretend she didn't hate her sister.

The clipboard was presented to her next. There were several papers to be filled out and a pen with her sister's lyrics across the side. "What's this for?"

Glenda pointed at the top of the first page.

Consent Form.

"For what? Where will it air?"

"Primetime if we're lucky. You should be excited. You might just end up famous yourself."

Shawna gulped and signed. *Yeah but for different reasons.*

She kept her hand as steady as she could and handed the paperwork back to Glenda when she was done.

"Are we ready?" Again with the fake smile and again Shawna had the feeling Glenda would pounce on her if she wasn't careful. More snake than human.

"I guess so."

"Let's roll." She motioned toward the crew. "Take a deep breath and smile for the camera."

CHAPTER NINETEEN
ERRORS AND CORRECTIONS

WHEN JOSH OPENED HIS eyes, he assumed he was dead.

Bright light blinded him and he thought: *This is heaven and everything is okay now. The nightmare is over.*

But the headache told him otherwise. It told him he was still very much alive and, if instinct was to be trusted, very much hung over. He rubbed his eyes. Dry and caked shut. His body was covered with cold sweat and his morning breath, assuming it was morning, registered as toxic.

He tried to sit up and stopped halfway, realizing for the first time that he was not in his apartment. His stomach threatened him. Bile rose in the back of his throat and he managed a single, sour burp.

What the hell happened last night?

He didn't remember much. One moment he was going over the shop's finances at McMurphy's, then, after the conversation with Dan (and a heavy dose of the creeps), he'd fled and . . .

"What time is it?"

He nearly screamed at the voice. Feminine yet edgy, nothing like Melissa's and thank god because that would mean she'd left her hospital bed.

He turned his head, fought a fresh wave of nausea, and thought maybe he was in heaven after all.

Trish lay across an unfamiliar bed. Her hair was tussled and her eyeliner had run, leaving behind jagged streaks. She sat up and her blanket sagged, revealing breasts he had imagined on more than one occasion. He stared. She did not cover them back up.

"Did we . . .?"

"Fuck? Yes. Twice in fact. Gotta give it to you, you're better than I would've thought. Great with your tongue too." She lit a cigarette.

He tried to hide his smile. He failed.

"What's so funny?"

"It's just . . . I didn't think this would ever happen."

"Neither did I. I mean I knew you *wanted* it to happen."

"You did?"

"There's a mirror behind the front counter. I caught you staring at my ass more than the inventory."

His cheeks reddened and he looked away. "Was I that obvious?"

"Afraid so. And controversial too."

"How do you mean?" He managed to balance on his elbows. The room spun almost as fast as his thoughts and he implored himself not to puke.

"You're my boss, Josh. In case you didn't remember."

He waved her away. "Oh, that. Well, not for long."

"How do *you* mean?" She set her cigarette down in a skull-shaped ashtray.

"Don't tell me you haven't noticed. When's the last time we had an actual sale? When's the last time we had a *customer*? Even the regulars have vanished." His legs swam with pins and needles. The sheet slid down as he readjusted. His hairy, pale chest was the antithesis of Trish's.

"Maybe it's just the economy, you know? Maybe we're in a recession."

"We're in a recession. There's no doubt about that. But that isn't killing the shop."

"Then what is it?" Her eyes lost focus. She looked everywhere but at Josh.

"What do you think? It's that pop bullshit and whoever's sending her albums by the dozen through our doors."

Trish nodded. "Her management team."

"Yeah, them. Something tells me that if I flushed every last disc down the toilet, they'd just be replaced the next day. We're dealing with something bigger than we can handle. It's time we cut our losses."

"Maybe we should embrace it, then."

"Embrace it?"

"Yeah, like, try and sell the stuff they gave us. Hell, we could make a fortune."

"Everybody already owns her album, remember? You said so yourself."

Finally she looked at him. And slid closer. "Sure, but her fans are rabid. They have to own *everything*. Maybe if we advertised more, let everybody know we have posters and cardboard cutouts and t-shirts . . ."

"T-shirts? When the hell did those come in?"

"Look, all I'm saying is maybe we ought to think it over. We fought the good fight and we lost. Now we can . . . I don't know . . . form an alliance or something."

"I don't think so."

"Listen to yourself. Aren't you the boss? The captain never abandons his ship. We can do like Esmeralda did. She's still selling her magic stuff but it's all in one corner now. The rest is books about Angie and tickets to her concerts. It's like a fan club in store form."

"No, okay? I don't want any part of that."

"Sure, you say that but I don't think you mean it. I think that deep down in that metal head heart of yours, you want to give in to her. Tell me I'm wrong."

His argument died in his throat when she slid closer. Mouth to mouth. She pushed him back and tossed aside the sheet. He was already erect at the mention of Angie's name. He hated her and everything she stood for but his body was on the other side of the argument. Trish took him into her mouth. All protest vanished. He stared at the ceiling and let her work her magic. It was over quickly. Not that he was complaining.

Afterward, she wiped her mouth and smiled. "Just think about what I said, will you?"

"Sure," he said, not because he actually planned on it but because his body still buzzed from her lips.

"I'm going to take a shower. Feel free to join me."

He watched her walk toward the bathroom. She left the door open. Soon he heard the shower running. Steam drifted into the bedroom.

He stood, looked at his clothes on the floor, a haphazard tower of fabric. Part of him wanted to take her up on the offer but he wasn't sure he could get hard again.

Until he did.

He was shocked to feel himself stiffen and rise.

But it made sense when he realized why his body reacted.

Across the way, next to a warped card table that was also the dining table, were several stacks of boxes. The closest one lay open, revealing the contents.

Angie Everstein CDs.

Hundreds upon hundreds of Angie Everstein CDs.

There were cardboard tubes of posters and a pile of the t-shirts Trish had mentioned moments before.

His cock pulsed, begged for release. The sight of Angie's face on the album covers excited him yet his stomach recoiled.

Trish was working *with* them. Angie's team. Part of him was certain that if he searched the apartment thoroughly, he'd find a tattered, black robe. She was *one of them*. Had been all along.

From inside the bathroom, Trish called for him. "You coming or what? Water's nice and hot."

He dressed and left without answering.

♪

Dan Peterson looked at his watch and thought: *you can do this*.

Days at the construction site ended around five or six, weather depending, but the crew would be working well into the night to finish the stage.

He had to wait until the sun was gone. Under the cover of darkness, he would tell the boys and their superiors he had to take a leak. By the time they noticed his absence, he'd be halfway out of the state.

He'd called his mother that morning while fighting a headache that was more of a migraine. She'd agreed to let him stay for a few days, though she'd bombarded him with questions. He dodged each of them while holding the crown of his nose and praying for the Aleve to kick in. But the pain still lingered. As did the fear.

He looked around as he sipped his coffee, which was one-third whiskey. Hair of the dog. The crew paid him no notice. The longer the project went on, their conversations turned benign. How their wives never wanted to have sex. How they wished they'd gone to college. Gone were the conspiracy theories and speculations regarding the stage.

That's because we're all being watched.

Dan knew that more than anyone. He'd been scolded before for running his mouth, after all. But at least he hadn't spilled any more beans since.

He froze mid-sip, the coffee-and-booze concoction stinging his tongue.

Something felt off. He thought back to the previous night but most of it was a drunken blur. He'd started this job as a heavy drinker but he was one step away from full-blown alcoholism. At least he had a good reason.

Had he said something he shouldn't have? He didn't recall any conversations but his gut told him otherwise.

He waved the thought away, pretending he was just being paranoid, set the coffee down and went about his business, trying his best to act casual.

Not for the first time, he noted the lack of noise. Bart Edelstein had not told any of his signature dirty jokes for weeks now. No profanity, no speaking aside from the occasional small talk. And he still hadn't seen a single damn animal. He wasn't talking just birds or squirrels. Even bugs seemed to stay clear. No flies or bees or beetles. It didn't sit well with him.

A shadow appeared on the ground before him. He was certain something had decided to visit the site after all. Something that was unlike any animal he'd ever witnessed. It was crawling up from the ground this very moment, ready to pull him under. Down and down until they reached whatever dark place in which it dwelled.

Except when the voice spoke, he realized the shadow was just a shadow and that someone stood behind him. Someone, no doubt, wearing a robe. "Mr. Peterson."

He flinched, closed his eyes, took a deep breath.

You can do this.

He turned slowly, offered his best yes-sir-of-course-sir smile.

Per usual, the face within the hood was obscured. The voice was male but that was the only detail he could ascertain. For all he knew, he'd spoken to this man a hundred times before. It could've been the same guy who'd given him that first warning.

First and last warning, he reminded himself.

"Yes?"

"You're not wearing your hard hat."

His headache still threatened him with every breath and the idea of thick plastic pushing against his scalp was sickening. "Sorry about that. Must have forgotten it."

"You'll need a replacement."

He noticed several of the boys not wearing theirs. "Is that necessary? The job's almost done, ain't it? And besides, what's going to fall on me?" He looked into the birdless sky. Nothing up there but dark clouds that refused to let the sun through.

"It's protocol," the robe reminded him. "Follow me."

The man walked toward the trailer they'd set up on the first day of work.

He followed. The guys watched as he passed, eyes wide with something like fear. The same stare he'd received on the way to the principal's office before he'd dropped out.

The trailer windows were tinted. He hadn't seen anyone aside from the Robes enter or exit. He'd assumed it was an office or a bathroom, but the Robes were not architects. And there were plenty of porta potties on the site.

The man reached the door, opened it slowly. It shrieked into the afternoon, loud enough to scare away birds, had there been any. Dan ought to make his escape now instead of nightfall. The Robes now outnumbered the workers. They could easily surround him.

His hands shook. He'd forgotten his coffee-whiskey on the ground. The headache crept along his skull.

"Mr. Peterson?" the man beneath the fabric said. "We must hurry. Time is running out."

Dan followed him into the darkness. He was prepared for a torture chamber on wheels, sharp objects lining every surface. Instead: black foam hanging along the walls of the trailer. Speakers as tall as Dan. No desk or blue prints. No sinks or toilets. Nothing but soundproofing and subwoofers, an audiophile's wet dream.

"What the hell is this?" he said, noting a distinct lack of hard hats.

"This, Mr. Peterson, is the corrections chamber."

"The what?"

Dan spun around and saw the door closing. Then came the undeniable sound of a lock clicking into place. He tried the knob and nearly screamed when it didn't budge.

The speakers crackled to life and a voice spoke. The same voice he'd just heard, though he wasn't certain how that was possible. Perhaps he stood outside and spoke into a microphone. "Mr. Peterson, I'm afraid you've gone against our policy. We did tell you to keep all onsite activity confidential, did we not?"

"Let me out."

"I'm afraid I can't do that. Not until we've administered your punishment."

He pounded the walls but his fists were soundless. "What the hell are you talking about? I kept my promise. I only slipped up once."

"Then how do you explain this?"

The speakers crackled again and he heard another voice, so familiar he had to touch his throat to make sure he wasn't speaking.

"It's the concert. Something's going to happen at the concert."

It came to him in a drunken haze. He'd been at McMurphy's, talking to his old pal Josh Meyers. Cuckold extraordinaire. Dan had told him everything.

It was a longstanding problem, running his mouth. His ex-wife and mother had never gotten along. They took every opportunity to make it known to Dan. He and Cherie had moved into his mother's house when Cherie had gotten knocked up. The plan was to stay there a year or two, pay off some debt and save for a house. They'd lasted three months. Animosity aside, the two women had agreed on one important point.

Dan Peterson had a terminal case of verbal diarrhea, would tell one what the other had said behind their back without thought. He could not keep a secret to save his life.

"I'm sorry," he said. "I'm stressed, is all. This job is taking a toll. I haven't had a day off in, what, two months?"

"You knew the hours would be long," the man said through the speakers.

"Please, just let me out and I won't say another word. I promise. Or hell, fire me. You can keep my last paycheck."

"Ms. Everstein does not believe in firing people, Mr. Peterson. She much prefers bringing people *together*."

He opened his mouth to ask what the hell that meant but managed only a squeal before the music started.

He preferred hard rock and heavy metal to radio pop. Nobody could sing anymore. It was all auto tune and robotic melodies. And when he did come across a vocalist with talent, they spewed lyrics about parties and cash-money-bills. But this song—it was different. Familiar.

Catchy.

"Forever with You."

His skin tingled and he forgot about his hangover, about running his mouth. He even forgot about the job from hell and the stage that was more than a stage.

There was only the song.

The lyrics were simple yet he was certain they held some hidden meaning. There was something beneath the music, some instrument or melody he couldn't put his finger on.

His finger.

The thought did not make sense yet it made the most sense in the world.

He raised his right index finger, studied it, though he wasn't sure why. He simply knew it was the right thing to do. As if it was what Angie wanted of him. And you did not disobey Queen Angie.

Queen?

Something wasn't right. Nothing was right. Everything was right.

The sane part of his mind, the part that was still able to reason, fought this new development but the battle was a short one. All reason receded until there was only the song again. "Forever with You" blared into his ears and into his soul and his right index finger seemed important again.

He opened his mouth, placed his finger on the center of his tongue, and, as if it were the most normal thing in the world, he bit down. He heard a crunch, as if he'd bitten through a carrot. His mouth filled with copper. He drank and ate. He repeated the process with the rest of his fingers but his hunger could not be filled. He moved on to his toes.

The pain was distant, belonged to someone else.

His stomach widened, pieces of Dan Peterson on the inside instead of out.

Angie sang to him, told him every secret that ever existed.

And outside, the crew worked like madmen, trying to finish the stage that was much more than a stage.

CHAPTER TWENTY
CHANGING FOR THE BETTER

STILL NO SIGN OF MIKE Mallory.

No vehicles aside from the K-9 rescue vehicle pulling over to pick up a dead raccoon. The woman, dressed in a uniform ten times too tight, looked around and, not spotting Shawna watching her, licked the carcass. Several times. Her chin grew stained with black blood. She tossed the mess into the back of the vehicle and sped off. Music blared within the van. Her sister's music.

It's getting worse, she thought. *That secret track or signal or whatever it is—it's getting stronger. Affecting everyone now. Tomorrow, half the town will be bopping their heads to "Forever with You." And by then it'll be too late.*

She walked through Essex Street, past tourist shops and thrift stores and overpriced restaurants. Nearly every window was adorned with flyers, many of them advertising Haunted Happenings and the Halloween parade, though posters for her sister's homecoming show gave them a run for their money. Angie's team may have been creepy but they had a knack for PR.

It was nearly noon. She hadn't bothered going to school. The thought of being trapped in classrooms, not unlike prison cells, was enough to make her want to scream.

Where the hell was Mike? He'd assured her he'd be watching at all times, but she was beginning to think that wasn't the case.

She went into her favorite comic shop to kill some time, crossed the street and bought an iced coffee, nearly about to give up when a vehicle pulled up to the curb fast enough to draw sparks.

It was not an RV.

It was a school bus.

The door opened and Miles Fuller stepped outside. This was not the same Mr. Fuller she'd once known. Not even the lunatic she'd seen through the window the day before. This Miles wore a sequined tank top instead of a button-down and a bow tie. This Miles wore leather boots instead of penny loafers. This Miles snarled instead of smiling.

"There you are, Ms. Everstein." She noted the transition from her first to last name. Less friendly and more formal.

"What's this about?" She nodded toward the bus. The driver, a spindly man that reminded her of a spider, watched the road without blinking, uninterested in Shawna or anything happening around him.

"You know damn well what it's about."

"I'm not skipping if that's what you mean." She took a step back, thought about screaming for help but the street seemed suddenly deserted. Where were tourists when you needed them?

"You could've fooled me. Let me guess. You're running a fever or you've been throwing up all night. Or better yet: you just needed a mental health day. Well, guess what? You don't *get* a day off. Not when your sister is working so hard for us."

"What is that supposed to mean?"

He closed his eyes and breathed in. "Can't you feel it? Can't you smell it in the air? The world is changing for the better. It's what we've all been waiting for, what we've wanted for eons even if we didn't know it."

Another step back until she was leaning against the Army and Navy store. She looked left and right. Six shops in either direction before she could turn a corner.

"Look, my mother let me take the day off, okay?"

He seemed to consider this.

"Angie's coming home from New York later and she wanted me to be there when she arrived. I swear."

A smile then. Not the caring, non-judgmental smile of the old Miles. This was more akin to a hunter with a clear shot. "You are a good student, Ms. Everstein, but you're a terrible liar. Your sister is already home, back in Salem. She arrived this morning. And she's dying to see you."

He grabbed her arm but she managed to push him away, managed to turn around and run into the spider-like bus driver who had been interested in their exchange after all. He lifted her without effort and tossed her into the bus. Her head collided with a window and she saw stars of every color, so many they were almost beautiful.

Almost.

♪

Sooner than later, Esmeralda told herself about a thousand times. It was the answer to most of the questions floating through her mind.

When should you finally listen to the doctor's advice?

Sooner than later.

When should you start taking those pesky high blood pressure pills?

Sooner than later.

When should you escape Salem, Massachusetts?

"Sooner than later."

Her own voice shocked her. The apartment had been deathly quiet. Her upstairs neighbor, a young single mother named Miranda with three children whose names she'd never bothered to learn, should've been driving her to the brink of insanity. Normally you could hear cartoons and arguments and the wheels of the computer chair those little brats insisted on using as a racecar. But now there wasn't so much as a footfall. The silence unnerved her.

As did the scent.

There was something rotten nearby. She'd checked every trashcan, every nook and cranny of her apartment, and could find no source. The stench reminded her of garbage on a warm summer's day, yet there was something sweet about it too.

Didn't they say that's what death smelled like? Rotten and sweet?

Instead of dwelling, she went on packing. Esmeralda Hopkins was not a hoarder by any means but she had acquired quite the collection of junk over the years. It came with the territory when you ran a witch store in the witch capital of the world. The back room of her shop— *not your shop anymore*—was microscopic. A few years ago, she'd resorted to storing her overstock in her apartment's spare room. There were countless jars of herbs and roots and other ingredients for spells. Most of which were total and utter bullshit.

Most but not all.

She hadn't always believed in magic. As a girl it had intrigued her but she equated it with Santa Claus. It was fun to buy into the myth but that's exactly what it was.

She'd held this opinion until college, when her roommate-soon-to-become-best-friend Jeannie Rogers had a few too many screwdrivers and decided to mess around with the dark arts. The night was hazy at best. All she had were glimpses that stuck with her.

A dim dorm room and a desk littered with snack food and a window that overlooked a foggy April night and a pile of vials filled with powders and a book of spells that could be purchased online or anywhere supplies are sold and a feeling of dread and certainty that something else was in the room with them, something distinctly *not* Esmeralda or Jeannie, something that watched with a thousand eyes and spoke with a thousand voices and bit with a thousand teeth.

She could not remember everything it had said—whatever *it* was. But she did remember one word. One terrible word she still heard on the darkest of nights.

Hell.

She'd heard the word *hell* and neither she nor her roommate-soon-to-become-best-friend had uttered it themselves. They spoke less and less of the incident as time went on and she was just fine with that.

She hadn't had another experience like that until years later, when a little girl by the name of Angie walked into her shop and asked about evocation spells.

The temperature in her apartment plummeted. The silence from above and her train of thought and that stubborn stench were too much. These supplies were part of her old life, one she planned leaving behind. Let the landlord figure it out. She would only take what she needed.

Sooner than later.

She closed her spare room door, walked back into the kitchen, reached for her suitcase and—

And froze when she heard the doorbell.

The door was mere feet away and a large window offered a glimpse outside. The white curtains were nearly transparent, so she could see the figure on her steps.

Esmeralda reached across the island and grabbed the largest steak knife she could find. She had not sharpened them recently but hoped it would do. The blade glistened in the overhead lights.

She opened the door and was greeted with a robed figure just as she'd suspected. It was dark beneath the hood but the voice was familiar. "Ms. Hopkins, may I come in?"

"No." She held the knife behind her back.

"Did I catch you at a bad time?" The woman's eyes were hidden but Esmeralda felt them scan her apartment, linger on the suitcase.

"Are you going somewhere?"

She paused for too long before answering. "No."

The figure stepped forward. Esmeralda stepped back. "Any vacation time will have to be approved well in advance. Short of a family emergency, I'm afraid time off would be denied. Tomorrow is an important day, after all."

"What's this about?"

"You did not show up to work yesterday."

"I'm glad you noticed. Now if you don't mind, I'd like to get back to . . . cleaning."

"We noticed. As I said, any time off must be *requested*."

"I don't work for you."

"But you do, Esmeralda. More specifically, you work for our queen."

Her fingers grew numb. If she held the blade any harder it would fall from her hands.

The figure pulled back her hood. Esmeralda wasn't sure what she'd been expecting. A monster perhaps. Something with deformed features and countless scales. Something that whispered the word *hell* when you weren't looking. But it was just the woman with whom she'd spoken on the phone. "Ms. Everstein requests your attendance at the shop today."

"For what?"

"A meeting to discuss our plan for tomorrow. We'll be selling tickets and hosting another autograph signing for much of the day. Then, once the homecoming show begins, we ask that you help with security."

"Do I look like a cop to you?"

Glenda smiled. Her eyes were wide and glazed over. Wasn't that how all cult members looked? For that's what this—*all* of this—was. A not-so-secret society who worshipped a pop star like she was a god.

Or a devil.

"Are you sure you're not planning on going somewhere?" She nodded toward the contents on the kitchen table: a framed picture of Jeannie and the only photo album Esmeralda had kept, from when she was a child and her parents could still walk up the stairs without risking a heart attack.

"Positive." Whatever this was, it seemed mandatory. She'd made a mistake by not leaving earlier, when she'd had the chance. The thing to do was attend the meeting and slip out afterward. They would be keeping a close watch on her.

"Glad to hear it." Glenda looked at her watch. "You ought to get going if you expect to be on time. You know how much Angie values being punctual."

"Who are you really?" Esmeralda narrowed her eyes, wondered if her fear was obvious. Her chest burned being so close to this woman.

"I told you over the phone already. I'm her manager."

"Manager? I don't think so. Managers help book tours and talk shows and—"

"And that's exactly what I do. She appeared on one last night, in fact. Of course, there is more to my role than the obvious. The nature of our relationship is . . . quite complicated. I do whatever she needs me to." She stepped inside the apartment. "And what she needs me to do right now is make sure you arrive to the meeting on time."

Esmeralda hadn't realized how large Glenda's robe was until that moment. The fabric flowed from the breeze outside. There was plenty of room for a weapon under there. There could be several knives to her one. Esmeralda nodded, loosened her grip. It felt like defeat. "I'll be there shortly."

A pause. Another cult-like smile. "Very well. We appreciate your cooperation in this matter. I'll inform Ms. Everstein of your arrival."

Glenda took one last look at the suitcase before leaving. The woman may have been brainwashed but she wasn't stupid.

From upstairs came what sounded like a quick gasp before the silence returned. Heavier this time. Like something had died.

CHAPTER TWENTY-ONE
A PERMANENT REMINDER

FIRST THEY HANDCUFFED HER.

Too tightly, Shawna might add, though she didn't. She didn't say *anything* until the bus arrived at school. All thoughts of rebellion vanished when she saw the new sign that had been erected overnight. Impossible. Such construction would take longer than twenty-four hours.

Gone was the Salem High plaque and the Nathaniel Hawthorne quote beneath.

In its place: a set of new words that made her bowels shrivel.

Angie Everstein Institute for the Gifted.

A handful of students stood outside, laughing and joking like it was just another school day. No one was fazed by the new addition. And that was the problem. Whatever was happening out there, whatever spell Angie was casting—no one seemed to care.

Miles caught her staring. "Beautiful, isn't it?"

She sat near the front, just behind the steering wheel. It was the first time he'd spoken since her abduction—second abduction in a week's time, she noted—and his voice startled her.

"Who approves something like that?"

The same people who approved the stage.

"Angie can be quite persistent." As if that answered all of life's questions. And for her followers, Shawna supposed, it did.

"I want to speak to my mother."

"Later," Miles said, instructing the bus driver to drop them out front. The man giggled, a strand of spittle hanging down his chin. His tongue hung out of the side of his mouth, dog-like, and a cloud of flies hovered above him. "After the pep rally."

He led her out of the bus and past the sign. The letters were intricate, carved into the stone with what looked like symbols of some sort. Symbols she'd once seen in a certain spell book.

The straggling students watched as Miles pushed her along. One of them raised his hand and pointed. "You're her sister!"

His friends' mouths opened like they envied her.

Of course they envy you. You're a blood relative. You get to see her anytime you want, which is never. But they don't understand, don't know what you know. They can't see what's happening.

Miles waved them away like mosquitoes. "Get inside, will you? The rally's about to begin."

"Sorry," the boy said. He stared for a moment longer, not once eyeing the handcuffs, before taking off toward the entrance, his friends in tow.

"You're lucky we're on time," Miles said as they climbed the steps and entered.

The sign was not the only new addition to Salem High.

There was a booth set up in place of the front desk. Two girls, wearing tight *Forever-with-You*-embroidered tank tops, stood behind the counter. On the other side, a line of students tapped their feet as the girls sold tickets to the homecoming show.

No, not sold, for the sign read *free*.

To the left, where there should have been football trophies, hung awards with her sister's name on each. Shawna thought she saw a Grammy and a CMA. Both unlikely since the former was months away and the latter had no pop category.

"How many tickets have you sold?" Shawna said, not wanting to know the answer.

"We've lost count." Miles pulled her around the corner and they stepped into the gymnasium.

Or what used to be the gymnasium.

Now it looked more like a temple or church of some sort.

The windows had been painted over with black and no one had bothered to turn on the lights. She couldn't remember the last rally but the crowd had been half the size. If you weren't on the football team or a cheerleader, then what was the point? But today it was a full house. Today wasn't about sports.

There was no space to spare in the bleachers. The surplus of students flocked to the center of the room. They formed a circle. And in the middle of that circle was a statue.

A statue of Angie Everstein. She was not alone in the sculpture. Her sister had made a friend. Angie was wrapped around what appeared to be a goat. A goat that walked upright on two cloven hooves. Shawna had seen a hundred such demons on metal album covers but none of them chilled her like this. Those were pure shock value. This was something else.

The gym was too quiet. No one spoke, mesmerized by the art installation. They held their phones like lighters, like a rock ballad.

She looked around for an escape but noted Robes guarding both exits.

One of them, appearing from nowhere in particular, parted from the crowd and whispered something into Miles' ear. He nodded, and for a moment so brief it could've been an illusion, his face contorted with concern. He was the old Miles again. The one who'd told her to keep writing and ignoring her bullies. The moment passed. New Miles once more. A full-grown glitter critter instead of a well-liked English teacher. He opened his hand, grabbed onto something.

A long metal rod with a circular symbol at the end. She'd grown up in suburbia, had never visited a farm save for a field trip in third grade, but she'd seen enough documentaries to know what a brand looked like.

Miles held the rod up. "You may be our queen's sister but you are not above disciplinary action. Skipping school and nearly missing a rally is unacceptable. We must ensure it doesn't happen again."

The crowd murmured in agreement and Miles addressed them for the first time.

"Are there any objections to this sentence? If so, please speak up now."

Silence again.

Shawna scanned her fellow students' faces, many of them unfamiliar. She was far from popular, gave the goths and punks a run for their money, but she did see one face that stood out among the others.

Mia smiled and winked as if they were in on a secret. As if, after Shawna's flesh was scarred with her sister's strange symbol, they'd be friends again. Maybe even lovers.

Mia could kiss that idea goodbye. Brainwashed or not, her former girlfriend was one of *them*.

Another Robe stepped forward with what looked like a blow-torch. They held it close to the edge of the brand and pressed the trigger. A small flame shot forward, heating the metal until it burned neon orange.

"That'll do." Miles turned to her. "Do you have anything to say for yourself?"

She shook her head. She could've bad-mouthed her sister. God knew she excelled at that. But here, in this crowd of critters, it was useless. No matter what she said, rebellious or not, she was about to get her very first tattoo. *Not a tattoo*, she told herself. A *brand*. And that sounded so much worse.

"Hold out your arm."

She resisted. Not because she was brave. Quite the opposite in fact. The pain, she imagined, would be beyond words.

The two Robes grabbed her right arm and held it forward. She closed her eyes, pictured a faraway place. The last Everstein vacation had been ten years prior, when her dad was still in the picture. Costa Rica for two full weeks. Her mother spared no expense. The finest of cruise ships and dining. They declared bankruptcy soon after. Since then, Shawna had boycotted all tropical destinations. Now, though, the country seemed inviting. A vast beach with crystal water and sand so fine it felt invisible. The tide tickled her feet. Rolling in and out.

In and out.

In and—

She smelled barbecued pork. She opened her eyes. Smoke rose from her forearm and the flesh bubbled and blistered. They held her still, made her watch.

The crowd laughed.

It made a terrible sort of sense then. What was it her sister had said?

It's about you, Sis. It's always been about you.

Forever with You.

She studied her new wound.

From somewhere nearby came a thud. Light spilled into the gymnasium and the crowd turned from giggles to shouts. Miles stopped the branding. She'd never seen him so bothered, so *annoyed*. Days ago, he'd been a patient man and teacher, hadn't yet become jaded by the educational system. Mr. Fuller had been her hero.

And part of his skull burst open before her. His eyes unfocused, as if his brain hadn't gotten the memo. He blinked twice, slid to the floor.

"Let her go," Mike Mallory said as he stepped into the gymnasium. He held a pistol, aimed it toward the two Robes, and they followed orders.

Shawna ran, gritting her teeth against the pain, tripping every few steps. Behind Mike were two familiar faces. Professor Foster and Curtis escorted her into the RV.

The Robes and the students followed but did not chase. They stood outside the gym and watched. From inside the building, though still dark, Shawna caught another glimpse of the statue. She swore it had turned around. Eyes that should've pointed in the opposite direction now peered toward her. *Into* her.

Then she focused on her forearm, skin swelling.

"Don't bother coming in today," Josh said to Trish through the phone.

"What? Why?"

"We're not opening. There's been . . . a family emergency."

"What the hell are you talking about? Is this about Melissa?"

He wished it was that simple. "No. Yes. I don't know. Just take the day off, okay? I won't even dock your pay." *Of course you won't. Even when the world is falling apart, you're still the same old Josh. A pushover for all the pretty girls.*

"If you can't make it in, why don't you have me take care of it?"

Fat chance of that. He wasn't sure any more Angie merchandise could fit within the walls of the store but he wasn't about to find out. "No. We're closing today and tomorrow."

"Tomorrow is Halloween."

"I know."

"Why did you bail on me? I thought we had a good night."

Earlier she'd been playful and dare he say it: normal. But now she was losing control. And that scared her. *Infuriated* her.

Good. Let her be scared. He imagined those boxes in her apartment, wondered how long she'd been working for *them*.

"Sure, we had fun. But it was just a one-night thing. Let's not make a habit out of this." A week ago, he would've given his left testicle to be with Trish. Now the thought repulsed him.

"You're making a mistake," she said.

"What's that supposed to mean?" The shop was dark despite the sunlight shining against the windows. Though he was alone, he felt otherwise. He studied the shadows for movement.

She hung up, a dial tone replacing her voice.

He set down the phone, wiped sweat from his face. He couldn't remember the last time he'd been alone in the shop. Probably when he'd first opened the place. Two years next month. Hard to believe. In the beginning, he hadn't expected to hire other employees. Business had been slow to pick up. Melissa had promised to help him, had putzed around the front room for the first month or so. Then she'd gone back to lying on the couch with a pile of adult coloring books on the coffee table.

Back then, she'd still used crayons.

He didn't *want* to stop seeing Trish. She'd been on his mind ever since she came in to interview. But she was no longer the too-cool-for-school girl with the nose ring and purple hair. She was a glitter critter.

He'd been telling the truth about closing, but he'd neglected to mention they were closing for *good*. Sure, he was giving up on his dream but that *dream* had turned into a nightmare.

And it was time to wake up.

"Okay," he said, rubbing his hands together. "Let's throw some shit away."

He tossed CDs. Records and stickers and posters. Next came the cardboard cutouts, except putting them in the trash didn't seem final enough. He set them in a pile in the alley out back, searched the office until he found the lighter fluid. On slow summer days, he treated the employees to burgers and dogs from a discount grill he'd won at a Yankee swap.

He drizzled the lighter fluid onto the pile of cardboard. From his pocket he retrieved a book of matches, lit one, flicked it.

The cardboard crinkled, grew black, turned to ash. Bits of Angie drifted into the air. The wind took them.

The cutout on the bottom of the pile gave him the most trouble. He thought there was something symbolic about that but he was too tired to mull it over. Instead he tore off a still-burning section that could've been an elbow or knee and held it over the surviving Angie's face.

"Sing about this," he said as she began to catch. Her eyes and nose grew deformed from the heat. Her fake skin crumpled but did not crumble. Not at first.

The flame burned through the middle of her lips so they seemed to part. He knew it was a coincidence, a trick of the eyes, but he felt certain he'd hear her voice.

To speed up the process, he stepped on her face. It broke apart beneath his feet and part of him wished it had been the real thing.

The other part of him, though, the part below his belt line, had a different opinion on the matter.

By the time he was done, it was nearly three o'clock. He did not want to be near this place come nightfall. He surveyed his progress. Every bit of glittery bullshit was gone. The metal and punk records were proudly on display again. Venom and Bathory and Napalm Death posters took precedence.

He shut the lights off, grabbed his keys, and locked the place up. It felt final.

Until he saw the envelope on his windshield. Until he lifted the wiper and opened the flap and stared at the contents inside.

Tickets to Angie's Halloween Homecoming show.

VIP tickets.

He tore them into slivers, tossed them like confetti. "You see that, you bastards? That's what I think of you and your fucking queen."

He half expected one of her little followers to appear. But Derby Street lay still and quiet. Not a tourist to be found. He was alone.

His phone rang. *Trish,* he thought. Luring him back to her apartment.

He answered without looking at the screen, ready to tell her off, except it wasn't Trish on the other line.

"Mr. Meyers?" Male. Familiar.

"Yes?"

"This is Dr. Girard form Salem Hospital. We met briefly yesterday when your wife was admitted."

"Is she okay?

"I'm afraid I was going to ask you the same question."

CHAPTER TWENTY-TWO
NOTHING IS NORMAL

"DOES IT HURT?" MIKE SAID.

"What do you think?" Shawna hissed through her teeth as he cleaned the wound. The RV was not stocked with medical supplies. They made do with hand sanitizer that felt like lava as it sterilized her new brand. The flesh was red, raised. A pentagram that wasn't quite a pentagram. The same symbol that rested beneath her bureau, carved into the floorboards as if they too were skin.

Mike folded two slips of paper towels, pressed them against her forearm. He sealed the makeshift bandage in place with Scotch tape. The center grew moist with blood, tiny beads peeking from beneath.

"Where were you?" She pulled her arm away and hugged herself. Childish maybe, but she didn't much care. "Didn't you say you'd be stalking me? If you planned on being late, you should've at least given me your phone number."

"He was getting *us*," Foster said, adjusting his glasses. They drooped down his nose as Curtis, driving recklessly, avoided potholes that would not be filled until spring. "And he couldn't give you his phone number. It's too dangerous."

"Dangerous how?" she said, though she already knew the answer.

"Because we're on their radar," Mike said, cutting in. "They've been watching us, keeping tabs. I'm almost positive they'd listen in to any phone call we were stupid enough to make."

"You really think their reach is that wide?"

"I think it's wider than we can imagine." He nodded toward the paper towels, growing soggy by the second. "I'm sorry about that."

"It's not your fault, I guess." He couldn't have predicted her favorite English teacher would abduct and brand her. Mike was doing the best he could with the resources he'd been given. Which were slim to say the least. "Thank you, by the way. For saving me."

He nodded and she could tell he was in that house with the girl without eyes. Watching the bullets in slow motion as they pierced her rib cage.

"They'll be watching us even closer now," Foster said. He sat at the kitchen table, barely big enough for the three of them. He looked out the tinted windows. Salem was alive with visitors. The traffic was deadly. There were too many onlookers to keep track of.

Everyone was in costume. Halloween started weeks early in her hometown. Vampires and zombies roamed the streets. Princesses and pirates held their parents' hands as they visited witch museums and brushed up on their history of public execution.

"What now?" she said when the RV had grown too quiet.

"We kill that bitch," Curtis said from up front. He plugged his iPod into the dash and hip-hop beats shook the interior. Probably something he'd recorded.

"What he said." Mike took a sip of ginger ale that was likely as warm and flat as the one he'd given her.

"I know that much," she said. "But what's the *plan*? We can't just go in guns blazing, right?"

"Afraid not." He belched under his breath. "Not after today."

"Your sister is staying at the Hawthorne Hotel for the time being," Foster said. "In the honeymoon suite. It's on the top floor—takes up the *entire floor*—and if what Mike says is true, her team will be guarding the place like it's the pentagon."

Penta*gram*, her mind corrected without her permission.

"But we can't wait much longer, right?" she said, wondering why Angie wasn't staying at home. But it made sense, didn't it? Money was no issue to her, so why sleep in a house that had been falling apart for a decade?

"Tomorrow," Mike finished his soda and crumpled the can. "We do it tomorrow."

"Isn't tomorrow too late?"

"It might *already* be too late," he answered. "And stop picking at it. It'll only get worse."

She fingered the paper towel. "I always wanted a tattoo. A skull or a monster or something with flames. Something that would shock my mom. Never thought I'd get branded first."

"Use it."

"Use it for what?"

"A reminder." He turned his leg to the side and rolled up the cuff of his pants. On the back of his calf was a long, jagged scar. The white flesh reminded her of a worm. "I look at this every morning and think: you tried your best but you didn't kill me."

"Is it from . . . that night?"

He shook his head. "Not quite. I was riding a bike."

"A bike tried to kill you?"

"I was seeing this girl—Jill. She was the love of my life. Still is, the more I think of it. We were together almost four years. The first two were great. The last two, I'd joined the force and brought it home with me every night. Sometimes it can't be avoided. You either internalize it, drive them mad with cold shoulders, or you get mad yourself. Get violent too sometimes. I did a little of both." He rolled down the cuff as if he didn't want to finish the story, though he did anyway. "Jill had a daughter. Sweet girl named Katie. Katie didn't know her father but from what she and I heard about him, he was a real asshole. He never taught her to ride a bike and she was getting to that age, so I took it upon myself. We were riding together on the sidewalk one day. She went up ahead, way too fast, just like I'd told her not to. A car came around the corner. Couple of teenagers blaring shitty music like this stuff." He pointed to Curtis. Curtis flipped him off. "Kids didn't see Katie when they came up on the curb, so I pulled her aside, fell on my ass and caught the fender on my leg. I had a cast for six months. I yelled at her that night—Katie—and she cried for hours. I apologized but the damage was already done. Next day, I made it my life's mission to cheer her up but it didn't matter much. Jill got smart a few months later and left."

"Is this supposed to be inspirational? Because it's not working."

"Not at all. I would've been better off getting run over. At least then I wouldn't have seen my two favorite girls backing out of the driveway for the last time. I wouldn't have seen a girl with her eyes torn out because some witch or whatever the hell she is decided to take over the world. But you do the best with what you're given."

"You're not very good at cheering people up." But in a strange sort of way, he'd done just that. She felt something new. If not hope, then something like it. It had been a long time since she'd been this close to anyone. Family had always been a touchy subject but maybe families didn't have to be conventional. Didn't have to be blood.

"It's got to be during the concert."

"What?" She tensed. The tender moment passed quickly.

Foster nodded. "Mike's right." He'd taken his glasses off, either to clean the lenses or he'd grown tired of adjusting them. His eyes seemed foreign without the frames. "It's the last place they'll think to find us."

"What if it's already too late? That signal has been floating around for six months. It's already infected most of us. You said so yourself."

"We'll cross that bridge if and when we come to it. There are ways to block radio broadcasts. Hackers do it all the time. But first things first: we need to remove the source before the source removes us."

She nodded, trying not to think of the specifics, trying not to imagine slitting her sister's throat or putting a bullet through her temple. Being torn apart by an angry mob of glitter critters.

She looked outside, at the Halloween fanatics. They pranced around the cobblestone street as if everything were normal but the longer she stared, the more she realized *nothing* was normal.

A grown man dressed as a ballerina lay on the ground while a German Shepherd lifted its leg and pissed onto his face.

A miniature Frankenstein laughed and pointed while a woman, presumably his mother, punched herself in the face over and over.

An impossibly tall Graf Orlock passed out brochures for a local haunted house, except whenever passersby accepted the pamphlets, he held their hands, spread their fingers, and sliced the in-between flesh with the paper edges.

Maybe Mike had been right earlier.

Maybe it might already be too late.

♪

Angie Everstein's Ye Old Magic Shoppe.

Esmeralda read the sign and thought: *This is a bad dream and you'll wake up and be your hopeless fat self again but at least you'll be safe.*

Simple things like high cholesterol, like looming strokes and heart attacks—those could kill you, sure, but at least they were natural. *Rational.*

Her fingertips grew numb. Wouldn't that be something? Falling down and having a coronary just before she could make her great escape. But she knew she wouldn't be so lucky as she crossed the street and stepped into her old place of business.

It was not the same shop she remembered. Dark shades blocked any sunlight brave enough to cast toward the windows. The walls had been painted black. As had the ceiling and front counter and every other surface. The lights had been replaced with torches—*actual* torches—that burned slowly in sconces.

The managers knew how to draw in business. She'd give them that much. A barricade had been set up on the sidewalk, a crowd already forming outside. Hard to believe she'd spent so much time here, explaining to tourists that magic was mostly harmless.

Mostly.

Outside, she could just make out the cheers from fans, screaming Angie's lyrics, excited for tomorrow's concert. A mound of tickets on the front counter threatened to topple over. They looked like a professional job, with Angie's face and a holographic pentagram superimposed over her features.

"You won't be needing those," said a voice from behind.

Glenda. Couldn't forget a voice like that. A voice that made your heart want to stop whenever it spoke.

"You were supplied with a VIP pass, were you not?"

Esmeralda turned. "Mine's at home. Wouldn't miss it for anything."

"Good to hear. The meeting is about to begin. It's right this way." She headed toward the hall and melted into the darkness.

Esmeralda's eyes still hadn't adjusted. She held the walls for support. The torches didn't help much. They made the shadows seem like living, breathing *things*. By the time she reached the back room, she felt nauseous.

What she saw when she got there didn't help matters.

The stock room had grown in size. She scanned the area, did the math, realized the dimensions were impossible. The paint smelled fresher back here, toxic. It dawned on her then. This room was larger because it was *two* rooms. The business next door, a failed frozen yogurt shop, had been vacant for nearly a year. Rents were rising in Salem and sometimes empty buildings remained that way. Angie's team had bought the place, torn down the neighboring walls for more space.

Not for the first time, she wondered how so much work had been completed in such a short time.

She didn't think on it too long, though. Her attention was drawn elsewhere.

Toward the gathering of Robes in front of her.

And the figure that stood among them.

Angie was naked and holding her hands toward the black ceiling. The girl shimmered like the air around her was liquid. Her eyes matched the walls, all pupils and no color. The pentagram from the tickets had been drawn onto her forehead, only the star and circle looked red, dripping down her face and into her mouth.

Her mouth.

Something seemed off about the way her lips were pushed out at odd angles. She whispered something so Esmeralda saw what her nerves already confirmed.

Fangs.

Her teeth had been replaced with knifelike fangs.

Someone grabbed Esmeralda's arm. Glenda again.

"Put this on."

If she had any chance of escaping, Esmeralda had to make them think she was on their side, feign complacency. She slid the robe over her massive frame.

Her skin itched and burned. The fabric smelled of mold and must and, she supposed, dead things. Underneath, her body broke out in a cold sweat.

Glenda smiled. "It suits you." She turned her attention to her shimmering queen and spoke words too soft to make out. Words that sounded more like chants. The others repeated the lines in unison. Voices low and raspy, sandpaper to Esmeralda's ears.

She wondered only for a moment what this gathering meant, what purpose it served, but she was given her answer in the form of a vision.

For a long time she saw only darkness. She had the distinct feeling of walking down a spiral staircase that did not end. She could keep descending for eons and never reach whatever was down there.

Then there was bright light in the distance, racing toward her like a train. Only the engine was not a low rumble. It was a long, panicked screech.

When the light reached her she was back in Salem, albeit across town. Gallows Hill. She hadn't visited the stage but she'd heard plenty about it. Her regulars said it was a massive eyesore but there was something else about it, some indescribable feeling.

It was, they said, like the thing was *alive*.

Esmeralda couldn't agree more. The way it jutted out of the park's trees like some prehistoric beast rising from the ground, the way it seemed to expand in the corner of your eye like the steel itself had a pulse—yes, *alive* was right.

Hungry, too.

Angie stood atop the stage. The light came from the pyrotechnics, a miniature fireworks display that could not have been legal. The screeches—plural now—came from the crowd around her. Or what was left of it.

Much of what she saw didn't make sense. Abstract in a way her mind couldn't process. Nightmare logic. But she saw enough to know the crowd was in pain. The ground was wet but the night sky was cloudless. It hadn't rained and, besides, rain wasn't *red*.

From the dream stage, Angie stared toward Esmeralda.

You did this, her reptilian eyes said. *You gave me the tools, taught me the tricks.*

That it was, then. What she'd feared this whole time. What she'd kept in the back of her mind because the thought so terrified her. Angie's songs were infecting people and tomorrow night, during the big show, the infection would spread. The ground would run red with blood. Salem would come alive with screams.

Minutes later, though it felt like years, the vision passed and she was back in the room with the Robes and the girl she'd once spoken with about invocation spells.

Esmeralda wiped her face. Her flesh felt cold and clammy and she thought she might vomit.

"It gets easier," Glenda said. "The more you see through her eyes, the more you like it."

The crowd began to scatter. The meeting was over. She followed the others as Glenda announced they would be given the rest of the day off. Tomorrow, after all, was their busiest day yet.

Esmeralda stepped outside and stopped listening.

She was too busy thinking about the storeroom back at her apartment. The boxes of overstock. Maybe it wasn't too late. Maybe she could stop what she'd seen.

Assuming she lived long enough.

CHAPTER TWENTY-THREE
THE MOTLEY CREW PREPARES

"YOU'VE GOT TO BE KIDDING me," Shawna said as they pulled up to the storage unit.

Mike told Curtis to pull over and park. "Afraid not."

"Is it even big enough to fit all of us?"

"You got a better plan? Your sister's followers will be looking for us. It's not safe for you at home. It's not safe anywhere."

She was too tired to argue. And besides, he had a point. Lack of space wasn't what had her blood pumping. It was those posters within the unit. The pictures of Angie's victims and the path of murders leading to her hometown. A history lesson she didn't wish to revisit. Not to mention she'd been zip-tied to a chair the last time she'd been here.

Curtis parked and let them off. "That'll be fifty even." He held his hand out and pretended to take their money. She appreciated the humor but her funny bone was out of commission. He wasn't laughing either.

The night had grown winter-like. In the distance she could hear the commotion of Salem proper. Crowds were growing. Hundreds had arrived today, hundreds more tomorrow. Halloween brought in a million pairs of feet to the city. How many would attend the concert? Surely not all of them, she thought, not feeling convinced.

The storage complex was on the other side of town, bordering Peabody and Route 114. In the distance, she could see the stage. It looked complete now. Complete and unnatural, like a tumor on the landscape.

A video screen had been erected, surrounded by what looked like strobe lights. She could make out movement around the construction site. Tiny black dots that reminded her of viruses under a microscope. The crew was putting on the finishing touches.

"Ugly thing, isn't it?" Mike said from behind.

"The ugliest."

She heard the storage unit door slide open. Curtis argued with Foster about something. The latter lectured the former but the former wasn't having it.

"Ought to be an interesting night with those two."

She shook her head. "What?"

He waved her off. "Nothing. Just talking out loud. Having second thoughts?"

She shrugged. "It's a strange concept. She's my sister, you know? She wasn't always the antichrist."

He nodded. "It'll be the toughest thing you'll ever do. Taking a life, I mean. There's nothing that can prepare you for it. I hope you like nightmares."

"You're not exactly selling this to me. Besides, I don't even know the plan yet."

From his pocket he pulled out a flask and sipped.

"I didn't take you for a drinker," she said. "Too uptight. Too *obsessive.*"

"I don't usually. Especially when I'm on the job. Back when I was on the force? Guys used to pound back a few cold ones on their lunch breaks like it was nothing. Can't say I blame them." He sipped again, wincing this time. "This isn't exactly a job, though, so I figure why not?" He held the flask up, cocked his head.

"I don't really drink."

"What kind of teenager are you?"

She gave in, took it from him. After all, she might die tomorrow. Bleeding out on the ground, surrounded by the world's newest and largest cult. Maybe they'd make her a sacrifice. Sliced open on stage while the world around her went to hell. What a way to go.

She threw her head back, took a large gulp, and spit it out immediately. Her tongue and throat burned. "What the hell is that?"

"Sambuca. Licorice flavored liquor."

"Tastes like piss."

"Close enough." He took back the flask, sealed it, and turned around. "Come on. It's time we discuss our plans."

"Finally." Not that she was in a rush. Hearing Mike discuss how she'd kill her sister, her own flesh and blood, wasn't high on her bucket list. But it had to be done, she knew. One life in exchange for thousands. Hiroshima on a much smaller scale.

Hopefully.

Inside the storage unit she noticed some new additions. The photos were still there, curling at the edges from the humidity. The sign out front advertised a weather-proof complex but the smell of mold told her otherwise. The map, with its hundreds of tacks representing the trail of death, had been bloated, the corkboard warped beyond return.

The damage was not what concerned her, though.

It was the guns.

More of them than she could count. Pistols and rifles and what she assumed to be semi-automatics. She wasn't an expert by any means but she'd played enough *Grand Theft Auto* to know this was militia material.

"Where the hell did you get all of this?"

"Don't bother asking," Foster said. "He won't give a straight answer. My guess is that they're stolen."

"It doesn't matter where they came from," Mike said.

Curtis rummaged through a nearby box. He picked up what looked like an Uzi and stared directly into the barrel. All street credit left the building. Dollar sign tattoo or no dollar sign tattoo, the producer did not scream responsible gun owner.

She looked at them then. Studied the group in detail for the first time. An ex-cop who may have lost his mind. A professor who'd discovered a subliminal killing machine. A hip-hop engineer who might accidentally blow his brains out.

And then there was Shawna, a lowly eighteen-year-old with a hearing problem and a demon for a sister.

A motley crew if she'd ever seen one.

A motley crew that was expected to stop the end of the world.

"You gonna leave us hanging?" Curtis said, closing one eye and mock-aiming his gun. At least the barrel was pointed away from him.

"Put that down before you kill us," Foster said. He cleaned his glasses and put them back on. The wire frames were bent, hung off his nose at an odd angle.

"It's not just guns," Mike said.

"How do you mean?" Foster shut the storeroom door. The draft lessened but the interior suddenly felt like a prison cell.

"We'll need to look the part. That's why we'll need these." He threw them each a hulk of fabric. At first she thought they were blankets. Maybe they were calling it an early night. They'd iron out the details in the morning when their heads were clear. But when she unfolded the material she realized there would be no such luxury.

Robes.

Four matching robes that looked authentic. She peered inside hers, found the tag, expecting to see the brand name, the size, the *made-in-China* notice. But there was nothing of the sort. Instead, only a symbol: the pentagram-like image from her sister's album cover. The same symbol that now graced Shawna's forearm. Something told her this hadn't been ordered through Redbubble.

"A disguise," she said.

"Exactly." Mike held his own up. "It's our only chance of getting close enough."

"You expect me to wear this thing?" Curtis said. "No chance in hell. I stopped trick-or-treating a long time ago."

Mike ignored him. "The show starts at approximately eight o'clock tomorrow evening, weather permitting. There is no opening act."

She pictured a goliath rainstorm blowing through Salem, ruining her sister's plans. But she'd seen the weather that morning, the television muted in her living room. No rain in sight. The memory seemed eons away. Another life altogether. In a way, she thought, it was.

She stopped listening for a while, thought about normal things, like how her bandage was starting to come loose, like how she ought to call her mother, let her know she was safe.

Bad idea.

Kristen Everstein may have shown her maternal side during their last argument but she might be hiding something. A strange thing, not trusting your own family.

This is your family now, she thought as Mike went over the plan in more detail.

Outside, the wind howled against the unit like something wanted badly to get inside.

CHAPTER TWENTY-FOUR
LAST DAY OF THE OLD WORLD

KRISTEN HUNG UP THE PHONE and breathed a deep drag of her cigarette. She'd only recently taken up smoking. Just a few a day, at first, then a pack, then two, and so forth. She had an addictive personality. You'd get no arguments from her on that point. Take one look at her credit card bills and you had your proof. But she wasn't about to argue bad habits tonight. There were more pressing issues.

Like one of her daughters going missing.

She paced the kitchen, waiting for a phone call that never came. She'd dialed Shawna a half dozen times, leaving as many messages. Each call took only one ring before her daughter's monotonous voice spoke into her ear. Which meant her phone was turned off. Next she tried Angie, asked if she'd seen or heard from Shawna. No on both counts.

Kristen would have to try the police next.

Except Angie had told her otherwise.

"You can't."

"Why the hell not? Your sister's *missing*. She skipped school and apparently had a fight with one of her teachers." She'd called Salem High earlier and spoke with first a truancy officer, then the principal himself. Though he would not go into details, he'd mentioned an altercation. They'd speak about it next week, he insisted, once things had settled down, but the situation looked grim. As in *getting-expelled* grim.

"I'm sure she'll come back soon enough," Angie said through the phone, cool and collected. Usually her voice was enough to calm Kristen, make her believe everything would be okay. Tonight it had the opposite effect.

"Are you hearing yourself? What if she was kidnapped? What if she's hurt?"

"Don't do anything stupid. I'll be over in a little while. Just wait for me, okay? I bet you anything Shawna will be back by the time I get there."

That had been two hours ago.

How dare she tell Kristen not to worry. She was a *mother*. Not a good one by any means but a mother nonetheless. She'd been mostly absent from Shawna's life since her father left the picture. Smart move on his part, she had to admit. She'd grown bitter with age. As a child, she'd dreamed of being a social worker, making a nice income and helping others to boot. But she'd dropped out of community college after learning of her pregnancy. Then came the news of twins. Their finances had been doomed from the start. A young mother, unprepared for the challenges of being a parent. She hadn't always done her best, or even close to it, but now, faced with this crisis, she'd decided enough was enough.

She dialed the police despite Angie's orders.

"I'd like to report a missing person."

"Name and information," said a voice that seemed entirely uninterested.

She listed the details, having to repeat several.

"How long has she been missing?"

She did the math. "Since about ten o'clock this morning."

Then came the line the dispatcher had likely spewed a hundred times over. You couldn't count someone as being missing until two days passed. *Bullshit*, Kristen thought. If Shawna had been taken against her will, she could be out of the state by now.

The voice droned on for another few minutes, reminding Kristen that her daughter was probably just hiding out at a friend's house after the argument.

Kristen nodded, then frowned. "Argument?"

"Yes," the voice said. "It's common for girls of her age to do this. Act of rebellion."

Her skin buzzed with a warning. "I didn't mention any argument."

A pause.

The line went dead.

"Son of a bitch." She chalked it up to stress. Maybe she *had* mentioned the fight. Maybe she was too scared to notice. It seemed like a perfectly reasonable theory yet it didn't feel right.

Kristen doubted Shawna was at a friend's house since Shawna didn't *have* any friends these days. As Angie's fame grew, Shawna had drawn further and further into herself. Her behavior went beyond that of a normal teenager. Kristen should've spoken up sooner, called a psychiatrist.

It was a long shot, she thought, but perhaps Mia would know where Shawna was. Perhaps they'd rekindled their friendship (though something told her it was more than platonic, another aspect of her daughter's life she'd chosen to neglect). Maybe Shawna was over at her house this very moment.

She dialed Mia. The girl picked up on the second ring and though her voice sounded slightly less robotic, it did nothing for Kristen's nerves.

"I haven't seen her," Mia said.

"Are you sure? Were you at school today? I heard about an . . . altercation."

Mia giggled.

"Is something funny? I must have missed the joke."

"It's just that . . . do you really think Shawna would ever fight anyone? She's the least imposing person on the planet. Hearing aids don't exactly scream tough."

"Don't you talk about her that way or I'll . . ."

"Or you'll what? Come over here and slap me on the wrist? Look, I'm not afraid of you and neither is Shawna, wherever she is. You know how many times she told me she hates you? She used to dream about running away. Said she'd hitchhike if she needed to."

"She wouldn't say that." *Of course she would.*

"Think what you want but don't hold your breath for her to come home. If she's still alive."

"What did you just say?"

Another giggle. "Can't you feel it, Mrs. Everstein? It's happening faster than we thought. Tomorrow is the last day of the old world. Queen Angie is coming."

"What the hell happened to you? You used to be so . . ."

"Normal? Lady, you really do only care about yourself. If you'd taken one moment to listen to your daughter or anyone else, you would've noticed the change that's happening. Try turning on the radio once in a while."

Mia hung up.

Kristen hurled the phone across the room. It hit the wall with a crunch. The screen shattered and she could see her credit card bill increase by the second.

"Was that necessary?"

Kristen nearly screamed as Angie stepped into the room. "You scared the shit out of me."

"Language, Mother."

She wrinkled her brow. "What?"

"Isn't that what you always say? No swearing in the house. It's the number one rule. You give Shawna shit for it all the time." She covered her mouth, opened her eyes wide in mock shock. "Oops, there I go, defying you. Except you won't say anything. Because I'm your favorite daughter, aren't I?"

"Now isn't the time for games."

"It's not a game. It's a fact. I'm the pretty and talented one. I'm the one who can actually fucking hear. I bet those aids cost an arm and a leg, huh? And considering your past spending habits, it's probably money you don't have."

Kristen cried. The tears were sudden and tickled her cheek on the way down. "What is wrong with you? You've . . . you've—"

Her daughter's voice shifted as she finished the sentence. "Changed." The high-pitched, slightly valley girl tone was replaced with something deeper, darker, something that bordered on demonic.

Kristen looked around the kitchen for . . . what? A weapon? Ridiculous. But her eyes didn't find it so ridiculous when they settled on the rolling pin to her left. An expensive marble model three times the price of a standard one. She'd used it maybe twice. But tonight it might come in handy after all.

Listen to yourself. She's your daughter, not a burglar.

Another shape stepped into the room. "You called the police," Glenda said.

Kristen nodded. "Obviously."

"Didn't we advise against that?"

"You don't control me." She stepped back until her legs touched the counter. The rolling pin was within reach but she'd need to turn around. She didn't like the idea of letting her guard down.

"That's where you're wrong, Mom." Angie stepped farther into the kitchen. Her green eyes shimmered in the overhead light.

Green?

No, that wasn't right. Her daughter's eyes were sky blue. It was a joke they'd shared ages ago, when their family was still a family. If you looked into those eyes long enough, Kristen would say, you could see the sun.

But the sun had gone down tonight, replaced with an odd green hue that reminded her of reptiles. Vanity contact lenses? Something Glenda had suggested she wear for the homecoming show?

"You'd like to think you're calling the shots," Angie said. "But we both know it's the other way around. We both know I'm in charge. The second I got picked for the show, your eyes lit up like a slot machine. You saw all your debt going bye-bye but that's not all you saw, was it? No, you saw a new house and a new car and a new everything. The life you'd always wanted. Not a care in the world. But you're getting antsy. You haven't seen a dime of that money. And if we're being perfectly honest, Mother Dearest, you never will."

The tears flowed faster. Mostly because Angie was right. She'd been banking on the money because without it she was, to put it lightly, fucked. She could no longer afford the mortgage of a house that was too big to begin with. Her husband had suggested they buy something smaller after his vasectomy. It would only be the four of them—five if they adopted that cat they'd been discussing. But Kristen's tastes did not agree. She wanted something big, something they could "grow into" even though they never had and never would.

She wiped her eyes and reached behind her just as someone grabbed her arms.

She screamed as the other two Robes restrained her. How had they gotten in? She'd locked the garage door, checked it twice. She was obsessed with such things, with keeping her too-large house secure.

"The change affects everyone differently," Angie said. "It's taking a lot longer with you than others."

"What change? Tell them to let me go. They're *hurting* me." She struggled to break free, felt her shoulder threaten to dislocate.

"You've got to get out more, Mother. How many times have you listened to my songs? Did you watch the entire show on mute?"

What was she talking about? Of course she'd heard Angie's songs, albeit infrequently. Modern music didn't do much for her. She was proud of her daughter, sure, but that didn't mean she had to like her songs. Too poppy. Too squeaky clean for her tastes. As long as Angie was bringing in the money, then she could sing death metal for all Kristen cared.

"You really should take in an interest in your daughter's career," Glenda said. She put a hand on Angie's arm and they shared a look, a moment, like *they* were family and Kristen was just a stand-in.

"She's right, Mom. It's time you give my music a good listen." She signaled the Robes standing behind Kristen. One of them held her hands in place while the other lifted something over her head. For a moment, she was certain it was the rolling pin. They'd bring it down against her skull and all that worrying over debt and bills would vanish.

Instead, the Robe placed headphones over her ears.

Kristen struggled. "We don't have time for this. We have to find Shawna."

"I couldn't agree more," Angie said. "Glenda is already on it. We have a feeling she'll try something stupid tomorrow night. She's a lot like you. She doesn't know when to give up." She told the Robe to press play.

Kristen opened her mouth but no words came. Nothing but a small rattle in the back of her throat. Not a scream exactly but a plea nonetheless. A plea for the music to stop. It spun into her ears, the volume much too loud, but hearing loss was the least of her worries. She gritted her teeth against the melody. Her muscles tensed.

"Beautiful," Angie mouthed, "isn't it?"

Kristen did not agree with her daughter's choice of words. The music was not beautiful in the least. It was boring and generic and horrible all at once. Because there was something *else* there, something beneath the lifeless lyrics that threatened her mind. Her entire body convulsed. A seizure perhaps. Something warm dripped out of her mouth and, eventually, she fell to the floor.

Her head bashed against the linoleum, vision turning white and black, white and black.

Wherever Shawna had gone, she prayed it was far away from Salem. Far away from her twin sister. She prayed she never turned on the radio again, never heard this abomination disguised as a song.

A stranger stood above her, howling with laughter. A stranger with green, lizard-like eyes that never seemed to blink. A stranger who, her dying mind reasoned, did not seem all that human.

A stranger who—

Forever with you.

—had rough, calloused skin and obscene cheek bones and—

I'll never leave your side.

—and long fangs the shape of spikes—

Forever with you.

—that could cut deep without a moment's notice, without any effort and—

You can never hide.

—and a face that reminded her of every nightmare she'd ever had or worse and—

♪

The stage was complete.

It had taken just under two weeks from start to finish, not a marvel of construction but impressive nonetheless. More so when you considered the manpower. The team consisted of a mere thirty members, all of them overworked, all of them presently dead.

Dan Peterson had been the first but the rest followed quickly. Gary Lawson purchased a nine-millimeter Beretta two weeks before the stage's completion. He was thirty-five and in excellent health when he lined up his family—two girls, one boy, and a wife ten years his junior—and pressed the barrel against their temples. He fired twice each time, just to be sure.

That left seven rounds for him, though he'd only needed one.

Jaime Martinez had joined the job illegally. He was living in a cramped apartment with his cousins, hoping to send the money back home to his immediate family. The pay was good and his wife and children would soon be able to purchase a home big enough for the four of them. While urinating in the second to last porta potty, just three hours shy of his last shift, he'd heard Angie's song playing in his head. The lyrics had been floating through his mind all day. The Robes insisted on playing her songs over and over while they worked. He found them annoying, sure, but they'd never bothered him quite like this. He grew angry in a way he couldn't explain. So angry he began to elbow the cheap plastic until his flesh tore and bled and bruised but, still, it was not enough, for the lyrics had attached themselves to the base of his skull.

He knelt down and submerged his head into the toilet. Then and only then did the song stop.

Jeffrey Gottlieb smoked three joints his last morning, two more than usual. It was just about the only thing that helped with his anxiety and today he thanked the cannabis gods for the good shit. It calmed his nerves right up until he saw the most interesting rock on the ground. It was large and heavy and vaguely star shaped. It reminded him of that symbol on Angie's album cover. He picked it up to show his coworkers William and Corey but instead bashed their skulls in before he could comprehend what he'd done. He stared in shock for a minute and half, about the same time it took him to smoke another joint, before he lifted the rock above his own head and brought it down.

A concerned neighbor, wishing to remain anonymous, had called the police after watching the scene. Two officers—Taylor and Perez—arrived a half hour later. Taylor, well over six feet and three hundred pounds, was imposing to say the least. His friends on the force called him Godzilla. He had forgotten to wear pants that day, though no one dared to joke about his white briefs, stained yellow from sweat. He'd come down with something the night before. A flu of some kind. His husband insisted he take the day off but Taylor had ignored him, holding a pillow over Chuck's face while he slept. He thrashed only for a few moments before he stopped moving altogether.

Perez had worn his uniform properly, save for his belt, which he held in his hand and studied intently during the drive. Moments after they arrived, he slid the belt around his own neck and tightened it. He choked to death slowly and painfully.

Taylor took no notice. Instead he exited the vehicle, questioned the crew, who pointed him in the direction of the concerned citizen, one Betty Hersh. He made his way across the street to the ranch-style house, knocking on the door several times before she finally answered.

She asked him if everything was okay.

Taylor nodded, eyes vacant, and assured her nothing would ever be okay again. He shot her once in the stomach, then used his night stick to finish the job.

All the while he hummed the nation's number one song.

The same song the group of robed figures hummed that night and well into the early hours of the morning while Salem slept fitfully. Many had already undergone the change but the majority of them would not fully transform until the concert.

The figures danced and sang and recited lines older than the trees themselves from a leather-bound book their queen had provided.

They paused only to catch their breaths and fuck and bathe in blood and repeat the process until the sun showed itself for the final time.

It was the last day of the old world.

Nothing but night from here on.

Cold, dark night.

CHAPTER TWENTY-FIVE
THEY REMIND ME OF MOUTHS

JOSH MEYERS HATED ROLLER COASTERS.

He'd never been to a theme park in his life, not even Six Flags or Canobie Lake. Sure, he could've just played the games or visited the other attractions but he'd still be able to *see* the rides, behemoths that seemed to stretch for miles into the sky. Just the idea made his palms sweat.

When he woke on Halloween morning, he thought for a moment his worst fear had come true. Someone had drugged him, carried his unconscious body onto the world's tallest roller coaster, and launched him on a death ride without strapping him in.

The world spun a dozen different directions and he vomited as many times, mostly on himself. The pain in his head was beyond description, temples ready to burst. He longed to find the nearest power drill and relieve the pressure.

When he finally managed to open his eyes he saw neither a theme park nor a roller coaster, but reality was, in a way, much worse.

He lay on his living room floor surrounded by empty beer cans.

The prior night came at him like a thunderstorm. After finding the tickets on his windshield, he'd gone to the liquor store and stocked up, drinking a pint of rum (or had it been gin?) on the walk home. He'd gotten plastered in record time and, from what he remembered, he made sure the world knew it. He could not recall what he'd screamed into the streets but they'd been along the lines of *Fuck Angie*

Everstein, that cold-hearted, manufactured piece of poppy bullshit.

Paraphrasing of course.

He'd had the distinct feeling his words did not go unheard. The streets were eerily quiet for this time of year. Perhaps the tourists were in their hotel rooms, resting up for the big day.

But it wasn't tourists watching him from every angle. It was something less definable, less *tangible*. He'd stared into alleyways despite his last bit of sobriety telling him to run. He'd seen nothing out of the ordinary but something had seen him. Then he'd gone to town on the rest of the booze.

Hence the mother of all hangovers.

He managed to get up, slipping on vomit several times, and hobbled into the bathroom, where he took a piss that mostly landed on his feet on account of the throbbing erection. It wasn't all that unusual. He'd woken with them almost daily since puberty but never this intense.

Never this *persistent*.

The arousal was against his wishes. His head hurt beyond description. He felt flu-like and fucking was the last thing on his mind.

He waited for relief after flushing the toilet but his erection held. He tried cold water, tried pacing his apartment, tried eating tasteless oatmeal after popping two Aleve.

Nothing worked.

He poured a cup of week-old coffee and heated it for thirty seconds in the microwave. It burned his insides but he could already feel the caffeine taking glorious effect. His boxers felt loosened and for a moment he thought he'd grown relaxed until he looked down and saw his penis had simply shifted direction.

There were a few drops of coffee left and he couldn't help but wonder as he looked back and forth between the cup and his crotch. It was hot enough to burn his mouth but not permanently so. Perhaps if he just splashed a few drops onto himself . . . maybe that would do the trick. Or better yet: brew a fresh batch and submerge his manhood into the carafe. That ought to take care of his problem.

He shook his head and dumped the coffee into the sink, let go of the cup.

What the hell was wrong with him?

He theorized only for a moment before he heard the voice.

Make that *voices*.

Not in his apartment but too close for comfort, just the same.

They giggled and whispered and hummed a song that was familiar at once. The same song that played on a loop through his head.

He locked his door, didn't dare look out the window at the back stairs, the direction from which the voices resided.

His stereo set-up was in the living room, took up *most* of the living room, though that wasn't hard to achieve in an apartment the size of a bathroom stall. He searched through his records for something loud and settled on a thrash band called Sodom. Original pressing. Worth hundreds on Ebay. Sure, he could've just streamed it for free but he was old school.

The power chords and kick drums drowned out the voices. He lay on his floor. The wood was cold and rough but he could've fallen asleep. *Would* have if it wasn't for the record skipping. The song distorted. He didn't need to look at the turntable to know the needle had gone rogue even though he'd replaced it just last month. He could hear the sound of his precious first pressing being scratched.

The music stopped.

The humming returned.

He covered his ears, searched for headphones until he remembered he'd left them in the car. "Stop it," he said. "Stop humming that fucking song!"

"Now why would we do that, silly?" the first voice said.

"Why don't you come out, Josh?" the second voice said. "We've been waiting all night and it's so boring and cold. Won't you entertain us?"

He peered through the window and immediately regretted the decision. There were two women on his back stairs. The first was Trish, though she looked like a stranger now. No more metal shirts and black eye liner. They'd been swapped for sparkles and sequins and glitter. So much glitter.

The second figure made him nearly faint.

Melissa caught him staring and beamed. "Josh! There you are. Let us in, okay? We've got a lot to do today and we need your help. We have to make sure everyone goes to the homecoming show."

"Go away."

Melissa snorted. "You'd like that, wouldn't you? If I went away and never came back. But we both know that'll never happen. You're the one who always backs down. Otherwise, you wouldn't be living in this shithole instead of a condo you bought with your own money. If you had any balls, you would've kicked me out instead."

"She's right," Trish said. "You're a pushover, so why bother fighting anymore? Just give in to our queen. It'll be easier that way. Trust us."

"I should've never married you," he said weakly, watery eyes not helping matters.

Melissa shrugged. "You know what they say about hindsight and all that." She held up her bandaged wrists. They were soaked in red. "It's so itchy, Josh. I can't stop scratching. I know, I know. It'll probably get infected. That's what you're thinking, right? You've got to relax." She bit into her right bandage, then the left, tore the fabric until the wounds were exposed. "They look cool in a way, don't they?"

"I love them," Trish said, taking the hands in her own. "Do you mind?"

Melissa shook her head. "Go right ahead."

Trish traced the edge of the slits. The stitches had mostly been torn out and the flesh had turned purple.

"They remind me of mouths," Melissa said. "And if they could talk, they wouldn't be *talking* at all. They'd be singing."

Trish smiled, nodded. "Oh yeah? What song would they sing?"

They turned toward Josh and hummed "Forever with You." The melody went through skin and bone and into his core. He slid back down to the floor and felt the world slipping away. Blackness prevailed, though the song still played in his head somewhere. His entire body went limp.

Save for one section.

♪

"Rise and shine."

Shawna opened her eyes and saw Mike Mallory standing over her. For a quick moment, her sleep still fading, she thought he was her father waking her for school. He hadn't abandoned his family after all. He'd been away on a business trip all this time. But he'd worked as a mechanic during the weekdays and as a gas station attendant on weekends. Worked his ass off while his wife insisted she *couldn't* work. While she spent their entire life's savings. He didn't go on business trips. Didn't go much of anywhere aside from bed and the couch during football season.

"You sleep okay?"

She rubbed crusted eyes and groaned and he was Mike Mallory again. "What do you think?"

"Nightmares?"

"A boat load."

"I know the feeling."

She wondered if his dreams had been filled with teenage girls of the eyeless variety. Her own had been much less obscene, yet somehow just as bad.

She'd dreamed of her childhood.

Nothing in particular. Just glimpses of birthday parties and family get-togethers. Angie getting all the attention, of course. Even back then, before the talent show—before the *talent*—she was still the prodigy of the Eversteins. But she hadn't been quite as malicious.

Because there was no Ethel, no creeping things. She was a different person.

The girl that would be on that stage tonight was not her sister. Not anymore. Her forearm itched and for a moment she forgot all about her new tattoo. She scratched the flesh and yelped as a scab tore off, fresh blood beading.

"You'll get used to it," Mike said. "The scar, I mean. It gets easier."

"You should write fortune cookies."

He laughed without smiling.

She stretched and stood, cracked her neck. "Why are we up so early?"

"I asked him the same thing," Foster said from behind Mike. "Shouldn't we be getting as much sleep as possible, considering tonight's events?"

Curtis groaned in response. He held an arm over his eyes and muttered that this was bullshit. Shawna couldn't agree more.

"It's not safe to stay in one place," Mike said. "We have to keep moving. They're on to us."

"How can you be sure?" Foster grabbed his glasses, placed them crookedly on his nose. "I don't suppose we can stop to get these adjusted on our way to the apocalypse?"

Mike ignored him and nodded toward the box of guns in the corner of the storage unit. There were three less than there'd been last night. "I put them in the RV," he said. "We have to get moving. Her management team seems to grow by the day but they're not the only ones we need to worry about. It's the fans too. The critters. They follow her every move, worship her like a god. And if you haven't noticed, she has more fans than we can count. So, until she's bleeding on the ground, we assume everyone is out to get us."

"Sounds like high school to me." Shawna finally got up. Her head hurt and she craved a cup of coffee.

The wind howled against the storage unit's paper-thin walls. She didn't like the lack of windows, didn't like not knowing what was on the other side.

"Come on." Mike grabbed the remaining weapons box. "Grab the door for me, will you?"

Shawna lifted the latch.

From the way Foster's face contorted, she had a feeling she wasn't the only one terrified of the outside world. It seemed safer to stay here and wait for help.

There's no help. You're *the help.*

She closed her eyes as the breeze invaded the interior. She expected to hear shouts and screams but there was barely any noise at all. Nothing but distant ocean waves and traffic. When she looked again, she saw the RV and not much else.

Until she stepped outside and spotted the stage across town. A crowd was already forming and it was barely nine o'clock. Less than twelve hours until show time.

Curtis was last to leave the unit. He stood beside her, nodded toward the stage. "How many people you think are gonna show up?"

She shrugged. "A lot, I guess."

"And they'll all be her fans, right?"

"I wouldn't go to a show if I wasn't a fan. Would you?"

He turned his Red Sox cap around so the brim shielded his eyes from the sun. "They're with her to the death, right? Officer Rambo said so himself."

"Yeah? What's your point?"

He lowered his cap to hide his eyes. "My point is we're gonna have a shit ton of raving lunatics that are mad as hell when we kill their queen in front of their eyes."

She hadn't thought about that until now. Mike hadn't mentioned an escape plan and she didn't feel like asking. Didn't feel like telling Curtis everything would be okay. Instead, she kept quiet and stepped into the RV.

CHAPTER TWENTY-SIX
PROMISING AN HISTORIC EVENT

IT WAS THE HEALTHIEST BREAKFAST Esmeralda had ever eaten. She resisted the urge for microwave burritos and cinnamon buns. Even managed to turn down the strudel with extra frosting. Instead, she settled on oatmeal and a grapefruit well past its prime. Grocery shopping had sunk to the bottom of her to-do list as of late.

The meal was as tasteless as it was unfulfilling but she did not suffer indigestion or heartburn. She even felt less winded when she stepped outside for her mail. The town was quiet. *Too* quiet. She lived three blocks from the city center. The donut shop around the corner normally drew a crowd this early and taxis loved to cut through her street to bypass tourist traffic. But there was nothing aside from a crow chewing something on the sidewalk. Something that was large and decaying and, she could've sworn, in the shape of a small human.

She went back inside and locked the door, checking the mail. A notice from the city reminding her of tonight's concert, as if she could've forgotten. An advertisement for Angie's Ye Olde Magic Shoppe. Her water bill.

It was not from the city of Salem, nor the Commonwealth of Massachusetts. The official seal in the upper left-hand corner had been replaced with a small symbol that looked very much like Angie's trademark.

She's taking over the town, one business at a time. Next it will be city hall, if she hasn't already. Salem is only the beginning.

She was expected at work by ten. Work being the stage. She'd been assigned ticket duty along with some of the other Robes, then on to security once the concert began. Leaving town in broad daylight was no longer an option because she was certain they were watching her. Last night, through her window, she'd spotted several of them pacing the street. Observing her house.

She threw the mail away, water bill included, and stepped into her spare room. The boxes were in disarray, several of them looking ready to topple over. Before bed, she'd searched for some supplies. She could have found them easily downtown but she didn't like the idea of leaving her apartment after sundown.

On the floor lay a candle, a large metal bowl, a taper, a jar of salt, and knot of sage. She lit the latter first, walking through her apartment and watching the small flame dwindle. The smoke drew patterns in the air. Most people liked the herb's smell. Took comfort in it. Not Esmeralda. Sage meant you had a problem to solve, a curse to reverse.

Afterward, she filled the bowl halfway with water and set first the taper, then the candle, down. Next she filled the water with a generous amount of salt and lit the candle. This was the part that always gave her trouble. You had to concentrate on your desired outcome but concentrating had never been one of Esmeralda's strong suits. Her mind would wander, as it often did, to worst-case scenarios. Instead of imagining a positive outcome, she'd picture a nightmare made real.

She took a deep breath, closed her eyes, tried to block everything out. The faucet trickled. The steady drip helped her concentration. Eventually she was able to enter a sort of trance. Her desired outcome was simple: undo what Angie had set in motion. Though Esmeralda had not lost her mind yet, like so many others, she knew it was only a matter of time. It was Angie's music, but more specifically, her *voice*. It did something to you. Changed you in ways she didn't want to imagine. If she focused hard enough, she could feel herself going mad. The song was always there, in the background, even when it wasn't playing.

So she willed her inner stereo to turn down its volume.

For a moment, it worked. But the moment passed quickly.

The phantom boom box cranked to eleven. The song played from unseen speakers. She hated to admit it but the song wasn't all that bad. She'd never paid it enough notice. The lyrics were simple, sure, but only at surface level. Listen closely enough and there was some hidden message to be found.

Forever with You.

She nodded. Yes. She was forever with Angie and Angie was forever with her. They formed a bond that could never be broken. Esmeralda had given her the tools to conjure whatever it was she'd conjured. She had, it would seem, created a monster.

She'd asked the girl if the spell worked a few days after Angie bought the supplies, when she'd visited the shop.

"So," she'd said, beaming, "did you evoke your little imaginary friend?"

"She's not imaginary. She's real. That's why I wanted to evoke her."

"Oh yeah? What's her name then?"

"Ethel." This said too quickly to be rehearsed. Too quickly to be improvised.

"Sounds like an old grandmother to me. Who names their kid Ethel? Yuck."

The girl's face turned from cute to hideous in less than a second. "Shawna said the same thing. Didn't believe me until we found Ethel and brought her back."

"Back from where?" She shivered, which seemed improbable. The air conditioner had recently shit the bed and it was mid-August.

Angie shrugged, her anger lessening some. "From wherever you go when you die but have unfinished business. That's where she was. She says it's dark and cold and in the background there are all these screams, like everyone else is begging to be brought back too. And if you scream loud enough, Ethel says, someone will hear you. Like I did."

Esmeralda gulped and frowned at a sour burp. She'd been forty pounds lighter then but her indigestion had still left much to desire. They made small talk for a few more minutes but she stopped listening after a while. Mostly because she was too scared to focus.

Now, ten years later, she thought of how good a leader Angie would make. It would be much easier to give in. Lie back and let the beautiful music work its magic.

She frowned. Beautiful? She hated that damn song and everything it stood for. And she did not live in a monarchy. She forced her thoughts elsewhere, toward her desired outcome: a world without Angie Everstein.

She opened her eyes.

The clock in the kitchen read nine-thirty. She couldn't be late.

Magic would not help her today. It may have calmed her, increased her focus, but she needed to take matters into her own hands. She left the candle burning.

♪

They listened to news radio for most of the afternoon. Foster tried shutting it off several times but Mike insisted on leaving it. He was on driving duty, got to choose their soundtrack for the duration of their trip. The stories turned from dire to worse.

"*A local boy hanged himself after setting his family on fire.*"

"*A group of four retirees traveling on a cruise stabbed several passengers with forks, one of whom suffered fatal injuries.*"

"*Nancy Perkins, fifty-four, gouged her own eyes out last evening after waking from a nap.*"

Shawna caught Mike wince at this last one.

It was not only the stories that worried her but the newscasters reporting them.

"Thanks, Sheila. Our faithful Queen Angie would like to remind you of her homecoming concert in Salem, Massachusetts tonight. She promises a historic event that will change the face of mankind. If you're in the area, or even if you aren't, please do attend. Those who opt out will be punished. The event is all ages."

Curtis finally shut it off late afternoon, Mike's protests be damned. "Had enough of that shit."

"About time," Foster said. He'd been typing something on his laptop for most of the day. "Can we have some peace and quiet for a little while?"

Mike grunted.

Shawna thought of the murders, connected dots she wished did not connect. "There's no pattern anymore."

"Come again?" Curtis said. His eyes were tired and bloodshot. Earlier he'd smuggled a bottle of vodka on board and managed to take three shots before Mike confiscated it.

"The killings. Before, they were farther away, got closer to Salem. We were the epicenter. Now they're happening *everywhere*. Near and far. People are getting killed on fucking cruise ships. You can kiss your patterns goodbye."

Foster nodded, typed something quickly as if taking notes.

"She's right," Mike said. "The signal may affect everyone at different times but it's starting to change people at a faster rate."

Curtis rubbed his eyes and swore under his breath. Then above his breath. "Shit, man. What if it doesn't work? What if all this is for not?"

"What do you mean?" Shawna said, even though she'd had the same thought countless times.

"I mean what if we kill the queen and it doesn't make any difference? What if we're still infected somehow? Like a virus or something. It's already in us, just waiting to incubate or whatever the hell it does. Maybe it won't *matter* if we kill the source. If you get rid of patient zero, it doesn't get rid of the disease. Right, doc?"

The professor nodded. "I suppose. But we can't assume it's the truth. If we kill Angie, it may not stop the signal completely. She has thousands of CDs in circulation, even more digital downloads. Streaming is a whole other can of worms. But it will certainly stop her from recording more songs. And besides, if her fans see her killed on live television, it will send a message."

"What kind of message?" Curtis's eyes were moist now. He blamed it on allergies.

"That not all of us are glitter critters," Mike answered for him, taking a left turn a little too fast.

They grew quiet for a time. The sun was shining less and less. She'd expected the day to crawl at a snail's pace but it had sped by like a jet.

"What're you working on?" Shawna said to Foster, nodding at the laptop.

"I've been documenting this whole thing. Maybe I'll write a memoir someday." He winced at the last word, probably hadn't been thinking of the future all that much.

"You really think anyone will want to read about this? I mean, we're all living it, aren't we? Sounds more like a horror novel to me."

He shrugged. "Maybe I'll turn my hand to fiction. That's what I wanted to be when I was a kid. A writer. The next Stephen King."

She ought to tell him about her own writing, her poems she'd hoped to one day publish, but then thought better of it. Because Mr. Fuller had been the one to boost her confidence, tell her the words were worth reading in the first place.

She thought of the way he'd taken joy in scarring her. The way he'd told the Robes to hold her still. The way his head had burst like an overripe melon as the bullet tore through his temple.

The RV stopped suddenly. "We're here," Mike said.

Here being Salem State Park, a collection of hiking trails and urban legends. Rumor had it there were plenty of witches left for dead in the park, many of which still haunted the grounds. She would've laughed if it didn't seem so possible.

Is this where you died, Ethel? Is this where they hung you and burned you and buried you?

"Let's pack up." Mike cut the engine and started unloading the boxes. It seemed ludicrous as she watched the group strap on holsters, then fill those holsters with guns that looked better fit for a first-person shooter. By the time they finished, they were makeshift action heroes in disguise, pulling tattered robes over their bodies to conceal the weapons.

Shawna's arsenal was much smaller. A single nine-millimeter pistol tucked into her right combat boot.

"You know how to fire these things?" Mike said.

She shrugged. "I play a lot of *Call of Duty*."

He did not laugh. Instead, he walked her through the process in detail and forced her to repeat his instructions aloud, verbatim. The pistol felt cold against her skin, made walking a hassle, but there was something comforting about it too. Knowing she could at least try to defend herself should the need arise.

And it *would* arise, she reminded herself.

"Let's get going." Mike waited as they exited the RV, then locked the doors.

"How far of a walk is it?" Curtis was already out of breath. He was not obese by any means, though he didn't exactly scream *fitness* either. He made his living sitting in a chair for days at a time.

"Five miles."

"Five *miles*?" Curtis wound back and kicked a rock. It ricocheted off a nearby pine tree and vanished into a pile of leaves.

"It's our best bet." Mike started walking.

He was right. The Robes would be looking for them in and around the stage but it seemed unlikely they'd hike through the woods at sundown. You'd have to be crazy, what with all the ghost stories and tall tales.

After only a few steps, the sun stopped following them. The shadows grew into skyscrapers, covering everything like a black blanket.

She thought she heard something skitter to her left, then her right, but each time she looked, there was nothing but rust-colored foliage and anything that might've been hiding within.

CHAPTER TWENTY-SEVEN
NO END IN SIGHT

FROM SOMEWHERE NEARBY: A CRASH.

Something like glass shattering, tiny shards almost musical as they fell to the floor.

Next: two voices, whispering at first, then laughing at the top of their lungs. Their footsteps frantic, like dancing. Whatever they were up to, they were excited about it.

Josh Meyers registered these details on a semi-conscious level. He wasn't out cold exactly but much of his mind was . . . occupied. The song had gotten to him in a way he couldn't explain. He knew he lay paralyzed on his living room floor. He also knew he was in grave danger. Yet he could not bring himself to move even an inch.

Instead, someone *else* moved him. He felt two pairs of hands grab his body and pull him until the surface beneath his back was no longer cold and hard. Carpeting. His bedroom, he realized. Someone had broken in and dragged him into his bedroom and now they were lifting him up and onto his comforter. The pain in his head was bad enough to register in his daze but one of the intruders lifted his neck and slid a pillow beneath it. If he could've opened his mouth, he would've thanked them.

Thanked them?

No, that wasn't right. They—whoever *they* were—had invaded his private sanctuary and could be holding him hostage. He did not deserve this fate. Not after what happened at his shop. Not after his failure of a marriage. His pulse spiked. Shop and marriage. Marriage and shop. Trish and Melissa. Melissa and Trish.

He opened his eyes.

And gasped.

His body became his own again. The pain was replaced with a new sensation. One located below his belt. His erection had not gone down in the least. The two mouths working at it didn't help matters much. Trish and Melissa caught him looking.

"Wake up, sleepyhead." Trish grabbed the shaft while Melissa worked the head.

He tried sitting up but each woman set a hand on his chest and pushed him back down.

"Not so fast," Melissa said. "Don't tell me you didn't fantasize about this a thousand times over. Your poor, depressed wife finally wanting to fuck *you* again instead of strangers. And that cute little metal chick you hired because she had a sweet ass. Tell me you didn't have wet dreams of us sucking you off at the same time. Tell me I'm wrong."

He was too exhausted to argue. "Just get off me, will you? I want you to leave."

"Sure, *you* want us to go, boss." Trish winked at him, tongue working vertical miracles. "But someone *else* doesn't agree." She grazed her teeth along the flesh. Not enough to hurt but enough to remind him who was in charge.

"She's right," Melissa said. "Just lay back and relax. Let us do all the work. Then, when we're through having fun, we'll bring you to the concert."

At the mention of Angie, the song began to play.

He looked toward the living room, where his ruined turntable had been thrown to the floor and smashed. The same went for his alarm clock. Which meant "Forever with You" did not play from any external source.

The lyrics entered some deep chamber of his mind and he knew there was no going back. Angie had won. He covered his face in disgust as Trish and Melissa quickened their paces. He begged his pleasure center to switch off but he was granted no such wish. He came quick and hard.

Trish moaned and smacked her lips. "You taste great."

He turned his head and vomited onto the bed.

"Not quite the reaction we were hoping for." Melissa took off her shirt and instructed Trish to do the same. "Our turn to play."

Josh grabbed the skull-shaped lamp from his bedside table. He'd had it since childhood, purchased on a trip to New Orleans, which he'd deemed the Salem of the South. It was perhaps his oldest and most prized possession, even more so than his record collection. No matter how tough things became, no matter what life threw his way, that lamp had always been with him. Lighting up the darkness, if only a bit.

But Josh Meyers did not have time to reminisce. He smashed the lamp against Trish's skull. She yelped and fell off the bed. Before she could get back up, he stomped on her chest. She did not fight back, made no attempt to get up. He stomped down twice more until she stopped breathing and moving.

He expected Melissa to claw at him but instead she held her stomach and laughed. Tears streamed down her face.

"Josh, honey, I didn't think you had it in you. She's taught you well."

"What the hell are you talking about?"

"Angie. She's in you now, part of your blood stream, and she's turned you into the man I wanted all along. What do you say we fuck for old time's sake?"

She started unbuttoning her pants. Josh raised the lamp, broken now, above his head and brought it down against her face. The first blow sculpted a second mouth into her left cheek. The second blinded her. She collapsed to the floor, on top of Trish, muttered something softly but the song in his head drowned out the words. He had a feeling it wasn't an apology.

He made it as far as the back stairs before the music overtook him. He could feel himself changing, giving all his energy to *her*. A pop star he'd loathed since she'd first won that shitty talent show. And now he would become one of her disciples.

His arms shook. He convulsed with something like a seizure. His last thought was of his broken record player, the sound of the needle scraping the vinyl. It meant something, he knew, some final warning from whatever was left of his mind. He looked down from the stairs of his third-floor apartment and realized that all stereos had an *off* switch.

He laughed at the notion, as blood leaked from his nose and eyes, as his erection jutted out once again, and all the way down as he dove off the stairs and headed face-first to the grass below.

♪

"How much farther?" Curtis said, not for the first time.

Mike and Foster told him to shut up in unison.

Though it was dark, the flashlights they'd brought from the RV offering only small beams of illumination, Shawna could tell he was sweating badly. He wiped at his forehead every few moments, holding trees to keep up.

Shawna didn't blame him. Her lungs and legs burned and she found herself in the rear of the group for most of the trek. It wasn't just exhaustion keeping her back. She was out of shape, had skipped her fair share of gym classes, but there was something else slowing her down.

She heard things in the forest. Things she could not blame on snapping twigs or their hushed voices calculating how close they were to the stage. These noises were unaccounted for: whispers and moans and words she couldn't make out. After telling herself it was just nerves, she finally gave *into* her nerves.

They were not alone in these woods. Something was following them. It kept to the shadows. Hid itself well. She got to thinking: these trees were ancient, from a time predating humans. She thought of all the things that might have climbed them. The ground beneath her feet had once belonged to a different continent, before it broke away and traveled the globe. How many other legs had walked its surface?

"You okay back there?" Mike said. Was that genuine concern in his voice? She couldn't remember what her father's voice sounded like. This was the closest thing to a paternal exchange she'd had in years. It almost warmed her.

"Fine." She wondered if the rest of the group heard the sounds as well. If so, they gave no indication.

She walked for a few more minutes, telling herself there was nothing following the group, not believing a single word.

The Robes had chosen the stage's location for a reason. Gallows Hill was steeped in local history and when you took into account the legends surrounding Salem State Park, you had yourself a goldmine of folklore. Except folklore implied fiction and the sensation along her buzzing skin felt anything but fake. If you *believed* the lore, this place was swimming with restless spirits, Ethel, perhaps, among them.

Her mind conjured creatures but her thoughts cut off when Mike hid behind a tree. He held a hand up high, signaled for them to keep back.

"What is it?" Foster said. He'd switched to a pair of sport-proofed glasses, a string attached to either end to keep them in place should he need to run.

"We're close," Mike said.

"Finally." Curtis sat down against a tree to catch his breath. From the sounds of it, he'd be waiting for a long time.

There came a steady drone of infinite voices. The crowd.

Mike cursed and she saw why as she took a few steps forward. They'd come at the concert from the wrong angle, steered off course along the way. The stage was to their left instead of dead center. They'd need to backtrack and she wasn't sure if they had time.

She walked up to his vantage point and lost her breath.

It was the largest gathering she'd ever seen. Forget Woodstock. Forget Coachella. They'd cleared enough trees to fit hundreds of thousands. You couldn't see a patch of grass or any ground. The concertgoers were packed so tightly they moved as a single organism. The lines wrapped around the corner and down the street. No end in sight.

"It's worse than I thought," Mike said.

She nodded. "They're going to be pissed when we kill their queen."

They still hadn't discussed the other part of the plan. The part that involved escaping. She didn't broach the subject. Because part of her knew the answer already.

There *was* no escape plan.

CHAPTER TWENTY-EIGHT
SHARP ENOUGH

ESMERALDA BROKE AWAY TO MAKE one more phone call.

She'd been placed on crowd control, keeping track of incoming concertgoers. Gallows Hill was filled beyond capacity. It was hard to imagine it had ever been a field meant for quiet observation. Now it looked more like a gathering for the pope, thousands flocking to Salem to catch a glimpse of their savior.

She made sure no one was watching, pulled out her cell phone, and dialed. The robe was tight against her body, the fabric thick and heavy. It was a miracle she hadn't fainted.

Come on, she willed. *Pick up.*

When Jeannie's voice played through her ear, she could've cried. "Hello?"

"Jeannie, it's me. Listen, I should be leaving later tonight. I just have to take care of something first. There's been . . . an emergency. A lot of strange stuff has been happening up here. Do me a favor, will you? Don't listen to the radio until I get there."

". . . you've reached Jeannie. I'm not here right now but please leave a message . . ."

A long pause, followed by a beep.

She sighed. "Hey, Jeannie. I . . ." Her mind scattered. The robe became a furnace and panic crept into the picture. She covered her eyes, stinging from sweat. Could she do this? Could she really do this? "I wanted to let you know I'll be leaving soon. It's a hell of a drive so

I'll probably have to stop somewhere to sleep. I can't wait to see you. Talk soon."

She hung up. What if something had happened to her friend? What if this . . . *epidemic* went beyond Salem? She imagined good ol' Jeannie, college roommate extraordinaire, as a group of glitter critters ripped her eyes out and ate them like candy.

"Ms. Hopkins," said a voice from behind. A voice that was undeniably Glenda.

She spun around.

"Is everything okay? I noticed you'd moved from your spot."

"Everything's fine. Just needed some air." She pointed to her hood. "I don't know how you deal with these things. They must way ten pounds."

"Oh, you get used to them."

They stood in silence for a moment. Not awkward exactly. She was too scared to feel awkward. Eventually, Esmeralda nodded toward the ocean of moving bodies. "It really is something, huh?"

"Not as much as we'd hoped but the night is still young. Our Queen won't let us down. Speaking of which"—she waved Esmeralda on—"Angie would like to see you before the show begins."

She faked a smile. This was what she'd wanted and feared most. She couldn't stop this massacre if she didn't get within arm's length of Angie but part of her still wanted to make for the highway. "I haven't finished my shift."

"You've been doing a great job," Glenda said. "But Angie requests your presence."

Another false smile, this one so wide it hurt her cheeks. "Lead the way."

She followed Glenda through the crowd, almost losing sight of her several times. It was hard work pushing through the critters, even along the side barriers. Eventually the numbers dwindled to the occasional fan or two, hoping to sneak a peek without actually attending the show. Glenda and Esmeralda entered the woods, what was left of the fading sun vanishing behind fall foliage. The stage was a few minutes' walk at least.

"Did I ever tell you about the first time I met Angie?" Glenda said.

She had several times but Esmeralda let the woman talk just the same.

"I'd been managing Lady Gaga for a couple years. That woman is talented. I'll give her that much. But after a while, it seemed like she didn't know what she wanted to be. Is she country or pop or R & B? Then comes along this young girl, barely a senior in high school, singing her heart out on stage in front of judges. She belonged at the top of the charts from the start."

Esmeralda let her take the lead by a few feet. Even beneath her robe, Glenda's ass worked the woods like a runway. A trained professional, always on for the cameras even when the cameras were off. It was a body to drool over, something Esmeralda could aspire to but never achieve. Glenda may have been past her prime in show business terms but she was still a knockout by everyday standards.

"I was seeing this actor. Jay Schwartz. Well, he changed his name to Gardner but he was Schwartz to me. Beautiful boy. Nothing serious but he could fuck for hours on end, which a woman needs every now and then. I'm sure you understand."

"Do I ever." She hadn't been with a man in nearly twenty years, grew winded when she touched herself let alone another human being.

"We'd just started making love when Angie came on the television and I didn't know what came over me. I rode Jay like a bull and next thing I know, his face is blue and he's begging me to let go of his throat but I didn't—I *couldn't*—until the song was over and by that time he was already gone. I slipped out of his place and took all my stuff. The papers said it was autoerotic asphyxiation. That's when I knew. Angie's voice—it's not just a voice."

"You're right about that." Esmeralda looked around. Nothing but trees and bushes. No sign of any other Robes. She slipped the chef's knife from her belt. The same one she'd threatened Glenda with back at her apartment. Still unsharpened. Still sharp enough.

Glenda went on about her faithful queen and the next stage of human evolution and a million other things but Esmeralda stopped listening. With one shaky hand, she grabbed a fistful of Glenda's bleach blond hair, and with the other, she slid the blade across her fake-tanned throat.

The blood poured quickly and freely down the front of Glenda's robe. She remained lucid for a moment, covering the wound and studying the streams of red as they cascaded from her throat. She did not scream, didn't even fall at first.

"I'm sorry," Esmeralda said. And she was. Killing was not something that came natural. Her stomach heaved at the dying woman before her. But she didn't have time to dwell. The stage was close and she'd need to get there before the show started.

If Queen Angie wanted to see her, Queen Angie would get her wish.

She hid the blade beneath her robe and walked toward the stage.

From behind there came a loud thud as the world's most popular talent manager fell to the ground.

CHAPTER TWENTY-NINE
THE INTERVIEW FROM HELL

MIKE MALLORY HELD AN INDEX finger to his mouth, told the group to stay quiet. Up ahead, standing beside a tree, was a Robe. Hood down, revealing a masculine face with stubble that bordered on a beard. He did not look their way. He smoked a cigarette, tipping the ash to the ground and watching as the wind took it away. Something told Shawna the man was not supposed to be this far from the show, slacking off before the house lights went on. It was heartening in a way, knowing even Angie's most devoted fans still evaded work once in a while.

"The hell's he doing?" Curtis whispered as Mike made his way toward the man.

"What do you think?" Foster looked at his feet and covered his ears.

The Robe hocked a loogie onto the ground, wiped his mouth with the back of his hand.

And gasped as Mike brought down the rock he'd picked up from the ground into the man's skull. Two quick bashes did the job. The man did not scream on his way down, only gasped as his face hit the soil.

"Come on." Mike tossed the rock onto the man's chest. He wiped his hands on his robe as if he'd just sliced some vegetables, made it look easy.

The trees thinned enough to see the mass of people once again.

Their collective voices were deafening. The video screens were closer and Shawna could see stock photos of Angie. Press pictures that had played on the news, at first, but they grew stranger after a while.

First: a photo of her sister, smiling mischievously at the camera.

Next: Angie holding what looked like a prop sword, a large boa constrictor around her neck.

The topless photos from the Internet.

Real-life versions of the paintings that had been erected at Salem High.

Her sister wearing a blood-red bikini, standing in the middle of what looked like these very woods, standing in the middle of a mass of *things*.

Shawna squinted, couldn't make out finite details, but knew they were not human.

Eventually the images faded, replaced with a video.

The crowd cheered at the sight of Angie's moving mouth, looking into the camera as someone off-screen asked her about her childhood. It sounded like Glenda.

The documentary, Shawna realized.

"I grew up in Salem, Massachusetts in a middle-class family," Angie said, voice echoing throughout Gallows Hill. Her eyes sparkled in the frame and her make-up was beyond professional. "My father left when my twin sister and I were very young. I don't remember much about him. He was there one day, gone the next. No warning or anything."

No warning? Oh, there'd been plenty of warning. Their father had begged Kristen to get a job, to stop driving their family into debt. He had his reasons—plenty of them—and he'd given *more* than fair warning. It may not have justified his decision, but Shawna couldn't say she blamed him.

Angie answered a few more generic questions. What made her want to be a singer? How did she hone her talent (without a single mention of Ethel)? What did it feel like winning *Harmony Club*?

Kristen Everstein was next up for the interviews. She smiled for the camera, pretended her life was grand and free of financial hardship and Shawna nearly believed her. The family photos set up in the background added to the façade. Normally they were kept in a box in the basement.

"Ms. Everstein," Glenda said from off-camera, "are you proud of your daughter?"

Kristen nodded much too quickly. "Of course. It's been delightful to watch her journey." *Delightful* wasn't in her mother's vernacular. She ought to have gone into show business herself.

"I can only imagine," Glenda said. "When Angie first started singing, did you ever think she'd make it this far?"

The frame skipped, a quick-jump edit. Perhaps Kristen had taken too long to answer. "I knew she'd do great things. I just didn't know *how great*. She's determined. Always has been. I can still remember hearing her voice while I made supper for the girls. It isn't easy being a single mother. I tried my hardest and her voice, so soft, so soothing—it always made things better."

Shawna rolled her eyes. The only family meal she could remember was overcooked macaroni and cheese served from a cardboard box.

A few more questions, a few more stock answers, and the interviewee switched. Shawna's pulse quickened as her own face adorned the screen. It was strange seeing her features stretched to their maximum. The make-up team had done a bang-up job. Gone were her blemishes and acne scars, the oil that made her face reflective. But her pig nose remained. As did the hearing aids, sticking out of her hair no matter how hard she tried to hide them.

"Shawna," Glenda said, "tell me a little bit about your sister."

A pause, eyes staring into the camera for too long without speaking. No fancy editing this time. Just raw footage that made Shawna want to cry despite the rising anger. She'd assumed the interview would air on television. At least then she wouldn't have to watch real-time reactions. Audience members booed and snickered and she heard the words *pig face* on more than one occasion. Derek's nicknames had caught on.

"What would you like to know?" Shawna finally said on-screen.

"To be honest, I'd like to know if it was . . . difficult growing up with her."

"Difficult how?"

"Angie Everstein is the world's biggest pop star. Her album has outsold Michael Jackson's *Thriller* and is on its way to being the most successful record of all time."

Shawna nodded. "I'm aware."

"So, what's it like? Living in her shadow, I mean. It must be hard watching all her success. Does it ever make you jealous?"

Yes, she'd wanted to say in real life. Yes, of *course* it made her jealous. It made her jealous every waking moment. Things had been tough enough before the talent show. Her *sister* had the normal nose. Her *sister* had the smooth skin. Her *sister* got the perfect tits. And then, as if the universe had decided to spit further onto Shawna's face, her *sister* had learned perfect pitch by way of a conjuring spell. It would've seemed like a bad joke if it wasn't the truth. But Shawna had kept herself together during the interview. She'd felt brave at the time but with her eyes magnified for thousands of onlookers, she just looked pathetic.

"I'm not jealous at all," her past self said. "I'm proud of her. She's worked her butt off and she deserves every bit of fame. Her singing didn't just fall into her lap. She trained for years. She's proof that hard work pays off."

The crowd erupted into laughter and more booing. Some threw cans and crinkled wrappers. Others let the screen know how much they hated her. She was, after all, a traitor after her escape from school. This was the lion's den and she'd stepped right in.

"Don't let them get to you," Mike said, placing a hand on her shoulder.

She pushed him away. "Too late for that." She wiped her wet eyes, cursed herself for crying. Then she took the lead, waved the group on.

But froze after a few steps when the interview abruptly ended.

When the house lights lowered.

When the pyrotechnics began.

She shook her head. *No.* Her watch read seven-thirty. A half hour until show time. Probably longer. No concert had ever started on time, let alone early.

"Ladies and gentleman," said a voice from the speakers. "Please welcome to the stage your one true queen, the lovely and powerful Angie Everstein."

♪

When Esmeralda heard the announcer, her chest tightened. She'd felt the sensation plenty of times, had described it in detail to her doctors while they'd adjusted her meds to push off the inevitable outcome. But here and now, with the crowd cheering and screaming, she was certain this was different. Her body wasn't just pleading. It was *telling*.

She leaned against the nearest tree, waited for air that never came. Her lungs worked overtime for no pay. She saw stars and not just those in the sky. She couldn't give up, even if her body was giving up on her. The stage was so close. She could see the cheering crowd.

Thousands of them. So much glitter it was nearly blinding.

She limped toward the back of the stage, pictured her desired outcome once more. Her belief in magic was complicated. She thought most spells were only half true. You couldn't say a few words and mix a few potions and think everything would work out. What it came down to was this: you had to make your *own* fate, your own *destiny*. And her destiny on this Halloween night was plain and simple: rush the stage and slice Angie's throat from behind, just as she'd done to her manager. Then and only then would Esmeralda allow her heart to stop beating.

Another burst of pain. She held her chest. She ought to hide the knife but that seemed like a mountain of effort. Every move was a struggle and she couldn't waste a single ounce of energy.

I'm coming, Jeannie.

Are you sure about that? Even if you manage to get to a hospital, it'll be too late. It's been too late for years. You're living on borrowed time and then some.

The back-up band stood shrouded in shadows. She saw only dim outlines of a guitarist, bassist, drummer, and keyboardist. They played ambient noise, something you'd hear on the cheapest of cheap Halloween soundtracks. It did not match the pop music that would blare through the speakers in mere moments.

She could feel the notes teasing her mind, letting her know she'd become one of them soon. Once Angie's real voice began singing it was game over. But she was too stubborn to give up or slow down.

The steps of the stage came into view, as did the screens, the speakers, the monitors. So close now. She pulled up her hood as she saw another group of Robes. They stood off to the side, watching the stage from behind. Something felt off about them. Shouldn't they be out there in the sea of fans?

She held the knife behind her back and walked forward with slow, deliberate steps, selling her new role. Angie may have been deceiving but she'd made a fatal error in trusting Esmeralda.

A twig snapped beneath her feet. The other Robes looked her way. The tallest of them stepped away from the group. His words were lost in the soundscape of the band. Probably telling her to get back to work. Precisely her plan.

She turned toward the steps that were only steps away.

She hid the knife as best she could.

She saw her desired outcome once more, the look on Angie's face when she fell to the cold metal stage, her reign finally over.

She froze when the tall Robe stepped in front of her, raised a pistol, and—

CHAPTER THIRTY
FINDING THE OFF SWITCH

CURTIS PULLED THE TRIGGER.

Even over the music, Shawna heard the report of the pistol. The bullet lodged into the Robe's throat. The hood fell, revealing a large woman's face.

Esmeralda Hopkins.

She held her wound to no avail. Blood leaked from the cracks of her fingers. Eyes wide, she charged them, mouthing something incoherent. Red bubbles emerged from her lips, popping with each syllable.

Curtis took aim again and fired. This time the bullet met her forehead, making her indistinguishable. She fell back and her eyes remained open.

Mike reached over and lowered Curtis's hand, which was shaking badly now. Tears distorted his dollar-sign tattoo. He shook his head and, despite his tough guy attitude, cried like an infant.

Shawna kneeled down, reached forth, and closed Esmeralda's eyelids.

"Did you know her?" Mike said.

"A long time ago." She almost told him this was the woman who'd given Angie her tools. In a way, it was just as much Esmeralda's fault as Angie herself. After all, she wore a robe. She was one of *them*.

When Shawna stood back up, Curtis held a second pistol, this one nearly twice the size of the first.

Professor Foster, who might have been the world's sweetest, most grandfatherly man, held on to his semi-automatic, pointed it toward the stage.

Mike, holding a rifle, nodded toward her. The gesture carried with it more words than the sum of all their conversations.

The band was finishing up their introduction.

It was time.

Through the trees she saw a figure enter the stage. There was no transition about it, no door through which the figure could've stepped. One moment there was empty space, the next a blond-haired, green-eyed girl.

Angie strutted toward the microphone and said one simple word. "Welcome."

The crowd did not cheer. They grew so silent Shawna heard her own heartbeat.

From her boot, she retrieved the pistol Mike had given her. It was pathetic compared to the rest of the group's artillery, more toy-like than deadly. But the weight of it was comforting all the same.

"Tonight is a special night," Angie said. Her voice seemed to emanate not from the speakers but from the trees, the ground, the earth itself. "Join me, won't you, in the dawn of a new time. A new *era*. Raise your hands if that sounds like fun."

The crowd obeyed. If there was a hand left down, it was lost in the thousands pointing at the night sky. Shawna took the lead, stepping forward. She heard the others following, rustling leaves as they went.

No more Robes appeared. They were all on the other side of the stage, just as mesmerized as the glitter critters at their one true queen.

"I'm glad you're all here," Angie said. "It means the world to me. Now, what do you say we play some music?"

The silence vanished, replaced with thundering applause loud enough to shake the ground beneath.

Shawna made it to the small clearing behind the lights. She wasn't sure how close the others were but she didn't have time to look back. There was only enough time to climb the back steps, taking them two at a time, reach the upper level of the platform, raise the gun and—

—and freeze as the band started back up, playing actual music this time. *Familiar* music. Music that led its listeners down a deep, dark, primal path. Music she'd heard countless times no matter how hard she tried to avoid it.

"Forever with you," her sister sang.

Angie had barely gotten through the first few lines before the change took place.

The air shifted.

The temperature plummeted.

The sky darkened.

The crowd erupted into something like a riot. She'd heard stories of looting and violence during times of disaster. Hurricanes and earthquakes brought out the worst in humanity but this was an entirely different beast.

The depravity was spread wide. Near the front of the stage, a woman removed her sequin pants and tied them around the neck of a small girl standing nearby. The girl's eyes widened, face turning first red then blue. She struggled for only a few moments before her body went limp. The woman took back the pants, waved them in the air like a flag but her victory was short-lived. The man standing behind her, graying hair and tweed blazer that did not scream *pop fan,* bashed her over the head with what looked like a baseball bat with several nails driven through its shaft.

There were other such scenes. A murder here, a rape there. Screams and pleas and cheers as if they were one and the same. Bone and flesh and blood. So much blood. It was hard to tell where the head bopping ended and the head removing began.

The chaos was not limited to Gallows Hill. In the distance, police cruisers flashed, lighting up Salem like Fourth of July fireworks.

Foster had only been half right. There may have been a secret track on the recordings but that wasn't the worst of it. Angie's producers, whoever they might have been, had added the frequency to mimic her *real* voice.

"Come on," Shawna shouted to the group, words lost in the commotion.

She sensed them gaining but sensed something else as well.

She turned her head and saw that the people in the crowd weren't the only ones affected by the world's most popular song.

Foster's glasses drooped too far down his nose as he stumbled toward her. The frames fell to the ground, crushed under one of his boots, though he didn't notice. He held his hands out, dropping the gun in the process.

"Professor? What're you doing?" She knew the answer of course. He was just as much a critter in that moment as the sea of fans behind her.

Curtis, too, was affected. He raised his pistols for the second time that night and fired. The first bullet struck a nearby tree. The second made contact with Foster's left leg. He went down hard, buying her just enough time to finish climbing the steps.

She eyed Mike as he kicked Curtis to the ground and tossed the pistols aside. He nodded toward her, met her eyes. *Go*, he said without saying it. *End this now.* He hadn't lost his mind yet but that would likely change any moment.

She obeyed.

Up the steps and onto the stage.

Past the band and around the speakers.

At the microphone now, Angie's perfect ass shaking in tune to the beat, when suddenly, without warning, the song stopped.

The band froze. Not a stray note or beat to be heard. The screams took precedence, occupying the silence. It was the worst thing Shawna had ever heard and that, recent events considered, was saying something.

"I was waiting for you," her sister said into the microphone. "I'm actually surprised in a way. I didn't think you had it in you."

"You thought I'd let you do *this*? Thought I'd let you end the world?"

"*This* is already happening. The world ended"—she looked at a small, sparkling watch on her left wrist—"about two minutes ago."

"Maybe," Shawna said. "But you're going to hell with the rest of us."

Someone near the front of the stage screamed in agony. A tall man with dreadlocks and a basketball jersey. A group of three surrounded him, lifted him by his limbs, and pulled. Shawna swore she could hear skin and muscle tearing as he, quite literally, fell to pieces.

"Beautiful, isn't it?" The back of Angie's head was, in a way, worse than the real thing. Shawna suspected that if her sister turned around, it wouldn't be her sister anymore. It would be . . . something else.

"Is this what you wanted? Is this why you took up singing in the first place?"

"It was Ethel's idea. Her life's *dream*. I just made it come true. She's here with us, Sis. All around us. And she's delighted."

Shawna shivered. A cool breeze blew through Gallows Hill, bringing with it the scent of the recently deceased. Blood soaked the ground and the trees and everything else. "Tell Ethel I never liked her voice anyway." She raised the pistol.

Angie turned around.

Shawna had been right. It wasn't her sister. It was something horrid, something deformed and misshapen created in the *image* of her sister. It was the thing she'd seen in so many nightmares.

Green, scaly skin.

Matching eyes.

Oval-shaped pupils more snake than human.

Jutting chin and raised eyebrows and pointed ears.

The teeth were the worst, for there were far too many. Dark with decay, hanging from her mouth like spikes.

"What are you?" Shawna said, forgetting for a moment about the pistol in her shaking hands.

"Something new," Shawna said. Her voice was not one but many. Countless whispers speaking in unison. "It's the music, Sis. The songs are . . . special. They changed me for the better. And everyone in the audience—everyone who survives the change—they'll be different too. New and improved. Humans 2.0. These are my children now."

It didn't look as though many would survive, Shawna thought, surveying the crowd once more. But the change was worldwide. Surely there would be enough to form an army.

"Make this easy on yourself," Angie continued. "Join us."

"You really think after all this I'd give in to you?"

Angie laughed. Claws on a chalkboard. "Of course not. You've wanted me dead since we were girls. Since *before* Ethel. I've always been the prettier one. The talented one. You're not a twin. You're a growth they removed from me. A tumor and nothing more. You—"

Shawna pulled the trigger. She hadn't been prepared for the recoil. Her arms lifted against her will and she fell back, elbows catching her fall.

The bullet sliced clean through Angie's left shoulder, leaving behind a gaping mouth-like hole.

Angie brought a crooked finger to the wound, collected some of the brown blood, and licked it off like candy. "You've got to work on your aim."

The Robes stormed the stage. Unlike the crowd, they had not lost their minds completely. They moaned in ecstasy but they seemed more lucid than the rest. Perhaps they'd been spared. Perhaps they'd been chosen.

Angie ordered them to stop. She grabbed the microphone, held it to her scaly lips, and sang.

The band did not join this time. Her sister sang a cappella, the notes haunting and beautiful despite Angie's new gravelly voice. *Voices*. The words entered Shawna's mind. Worse than the recording studio. This was direct from the source and there was no *off* switch. No obvious one, at least.

Shawna tried to reach for the pistol. She'd dropped it during her fall. It couldn't have gone far but her hands did not feel the cold metal.

That's it, her sister seemed to say while singing "Forever with You." *Give in. Stop fighting and maybe you'll become one of us if you're lucky enough. If not, you'll just lose your mind. Either way, I've already won. What is it your little bullies call you? Pig Face? Well, Pig Face, it's time to start oinking.*

Shawna's skin grew cold, then hot. Her insides churned. Warm blood trickled from her eyes, her ears, her mouth. A headache formed in the back of her head the likes of which she'd never known. She rubbed the flesh but there was no relief. She saw in her mind all the lives she could end. All the carnage she could create. What she'd seen down there in the crowd—it was nothing. Just an appetizer for the main course.

She smiled as the song went on. It wasn't all that bad. Quite catchy, the more she thought about it. Her best plan of action was to lie back and let the melody do its job. Better just to give in. She'd fought long and hard but in the end it hadn't mattered. In the end there was only Angie Everstein.

From behind, she vaguely felt someone touch her temples. Or perhaps that was part of the change. Her body was giving up all control and soon she'd join the crowd in their debauchery.

Next, the music was turned down, as if by some cosmic volume knob, before it mostly vanished altogether.

She turned her head and vomited onto the stage. The headache receded but it still clung to her like a scar. Gone were the screams and pleas but more importantly, gone was her sister's voice. Looking up, she saw Mike. Both his ears bled. Not from the music, she realized as she stared at his pistol. He'd taken matters into his own hands, had fired close enough to cause damage. He'd pulled out her hearing aids and for the first time in all of her life, Shawna thought her sister looked scared.

Angie stopped singing, her deformed mouth hanging in an open O.

The solution—the *off* switch.

Shawna's curse had proven to be a gift.

Mike fired his rifle as the Robes advanced. He took them out until there was a pile of steaming and singeing fabric. There were others in the audience, climbing the sides of the stage. The fans took notice too. Any moment now, she and Mike would be torn apart by a sea of glitter critters.

Shawna found the pistol near her bruised elbow. She grabbed it, pointed at the thing that was her blood but by no means her sister. She closed one eye, steadied her arm as best she could, and pulled the trigger once more.

Angie fell from the stage and into the crowd.

Shawna couldn't be sure but she swore the bullet had splintered her sister's throat. Or maybe it was wishful thinking. There was no *time* to think as Mike lifted her from behind and carried her around the side of the stage, through the woods, and into a large vehicle. At first she thought it was the RV but it was much too decadent.

The words on the side and the picture of her sister—sans her new reptilian features—told her this was the official Angie Everstein tour bus.

"Where are Curtis and Foster?" she said as they entered.

Mike did not answer as he closed the doors and turned the keys.

She turned her head so they locked eyes. "Where's Curtis and Foster?" she said again, nearly forgetting he was like her now. Without one of life's most precious senses. He said nothing, shook his head *no*.

She didn't ask where he'd gotten the keys. She didn't ask if he'd seen the bullet lodge into Angie's throat. She didn't ask anything as they drove away.

In the rearview mirror she saw Robes and critters alike, jogging after them, though not fast enough. The bus accelerated and they faded into the background.

She made to place her hearing aids back in, then thought better of it.

Silence had never sounded better.

EPILOGUE
BRAVE NEW GIRL

MIKE MALLORY KNOCKED ON THE door and stepped into the bus. "You coming or what?" His voice had started to slur after his ear drums had ruptured.

"Be right out."

She sensed him lingering. She'd never been on the other side of hearing loss. Even after six months, she still hadn't grown used to it. She turned away from the mirror and nodded. "Be right out." She formed the words slowly, deliberately, so he could see their shape.

He nodded back to her. "You'll do great."

"No pressure."

"None at all."

He closed the door and in the background she could just make out the rows of people gathered outside. Not an army by any means but their ranks were growing by the day.

She stared into the mirror at the dark bags under her eyes. They'd spread outward these past few months so that she permanently looked exhausted. She'd been in a constant state of tension for as long as she could remember, before *and* after the apocalypse. She hadn't grown used to *that* either.

The world had not ended as she'd expected.

There was no great explosion or disaster, no missiles launched, no World War III. It had been a battle of a different kind, one that still raged. Hence the crowd outside.

It was unclear if Angie had been terminally injured. There had been no new songs released. Their group took turns checking the radio for signs of survivors, killing the volume whenever "Forever with You" came on, which was most of the time. Even if her sister was dead, the damage had been done. The song would live on forever, as all music did. The secret track, even if it wasn't so secret anymore, was out there, in the atmosphere. Radio waves were everywhere, invisible information that traveled every which way. She shivered at the thought and not for the first time.

But there *were* survivors.

Individuals such as herself who were hearing impaired or those like Mike who had taken drastic measures to escape the change. Others were lucky. Earplugs didn't do the trick, only slowed the song's effects. Noise canceling headphones, on the other hand, were a godsend. At least until the batteries ran dry. They had a stockpile but it grew smaller by the week.

According to most of the popular radio stations, those that Angie now controlled, her army was flourishing. They spoke of Queen Everstein being alive and well, recovering more and more each day. Soon, her management team promised, she'd be singing as if nothing had ever happened. It could've been propaganda, comforting words to prevent panic in the new world, or maybe it was the truth. It was the latter theory that kept Shawna up most nights.

They were outnumbered. Glitter critters ruled the world. Their group of rebels was determined, sure, and growing, but it was a speck in the grand scheme. It seemed like a fool's errand to form an opposition. But what other choice did she have? If she was going to give up, she would've done it that night at Gallows Hill. Fighting back was the only option. If they could stop the signal from spreading, there was still hope, no matter how miniscule. They'd already managed to destroy three radio towers near their site. Far from a victory but it was a start.

She finished applying her makeup, satisfied she appeared somewhat human. You couldn't give an uplifting speech looking like you'd been awake for months.

She cracked her knuckles, took a deep breath, and stepped outside.

The sun was blinding and the temperature warmed her skin. Spring had been slow to start but she felt the promises of better times. She could've almost forgotten the world had ended.

Almost.

A podium had been set up outside the tour bus, the exterior of which had undergone a renovation. Someone (Mike, she suspected), had painted a large red X over her sister's face. The crowd stretched nearly to the wall of the gated community they'd claimed five months back. Winter had been rough, the New Hampshire mountains bringing snow by the foot, but they'd managed to fortify their home base.

Not for long, she thought as she stepped up to the podium.

The critters would find them. This hideout would not remain hidden forever.

She cleared her throat and the microphone screeched with momentary feedback. Half the crowd winced. The others stared and stayed still. Martin Pineau, a medical engineer, stood off to the side. She and Mike had found him not long after Gallows Hill. He was steadily creating hearing aids for the group. Just a matter of time and supplies. Neither of which were plentiful.

The crowd grew impatient. They wanted good news, something to make them forget they could die at any moment. Mike caught her eye and winked at her.

"Good afternoon," she said.

The crowd clapped in response.

"I'm sure by now you've heard that Angie may be alive and recovering."

A few *boo*s in response. Those that couldn't read lips looked to those that could for translation.

"It could be a lie but we have to assume it's the truth. We have to prepare for the worst."

She had their attention now. A strange feeling. Six months ago she'd been the almost-deaf girl everyone bullied. Now she was one of two world leaders. She wondered if her mother was still alive and if she'd be proud. Despite their differences, Shawna liked to think so.

She went on, telling the people what they wanted to hear: that there was an end to this. That they would find a way to rebuild and repopulate.

She'd grown good at lying these last six months.

In the distance a makeshift sign caught her attention. A man with a red beard and eye patch held it high. She stared at it for most of her speech, thinking about the days ahead, wondering if she'd ever come face to face with Angie again. What if her sister sat in a studio this moment, recording her follow-up album? Scheduling her first world tour.

Shawna tried to silence the thoughts, for silence, she'd learned, was the most powerful weapon in the world. The words on the sign echoed this sentiment.

Hear no evil.

Acknowledgment

Thanks go to the usual suspects, those being Emily Lacey, Ryan Beauchamp, Max Linsky, Scott Cole, Adam Cesare, Matt Serafini, Aaron Dries, and approximately 1.5 billion others. Thanks, too, to Grindhouse Press for their continued support and for calling me out on having two characters named Derek. There can only be one.

Patrick Lacey was born and raised in a haunted house. He currently spends his nights and weekends writing about things that make the general public uncomfortable. He lives in Massachusetts with his wife, his over-sized cat, and his muse, who is likely trying to kill him. Follow him on Twitter (@patlacey), find him on Facebook, or visit his website at https://patrickclacey.wordpress.com/

Other Grindhouse Press Titles

#666__*Satanic Summer* by Andersen Prunty

#055__*Merciless* by Bryan Smith

#054__*The Long Shadows of October* by Kristopher Triana

#053__*House of Blood* by Bryan Smith

#052__*The Freakshow* by Bryan Smith

#051__*Dirty Rotten Hippies and Other Stories* by Bryan Smith

#050__*Rites of Extinction* by Matt Serafini

#049__*Saint Sadist* by Lucas Mangum

#048__*Neon Dies at Dawn* by Andersen Prunty

#047__*Halloween Fiend* by C.V. Hunt

#046__*Limbs: A Love Story* by Tim Meyer

#045__*As Seen On T.V.* by John Wayne Comunale

#044__*Where Stars Won't Shine* by Patrick Lacey

#043__*Kinfolk* by Matt Kurtz

#042__*Kill For Satan!* by Bryan Smith

#041__*Dead Stripper Storage* by Bryan Smith

#040__*Triple Axe* by Scott Cole

#039__*Scummer* by John Wayne Comunale

#038__*Cockblock* by C.V. Hunt

#037__*Irrationalia* by Andersen Prunty

#036__*Full Brutal* by Kristopher Triana

#035__*Office Mutant* by Pete Risley

#034__*Death Pacts and Left-Hand Paths* by John Wayne Comunale

#033__*Home Is Where the Horror Is* by C.V. Hunt

#032__*This Town Needs A Monster* by Andersen Prunty

#031__*The Fetishists* by A.S. Coomer

#030__*Ritualistic Human Sacrifice* by C.V. Hunt

#029__*The Atrocity Vendor* by Nick Cato

#028__*Burn Down the House and Everyone In It* by Zachary T. Owen

#027__*Misery and Death and Everything Depressing* by C.V. Hunt

#026__*Naked Friends* by Justin Grimbol

#025__*Ghost Chant* by Gina Ranalli

#024__*Hearers of the Constant Hum* by William Pauley III

#023__*Hell's Waiting Room* by C.V. Hunt

#022__*Creep House: Horror Stories* by Andersen Prunty

#021__*Other People's Shit* by C.V. Hunt

#020__*The Party Lords* by Justin Grimbol

#019__*Sociopaths In Love* by Andersen Prunty

#018__*The Last Porno Theater* by Nick Cato

#017__*Zombieville* by C.V. Hunt

#016__*Samurai Vs. Robo-Dick* by Steve Lowe

#015__*The Warm Glow of Happy Homes* by Andersen Prunty

#014__*How To Kill Yourself* by C.V. Hunt

#013__*Bury the Children in the Yard: Horror Stories* by Andersen Prunty

#012__*Return to Devil Town (Vampires in Devil Town Book Three)* by Wayne Hixon

#011__*Pray You Die Alone: Horror Stories* by Andersen Prunty

#010__*King of the Perverts* by Steve Lowe

#009__*Sunruined: Horror Stories* by Andersen Prunty

#008__*Bright Black Moon (Vampires in Devil Town Book Two)* by Wayne Hixon

#007__*Hi I'm a Social Disease: Horror Stories* by Andersen Prunty

#006__*A Life On Fire* by Chris Bowsman

#005__*The Sorrow King* by Andersen Prunty

#004__*The Brothers Crunk* by William Pauley III

#003__*The Horribles* by Nathaniel Lambert

#002__*Vampires in Devil Town* by Wayne Hixon

#001__*House of Fallen Trees* by Gina Ranalli

#000__*Morning is Dead* by Andersen Prunty